To Wilma,

Thanks for
your support.

All the best.

Kirby
TEBB!

MY BOX OF JEWELS

By
Kathy R. Jackson

Order this book online at www.trafford.com
or email orders@trafford.com

Most Trafford titles are also available at major online book retailers.

Printed in Victoria, BC, Canada.

ISBN: 978-1-4269-2455-2 (sc)

Library of Congress Control Number: 2010900053

*Our mission is to efficiently provide the world's finest, most comprehensive
book publishing service, enabling every author to experience success.
To find out how to publish your book, your way, and have it available
worldwide, visit us online at www.trafford.com*

Trafford rev. 02/16/2010

 www.trafford.com

North America & international
toll-free: 1 888 232 4444 (USA & Canada)
phone: 250 383 6864 ♦ fax: 812 355 4082

For the memory of my maternal grandmother,
Ouida Mae Williams Gooch.

PREFACE

I read a lot of books, mostly Christian fiction, and during my readings I discovered a void. While many of the plots develop and unfold in an African American Protestant setting, none included the African American Catholic. Yes, I enjoyed everything I read but I longed for a story with African Americans of my and millions of other African American's faith, Catholic. Therefore, I decided to write a series of fictional books about an African American Catholic family. I'm currently writing the second book.

But more importantly, I would like to thank God for giving me the time and talent to achieve such a task. However, without the support of my family, friends and church communities, I would have never been able to do so. Instead of listing a vast number of names, I'll just say, thanks to everybody who encouraged and helped me see my dream become a reality.

PART I

ST. LOUIS

'When God takes from your grasp,
He's open'n your hands to receive sumthin' better.'

1

GRANDMA PEARL

This is one'a my favorite places. Sit'n out on my front porch watch'n the fancy cars and beautiful people pass by. I make it a point to always sit and clear my head at the end of er'y day. No television, music or conversation just sit and reflect on the day's activities, begin prioritiz'n tomorrow's agenda or just think about whatever pops into my head. For instance, don't you just hate it when parents name they children names that have characteristics linked to them and the child is nuth'n at all like they name. My niece has a beautiful daughter named Angel, about 4 years old, and if that child ain't the devil, I don't know who is. You can tell her to "stop" and the next minute she'll be do'n the very same thing again. I told her mama, "Y'all just don't know how to discipline children. Most'a times, all you need to do is whup they butts. Get you a skinny leaf switch from the yard and wet the tips. I guarantee you , it'll only take two or three good licks to get yo' point across. Gone forever, the undesired behavior." I'm a firm believer that kids today, need more discipline. Period.

Country folk, mostly from Mississippi, Georgia and Arkansas, often name they children with hopes of influencing peoples' opinions about they characteristics. Sadly enuf though, when the child's behavior doesn't measure up, you wonder, "Why did they choose *that* name? What was they mama think'n? Like the other day, I read an article in the local community newspaper about a young black man named, Success Jamieson. Jamieson was sentenced 15 years to life for the murder of an elderly Southside man and for burglarize'n over twenty homes in North County. It was report'd that Jamieson confess'd, in a fit of rage, he accidentally kill't the victim when he discover'd the man only had $25, hardly enuf to satisfy his $100 a day drug habit. For this act of cruelty, the only type of success Jamieson will likely achieve is the ability to bench press 250lbs and the art of master'n how *not* to drop the slippery soap. Perhaps he should have been named "Looser".

Now me, I didn't have a problem disciplining my children or my grandchildren. I'm from the old school and pride myself in know'n how to raise children. The old African proverb, **it takes a whole village to raise a child**, is true. There's no way I could'a raised my children without help from neighbors, relatives, friends and last but certainly not least, my church community. The bible says, we's all one body in Jesus Christ and I think it's time we start act'n like that.

People say I'm friendly, outspoken, and critical of others while yet at the same time they call me funny, smart and very kind hearted. If someone ask'd me for a self- description, I would say first, I'm a Christian and second, my work experience has made me very observant. Together they make a unique combination. I tell it like it T-I-IS. Tell you what God loves, the truth. My one simple rule of thumb is to always strive to be more Christ like. That's a hard goal to attain when society is constantly reveal'n images of earthy, ungodly desires. Don't get me wrong, by no means am I infallible but I do try my best to be mindful of the choices I make.

Decisions are made based on the information and life experiences that we have at the time of the decision making process. The decision I made five years ago may be totally different than the one I make today, ev'n given the same circumstances, but please know, er'y one of my decisions is made with God in mind. Yeah, I got me some property, a couple of degrees, a good job and I know how to speak Ebonics and the Kings English, and tend to mix the two quite eloquently, I might add, but ain't nuth'n like know'n and believe'n the Lord will provide your er'y need, if you keep your eye on the prize, Him.

My grandkids, nieces and nephews like to sit around and look at my family photo album. Seems like er'y time they ask me who the people are in the picture, I get to reminis'n and tell them 'bout the different situations we done come through. Nowadays, they got that digital camera where all the photos be in your computer. Hell, that ain't no fun, er'ybody crowded around the computer to look at pictures. I tell ya, this here picture album is the history of the Johnson clan. In order to keep from have'n to repeat myself ov'a and ov'a, and to make sure they get the story right, I decided I would pick out some family pictures and talk 'bout the people in 'em as I sit here on my porch each ev'nen. Then, that way, the family can share memories for many generations to come. It could be a talk'n picture album.

I hope I can work this thang. As a general rule I only know two things about electronics, off and on! O.K. Here we go, I got it now.…. RECORD.

The first picture I see when I open the picture book is me, 'bout nine or ten years old, sitting on the porch with my Mother in the background. You can't see her face but I remember that old green duster she used to wear all the time. When I was a young girl, I would daydream about my future for hours on end. Sometimes, I would imagine myself as a doctor. Other times a lawyer, teacher or nurse but no matter what the profession or residential location, my dream always included a husband, two or three children, a house, dog and a yard complete with picket fence. Unlike my baby sister Tootsie, I nev'a want'd more than three children and I only want'd, boys. Well, that ain't how it came to be. I had two girls first, then, I got my baby boy on the third try. Let me slow down, cause I'm get'n ahead myself. I'll introduce ya'll to *my* family a bit later. Right now, I think it's best I focus on me and how I end'd up in St. Louis.

Forgive me if I mix up dates. I sometimes get *senior moments* where I can't remember for the life of me, the sequence of things or what I was talk'n about. You have to remember, I'm almost seventy-five years old now. Anyway, let's get start'd with the story cause I wanna finish the first part 'fore it get dark and the mosquitoes start bite'n. I still gotta take a bath, do my hair and change clothes 'fore my ride gets here. Good thing I got wash and wear hair! It was a gift from God and my parents.

I was born to Ouida and John on January 13, 1936. I come from a large household. Hell, er'ybody had huge families back then. There was no such thang as birth control. And ev'n if it was, who could afford it? Anyway, we lived in Mississippi on a farm outside'a small town call'd Sumner. You probably nev'a heard of it but for point of reference, it's located about 30 or 40 miles from Oxford, home of the University of Mississippi. And it's the same place the murder trial of Emmett Till, a young boy from Chicago who was lynched for whistle'n at a white woman, was held. Ironically, in Sumner, they had a sign posted, just as you enter the town that read, "Sumner, a good place to raise a boy."

I have six brothers and one sister, all by the same parents. We range from 1-3 years difference in age. I'm the oldest, so my sister and brothers come to me for advice. Always have, ev'n back then on the farm. My parents were sharecroppers who somehow, managed to keep the family afloat. They eventually saved enuf money to buy some land with a small house on it.

Don't get me wrong, we didn't have what you call amenities, by no means but we did live a comfortable life compared to some'a our neighbors. More importantly, our parents drilled Christian morals and values into us. No, we didn't have inside toilets, run'n water, electricity or a telephone but Mother insist'd that our clothes be clean, ironed and not tattered, our house was to be neat at all times and we had plenty of food to eat. My parents routinely told us how important the bible coupled with a good education is to black folks. Mother would say, er'y time we get sumthin', white folks wanna take it away. Education the one thang they can't take away from you. No one can rob you of your knowledge.

My father was a country preacher who traveled the countryside three or four days a week visit'n the sick and spread'n the good news of the Gospel, Jesus Christ. I used to love to go with him when he made his rounds but unfortunately, the opportunity didn't present itself as much as I would'a liked, cause I was the oldest. You see, Mother was frequently pregnant or sick, so the bulk of the chores or the distribution of such, normally fell on me. Mother, who nev'a allow'd us to call her Mama, retain'd the title of cook but I gradually became the housekeeper, ov'aseer, negotiator and family mediator.

2

NEW BEGINNINGS

I got a lot of pictures in this here picture book but I ain't got not one single one of my Mother look'n right at the camera. She nev'a did like to take pictures. As far as I know, nobody in the family got a picture of her!

Things took a turn for the worse when I was about twelve. In December 1948, Mother was 7 months pregnant, with child number nine, and got really sick. The doctor came to visit, told her that she was threat'n to lose the baby and order'd her to go to bed and rest up for a few weeks. But Mother nev'a would listen to the doctor and by no means was she gonna take it easy. She continued cook'n and sew'n as always. She ev'n made suits for two'a my brothers. Now as I look back, I think Mother knew she was dying but what'n about to leave this earth without *all* her children have'n the proper clothes to wear to her funeral. The strength that it took to make them suits wiped Mother out, cause as soon as she finish'd, she took to bed and nev'a regain'd her strength. After about 3 or 4 days, with increase'n hemorrhage'n, Mother protested but we sent for Dr. Hightower again. When the doctor came, he examined her and said she need'd to go to the hospital right away.

Me, my father and Mother rode with Dr. Hightower to Grenada Hospital, ov'a an hour's drive away. By the time we arrived, Mother was already unconscious so they immediately took her to the colored section of the hospital for treatment. We stay'd in the wait'n area for two hours before the nurse call'd for my father. When he return'd, he told me, "In an effort to save lives, the doctor had to do an emergency c-section but

Mother and the baby died dure'n surgery." Tears roll'd down his face, it was the first time I ev'a saw my daddy cry. If I live to be a hundred, I'll nev'a forget the sadness in his eyes that day.

Chile, once the doctor finish'd his rounds and we start'd back home, that was the *longest* ride I ev'a experienced. It seem'd to last forev'a. With each beat'n moment I felt as if my heart would break in half from so much sorrow. I ev'n found it difficult to breathe and I couldn't help think'n, we ain't got no mama no mo', what us gon do? Mother had siblings in Detroit, St. Louis and Chicago and each was will'n to take some'a her children but not all of 'em. Reverend Daddy, as we affectionately call'd my father, was so distraught by Mother's death that he couldn't think straight and thereby instruct'd *me* to decide what should happen to the children. I was closest to Mother and knew she would'a nev'a let her children be separated. She regularly remind'd us that all we could count on for sure was God and most'a the times, our family. So, I what'n 'bout to let my brothers and sister be divided up like some leftover chicken from the annual family picnic. No, I what'n have'n it! I was determined for us to continue live'n as one big happy family. And that's exactly what we did. Ev'n though thangs got rough and we sometimes didn't know how we would make it to the next month, we persevered.

Yeah, we lived in a small house but it was fill'd with a lot of love. Initially, it had two bedrooms but another one was added when our family size increased to five. Mother thought it fit'n for me, the only girl, to have my own room since we had two boys in the family by now. More children were born but we nev'a did add any more rooms, rather we stacked the beds with poles and lumber on top'a one another, sometimes, three beds high.

Our house sat on three acres, most'a of which, we used as farmland. It was a simple frame house with many windows. An assortment of flowers greet'd you as you approached the house. A big white porch surrounded the entire front'a the house with two rock'n chairs and a swing on it. When you walk'd in, there was a small entry way then a bedroom on the left and right. Reverend Daddy and Mother occupied the smaller room on the right, while the boys' room was on the left. Further down the hall, smack dab in the middle of the house, is the dine'n room/live'n room/multi-purpose room, all rolled into one. Actually, this is the room two of my brothers often slept in before they moved into my father's room after Mother died. Likewise, this is the room where we had bible study.

The kitchen was the largest room, span'n the entire width of the house with an enormous fireplace that we used for cook'n and heat'n. Reverend Daddy made sure the boys kept a large supply of wood on hand. In fact, that was one of they daily chores, chop and bring in firewood, after they fed the chickens and hogs. Located immediately behind the kitchen was my room, the add-on. There was a back door that took you to the "out house" from my room. Ev'n though I enjoy'd the privacy of have'n my own room, they woke me up many'a night when somebody had to go use *it,* just simpler to cut through my room instead of walk'n all the way around the house.

We may have been cramp'd in our little house but we had some memorable times there. I remember one time I got up at my usual time, around 5:30 a.m. or so and began my normal routine. It was awfully cold outside. I could tell cause I saw my breath in the house. I grab'd some firewood to perk up the fire that had cooled down dure'n the night. Then I stood in front of the fire, facing opposite, til my backside was good and toasty. It wasn't til then that I could move freely about the house without my body shake'n and my teeth chatter'n. Since Mother's death, cook'n was added to my responsibilities. I *thought* I knew from watch'n Mother cook, how to cook things like soup, beans, rice, fried chicken, eggs and biscuits. However, drop'n vegetables in a pot, cut'n out biscuits and watch'n somebody fry chicken is not the same as prepare'n the meal yourself. But with trial and limit'd error, cause we couldn't afford to waste any food, I became a decent cook. This particular morn'n I was make'n pancakes, my brothers' favorite breakfast food.

I made about ten pancakes before I summon'd er'ybody to the table to pray over the food. Just as we joined hands and got situated my father start'd "Let us bow our heads in prayer," there was a loud thud at the back door. It scared us half outta our seats. No way, Reverend Daddy was gonna have his prayer interrupt'd, shorten'd maybe, so he continued on, "Most good and gracious God, we thank you for bring'n us together one more time. Please bless the food, bless the people that prepared the food, bless those who will partake of this food and bless my brothers and sisters who are not fortunate enuf to have food. In Jesus' name,"....... in unison we replied, "Amen." Then my father motion'd to my eldest brother, who sat closest to the door, to open it. To our s'prise, in falls a white boy. "Don't nobody say nuth'n'", Reverend Daddy command'd us all with his eyes. We remain'd silent as he approach'd the stranger. It was so quiet in there you could hear a mouse piss on cotton. It look'd as if the boy had been beaten, to me. Reverend Daddy bent down and took his pulse, then said, "He's got a strong pulse. Let's get him in a bed". Nowadays they tell ya' not to move an injured person, wait for help. But back then you could lie on the ground for days wait'n for help to arrive. I mean the ambulance.

Anyway, each of us got up and start'd prepare'n to care for the unexpected visitor. Within minutes us girls had assembled a make shift hospital in the multi-purpose room while Reverend Daddy and the boys took the stranger's coat and boots off in my room. Tootsie was put'n the finish'n touches on the linen as Reverend Daddy and my brother enter'd the room carry'n the mysterious visitor. I had told her to put a old yet clean blanket on top'a the fresh linen so that after we wiped him off and changed his clothes we could roll up the soiled things in the old blanket and wash 'em all together. I got one of my nightgowns and put it with the bowl, clean rags, homemade saave and store bought mercurochrome (it don't burn like that other red stuff), that I had placed on the crate next to the bed. I figured a gown would be better than a pair of long johns cause the gown would allow us easy access to his wounds, if necessary. I remember think'n; the first thing we need to do is wipe him off. With all that blood er'ywhere we couldn't tell how bad the injury really was.

When they laid him in the bed, he look'd to be asleep but I knew that was not the case, he was probably unconscious. As I watched him, I instinctively thought back to Mother and our ride to the hospital but then I purposely push'd the memory aside cause this young boy need'd my undivided attention. There was no time to daydream. I yell'd into the kitchen for someone to keep an eye on the pot in the fireplace and to bring it to me as soon as the water start'd to boil. Meanwhile, me and Tootsie began cut'n off the clothes that we couldn't otherwise remove. A few minutes later one'a my brothers came in with the water. I told him to pour some in the bowl, place the pot on the floor and then send for, betta yet, go get the doctor. Later I found out Reverend Daddy had sent for the doctor ev'n before they brought the injured boy into the multi-purpose room. Luckily, his wounds what'n as bad as they appeared to be. After we clean'd off his face, there was a cut about 3" long across his fo'head. If I had to compare it to sumthin' today, I'd say it look'd like *Harry Potter's* scar. The cut wasn't deep and it didn't need stitches but it bled a lot. Howev'a, once I applied the right amount of pressure, the bleed'n stop'd. His arms had minor cuts and his legs were badly bruised but neither seem'd to be broken. He smell'd absolutely awful though. Like a mixture of old blood and wet dogs. I ain't try'n to be mean or nuth'n but you know how chil'ren smell after they been play'n outdoors, like puppies, well couple that smell with some old blood. Chile, I was tempt'd to throw some of Reverend Daddy's *smell good* stuff in the water we was use'n to clean him up with.

I gotta pause for a minute, somebody calling me to the telephone. Hold on, I'll be right back! Five minutes later.... O.K. that was my niece. She want'd to know if I still need'd a ride to the concert tonight. What's the matter with these young folks today? Don't she know if I had'a changed my mind I would'a call'd her way 'fore now. The concert is in a few hours and *Yolanda Adams* is my favorite gospel singer. Anyway, where was I.... Oh, I know, I was tell'n you the part about us clean'n Sam up. That ain't his real name but that's the name we gave him.

When Tootsie and I got through clean'n, bandage'n and change'n Sam, he look'd a hundred percent betta and his breath'n seem'd to be regulated. Mind you I'm not a doctor but I was used to care'n for my brothers whenev'a they got sick or had sprangs, bumps, cuts and bruises. Initially, I figured him to be a young boy cause he didn't look to be tall as me and I'm only 5 feet, 2 inches, but after get'n a closer look, I realized he was much taller and guess'd him to be in his early twenties. I was nineteen at the time, just graduated high school. Took me a little longer to finish school cause of all'a the responsibilities at home, but I did. Ev'n though I didn't wanna leave my patient unattend'd, I also knew it was essential that he get nourishment. Therefore, I went to prepare some'a Mother's "cure all" chicken soup, in case he woke up.

I look'd in on him frequently. About an hour later when I came back in the room carry'n a tray with soup and bread, he was wide awake, look'n puzzled and confused, like a deer in headlights. I'm sure it could'na been more than a few seconds of him wake'n up. He attempt'd to lift his head but instead grab'd it with his hands as if it would tumble off without his support. I could tell he was in a lot of pain. I placed the tray on the crate and proceed'd to straighten his covers. Since I was unsure if he could understand me, I start'd the conversation off real slow, using hush'd tones. My name is Pearl. Do you understand what I'm say'n? He slightly shook his head yes with a crook'd smile but he didn't try to talk. So I continued. You show'd up injured at our back door a few hours ago and we brung you in here to care for you til Dr. Hightower come. You hungry? He replied, yes, by blink'n his eyes and slightly smile'n again. I smiled back and commenced to feed'n him the "cure all" soup. Don't ask me how, but I knew from that very moment on that we were destined to be lifelong friends. Christians say God put people in your life for a reason, season or a lifetime and I truly believe that!

Sam managed to eat about half of the soup before he dosed back off. This time he was sleep, not unconscious. It was just about then that I heard my brother Bubba return. Reverend Daddy had sent him to fetch for the doctor dure'n all the commotion. When I got in the kitchen I could tell he was out of breath. I told him, slow down, catch your breath first. It took him about 30 seconds before he could talk. Then he said, " Dr. Hightower was on his way to deliver a baby but gave instructions for Pearl to make sure she stop the bleed'n, clean the wounds and put some'a Mother's saave on 'em. He also said that he would come as soon as he could but it probably wouldn't be til tomorrow". Sometimes, depend'n on the doctor's schedule, we could wait two or three days before he came. If Sam's conditioned got any worse, we will definitely take him to the hospital.

I decided to sleep in the multi-purpose room incase he need'd anything throughout the night but he slept through the night without wake'n up. S'pris'nly, Sam was much better in the morn'n. I guess the soup and rest did him a world of good. I was glad he had some color in his skin cause the day before he was look'n whiter than a fish belly. At first, we couldn't make out nuth'n he was say'n. But after he ate a light breakfast and drank some warm milk, he began to speak clearer. Sam told us his real name is Ashley Wilcox and he's from Biloxi but goes to the University of Mississippi in Oxford. Now, you see why we call him Sam. Ashley just doesn't fit a man. Anyhow, he said the last thing he remembers is, while ride'n his horse, (he prefer'd horseback to train) he heard an unfamiliar sound, look'd up and saw a big piece of rock fall from a boulder but before he could react, it hit him across the face. He fell off the horse and slip'd down a rocky hillside. That's how he got all bruised up. Somehow, after several attempts, he managed to retrieve his horse, pull himself onto the saddle and start to head home but he felt really dizzy so he went to the first house he saw and fainted from pure exhaustion on the steps.

The doctor came later that ev'nen. Said I had done a good job look'n after Sam and he was fit to travel again. Sam decided he would get another good nights rest before head'n out in the morn'n. We stay'd up half the night talk'n about any and er'ythang. I was s'prised he spoke so freely to me. Back then white folks in Mississippi usually didn't have much to say to coloreds, unless it was a command. Howev'a, tonight the color barrier seem'd to disappear and we talk'd as if we was two friends catch'n up on the events in each other's life. Sam kept say'n how grateful he was for all we did for him and that he owed us a favor in return. I told him God instructs us to feed the hungry, care for the sick, and clothe the naked. We was merely obey'n our Father's teach'ns and that's favor enuf for us.

That night I slept in my own room and heard Sam leave before the sun came up. He left a note in the kitchen.

I'll never forget what you folks did for me. God bless you all.

Your friend,
Sam, "Ashley Wilcox"

Secretly, I hoped and pray'd he would keep his promise and stay in touch, cause I intend'd on keep'n mine. I couldn't wait to start my first letter to him.

Whenever black folks in Sumner, other than my family, used to see this picture of me and Sam, they would say, "Who dat white man you hold'n hands with?"

Life on the farm continued the norm til round about 1965 when one of Mother's brothers in St. Louis died and outta the blue left his house to me. Chile, can you believe that! I, Pearl Ann Johnson inherited property. Yes it's true Uncle John Boy had always been my favorite uncle but I had no idea I was his favorite niece. And I sure as hell didn't think he would leave me his house but that was right on time cause our little house in Sumner had recently fell victim to the Klan. They not only burnt a cross in our yard, they burnt our house to the ground. All cause

Reverend Daddy was trying to support his family by make'n a little change on the side repair'n cars. They was jealous of our success.

Thank God er'ybody got out in time and no one was hurt but we still had no place to go. God knew the only way I was ev'a gonna be able to get some land was if somebody gave it to me. He also knew we had to leave Mississippi quick and in a hurry cause rumor had it the Klan might come back and lynch one'a us.

Just goes to show you how awesome God is. He'll make a way outta no way!

3

US HERE NOW!

Here's a picture of me and Tootsie lean'n against Reverend Daddy's new car.

After the Klan burnt our house, Reverend Daddy decided to give up preach'n, sell the land and take the profits to start a little business in Atlanta. I was 28 at the time and Tootsie was turn'n 18 the next month. All the boys had left home by then, so since I had just inherited some property and need'd help with my new house, it was decided that Tootsie would come live with me. It didn't take long for us to gather up our things cause mostly er'ything was destroyed in the fire but Reverend Daddy's church, Deliverance AME, donated basic items like clothes, shoes, toiletries and money to help us get back on our feet. Er'ybody was so helpful. Sam ev'n sent a few dollars in the mail. I thought it would be a good idea to take the train and enjoy the scenery but Reverend Daddy said "I'm drive'n y'all to St. Louis cause I don't know how long it'll be 'til the next time I see my little girls."

Chile, ain't nuth'n like ride'n in a car with a person much older than you drive'n. They easily loose concentration. I've witnessed old people nonchalantly pass up an exit, slow down at green lights and get this, ev'n try to start the car when it's already on. Most'a the time they do this cause they concentrate'n more on the conversation in the car than drive'n the car. Be'n nosy, try'n to keep up with the conversation and ain't nobody talk'n to them. Reverend Daddy is no exception. We laugh'd and poked fun at his drive'n skills all the way to St. Louis. It took us about 12 hours but we safely arrived at my new home on his birthday, June 29, 1965. I remember cause that was the first day that I ev'a wrote in my journal and I been keep'n a journal er'y since then.

That house was the biggest I had ever saw in my life. It was located on Page, east of Union, 5247 to be exact. If I had'na knowd betta, I would'a said rich people lived there. It had three levels; four if you count'd the basement. Five bedrooms, two baths, an enormous kitchen with a dining area and a big fenced in back yard. In the front'a the house, flowers and white rock surround a lone tree. The front yard was so small you could cut the grass with a pair of scissors. And, children ran freely up and down the block. Mind you, in Sumner, our nearest neighbor was 'bout two miles up the road and here in St. Louis you could hang out yo side window and literally touch yo neighbor's house. I couldn't believe it! I wasn't use to live'n this close to other people but eventually my shyness wore off and I ventured out to see St. Louis.

My first adventure was the food. St. Louis has its own style of cuisine, especially Chinese food. They have items that you can't get elsewhere, at least no where I've been. Chinese restaurants in neither Atlanta nor San Francisco knew what I was talk'n about when I ask'd for a St. Paul sandwich or a order of Duck & Noodles? Actually, the St. Paul sandwich is egg foo young, without the gravy or the plate. The egg pattie is made with your choice of beef, pork, chicken or shrimp and served on two pieces of white bread with pickles, onion and mayo. Add a box of pork fried rice and a Orange *Whistle* soda and you had a meal for 'bout $1.50 back then.

Nowadays there's a *China-man* er'y few blocks or so. Why they call it a *China-man*, instead of a Chinese restaurant? Don't ask me, you know how us black folks are. Anyway, the food is always cooked to order. Thereby make'n the ingredients fresh, the service fast and the price within your budget, "cheap". Keep in mind, these are not typical dine-in restaurants but rather *small* carry out eateries. If five people are in the place at one time, it's more'n likely you're stand'n in somebody's personal space. Despite the close quarters, people still go cause the food is soooo good! They ev'n give you a free soda if you spend ten dollars. Er'y time natives, at least the black folks I know, return to St. Louis, the one thing they absolutely must do before return'n home is eat some *China-man*, bar-b-que and *White Castle* burgers. Often times they ev'n horde up a big package to take back home. Reverend Daddy always ask me to bring him some Duck & Noodles when I come to Atlanta.

Another thing that struck me as odd back then was the proximity of a lot of churches and schools to liquor stores. In the city, it's not uncommon for them to be located only a few feet apart but in Sumner, the church and school sometimes would share the same space. Mississippi was a dry county but they secretly sold moonshine way back up in the woods. We didn't have no package liquor store. RayRay *might* put yo' corn whiskey in a paper bag but that was the closet resemblance to a store as you got.

Chile, look at this picture of me, Faye and Pam at the club. It was Faye's 30th birthday party and we thought we was look'n good in those match'n outfits!

The nightlife in St. Louis was both fabulous and appeal'n to a small town girl like myself. Faye, my hangout buddy, had to frequently remind me to close my mouth cause it would be gap'd open with astonishment as a result of sumthin' I saw or heard while we was out. To me, the get'n ready part was almost as exciting as the bars themselves. Back then men and women alike were taught to be mindful of their appearance, especially they hair and dress, whenev'a we went outside'a the house. It's true women wore rollers and rags on their heads, tied-up shirts, cut-off shorts and such when at home. And the men usually had on overalls or khaki pants with cotton or flannel shirts. But when it was time to go to the bars, it was a totally different picture. Er'ybody was sharp. I mean clean down to the bone. The women hair was fried, dyed and laid to the side and the men had theirs trimmed or processed. Suits was the clothing of choice for the brothers and the sisters mainly wore calf length skirts with blouses or sweaters and kitten heels. Remember, this was still the conservative dress era, just right before mini skirts and leisure suits hit the scene.

Depend'n on the type of individual you want'd to meet or socialize with determined the places you usually went to. At the time there was a lot of bars in St. Louis but *Sorento's* and *NBC* were the two most popular ones, both were black owned and each catered to a distinctly different crowd. *NBC* was located on Easton Avenue, later named Martin Luther King, Jr. Drive. The crowd at *NBC* tend'd to be a little bit older and more stable, so to speak. If a girl was look'n for what we call'd a "Scullen Mule", that's an uneducated man who work'd hard at the *Scullen Steel* factory and made as much money as most professionals, she could find him at *NBC*. But the down side to marry'n a "Scullen Mule" was, the men work'd like a mule and died young, sometimes as early as age fifty. Postal and gov'ment workers lived much longer and were also considered good catches.

The other bar, *Sorrento's* was located on Taylor and they catered to middle class, up and come'n young blacks like businessmen, doctors, lawyers, nurses and teachers. Music, drinks and conversation always flowed smoothly at both bars but seldom did I see anyone dance. Back then bars was not for dance'n. Occasionally, a girl would dance on top'a table or a couple would dance in the aisle if they got drunk enuf but as a general rule, if you want'd dance'n, you went to *Club Riviera* on Delmar. *Club Riviera* was known for bring'n in big name acts. When black performers finish'd gigs at white establishments like the *Fox* on Grand, which barred Negroes, they would go and play at *Club Riviera* so that they own people could come see 'em perform. I saw *Dizzie Gillespie* and *Miles Davis* there. Also er'y year, Miss Fannie's Ball was held on Halloween at *Club Riviera*. Ev'n though the ball was on Halloween, we nev'a once wore costumes. We wore our regular partying clothes but the cross dressers came out in full force. Since it was illegal for men to impersonate women back then, gays used the premise of Halloween to cross dress without get'n arrest'd. Chile, it was sumthin' to see! It was difficult for me to pick out the cross dressers from the women cause they look'd just as good, if not betta, than the real women. You know, they *still* have that annual ball to this day.

None of the bars or clubs sold food back then but you could get sumth'n to eat on the Pig Ear Wagon, which was really a truck. It would be sit'n at the corner of Union and the Hodiamont tracks er'y Friday and Saturday night wait'n for hungry patrons. Not only could you get pig ear sandwiches, you could also buy hot tamales, polish sausage, *So Good* or *Old Vienna* brand potato chips and *Vess* sodas. I know the peoples who own'd that truck and they say it was very profitable, ev'n enuf so to purchase a new Buick, which they paid for in cash.

The bars in St. Louis closed around midnight but if you wasn't ready to go home, you could go to East St. Louis, Illinois, which is right across the river and party 'til the sun came up. We rarely went to the eastside but we always went "bar hop'n", as we used to say, from one place to another. What fun we had! Unfortunately, Faye died in an automobile accident a few years back….. I stop'd go'n to bars and clubs a long time ago but think'n back on those old times brings about smiles and tears.

I'm glad I got the chance to experience both but I truly miss my run'n buddy Faye, she was my *play* sister.

When we first got to St. Louis, Sam used to visit at least once the year but after I got married, he didn't visit as often but that what'n cause we what'n friends no more, it was just outta respect for my husband. I was a married lady.

4

BLACK CATHOLICS...
NO SUCH A THANG!

Look at this picture! The first time I ev'a saw a nun, I thought she look'd just like a very large penguin. Here is a picture of me and a nun in front of St. Englebert Catholic church.

As you already know, many things in St. Louis amazed me but nuth'n was as fascinate'n as the way they worshiped the Lord. We was always going to one church or anuth'a in Sumner, remember my daddy was a preacher, but in St. Louis, I felt like a fish outta water. They had mo' people in one church than we had population in our whole town. I was very uncomfortable, felt like people was always stare'n at me and don't let me start talk'n about the clothes they had on. Chile, you would swear you was go'n to a fashion show. The little country outfits we brought from Sumner was no match for city folk church clothes, so Tootsie and I decided to stay home and have bible study on Wednesday ev'nens. That way we wouldn't loose touch with the word of the Lord and we could still wear them two sisters, Poly and Ester. Within three months time, we had about 8 regulars who came to our bible study sessions. Most'a the people that came were folks we knowd when we lived in Mississippi. Like us, they too had moved to St. Louis in hopes of a betta life. We had those regular bible study sessions for almost three years before I found a church I could be comfortable in.

Sometimes after bible study a few of us would hang around and reminisce about home or talk about the strange things we saw in

18

St. Louis. Earl, who was also from Sumner and call'd hisself *dating* Tootsie, told us how he accidentally went to a Catholic church the Sunday before. Just so happen, he mistook it for the Baptist church (across the street) and went in. He say it took a minute for er'ythang to register cause the first thing he saw was black people in the pews but once he look'd up and saw so many white folks and the music start'd, he knew he definitely was in the wrong place. He said, at first, he was gonna leave but the Holy Spirit told him to stay, so he sat right on down.

For the life of me I couldn't understand why black people would wanna worship with white folks? I know we's all God's children but I had nev'a heard of us go'n to church together. Period. I take that back, the master would sometimes make the slaves worship with him on the plantation, aside from that, I ain't heard nuth'n about us worship'n together. If a black person was at the white church in Sumner you can bet it was not to worship but rather they was work'n in the yard or cook'n out back. Howev'a Earl made the whole experience sound so interest'n. He ev'n said they was recruit'n souls to convert. You could learn how to become Catholic free! Ain't many things in life free but religion is still one'a 'em. I always been curious and thirsty for knowledge so I decided to go to *that* church for myself, just to see what it was all about. To my amazement, I was thoroughly impress'd. What I liked most was that the minister (they call'd him a priest), didn't holl'a at me but rather spoke in normal tones when he said the homily, which I sumize was the same as preach'n on the scripture. They ev'n had these little books that you could follow along with, the Missal. That way, you didn't feel too outta place cause you could keep up with the order of service. And get this, the entire service was over in 45 minutes!!! I question'd if that was long enuf cause at all'a the Baptist churches I ever went to, the service lasted at least two and a half hours. Then you break, have dinner and return to ev'nen service at about 5:00 p.m. for a couple more hours. It was an all day event. Chile, I couldn't believe Catholics were done worship'n within an hour, go figure!

Anyway, as I was leave'n the church, someone gave me a card and ask'd me to consider join'n or if I wasn't Catholic, to convert. I fill'd out the card that day before leave'n the church. Don't ask me why I did it, I don't know. I guess it was more out of curiosity than anything else cause I surely couldn't see myself become'n a member of *this* church. I didn't like they music or sing'n which was very important to me at the time. Well anyhow, a few days later, a nun named Sr. Mary Kathryn Louise, (can you say that fast three times) call'd and invited me to come sit in on one of her classes and afterwards have a talk with her. I accept'd the invite and to my s'prise, Earl was one of the students in her class. He had nev'a told us he was take'n instructions to become Catholic and I couldn't wait to ask him, why he kept it a secret? I thought, perhaps it was the same reason why I didn't tell anybody that I was come'n here today. I didn't want to be prejudged or call'd a traitor by my black folks. The majority of black folks (and me, at first) think only whites are Catholic. Ev'n today, when I say that I'm Catholic, frequently Protestant blacks are astonish'd. They ev'n go as far as say'n, "I ain't nev'a heard of or met a black Catholic, I didn't think there was such a thing." I have to tell 'em, there are millions of black Catholics in the United States and also the major religion practiced in Africa, is Catholic. So, be'n black and Catholic is not as rare as you may think.

To make a long story short, I liked the universal teach'ns of the Catholic Church and therefore decided to convert. No matter where you live, here or in another country, all Catholics around the world study the same scripture read'ns and have the same order of service er'yday. You can follow along in Europe, Asia or Africa just as if you were right at your own parish here in the United States. That's powerful and amaze'n to me. The Baptist ministers on the other hand, are free to preach on whatev'a scripture they select without regard to what other Baptist ministers are teach'n that day.

Another thang that I like about the Catholic faith is that it is very traditional and regal. It has remain'd basically the same for thousands of years. I personally like all the pomp and circumstance; to me, it further enhances the Catholic tradition. Shortly after I began Catholic instructions the Pope convened the Second Vatican Council wherein all the Cardinals of the Catholic Church came together to discuss and change the order of service to include full and active participation of the assembly. In other words, lay individuals, us church folk, were now allow'd to participate in the mass like nev'a before. The mass was originally spoken in Latin but now it was said in English (or the language of your country) and we, the congregation could assist in the read'n of scripture and the distribution of the Eucharist, commonly known as communion. Unlike Protestants, Catholics receive the living body of Christ through the Eucharist at *er'y* mass not just the first Sunday of the month. Me, myself, I need Christ er'yday, once a month is not enuf for me.

Wait a minute; please don't get me wrong, I don't think my religion is betta than yours or anybody else's. I look at religion like this, we all try'n to get to God but have different routes that end up at the same place, eternal life. For instance, if you ask four people for directions to the *Fox Theater* you may get four different routes but they all gonna take you to the *Fox*. You just have to decide which route is best for you. The same concept holds true for religion, you have to decide which route to the Lord is best for you, be it Protestant, Catholic, Jewish or whatev'a. Er'ybody should have a relationship with the Creator. Whether you call him God, Allah, Jaweh or George, it doesn't matter to me as long as you have a relationship with Him.

I been Catholic now for more'n 40 years and plan on dy'n that way. I am very active in the African American Catholic community of St. Louis and all of my children are baptized and was raised Catholic. Like I told you before, the Catholic Church went through changes with Vatican II but the African American culture has really influenced parishes in the black communities. The images of Christ that *we* display mirror us, not them white folks. Which is what the bible and history tells us anyway. Also, the music and songs amplify black gospel roots. You'd be s'prised if you visit'd a Catholic church in a predominatly African American community today cause you won't hear the *woo woo* songs traditionally associated with Catholics and also the congregation is very diverse. You know, Blacks, Whites, Hispanics, Asians, etc., all worship'n together with special emphasis on the Afro centric. Catholic churches in white communities still have 45-minute services but the Catholic parishes in the black communities now have one and a half to two hour services that include more song and fellowship reflect'n our heritage. Mind you, the order of the mass and the scripture read'ns are the same as always, traditional and universal. Remember, that's a big part of what makes us Catholic.

Well I'm a have to stop for right now, cause I need to start get'n ready for the concert tonight, *Yolanda Adams* is at the *Fox*. Me, Tootsie, our kids and sometimes grandkids, make it a point to get together at least once a month to go to a concert, a play, a movie or just out to eat at a nice restaurant. We have ev'n gone on family vacations together.

I look forward to and truly enjoy the time I spends with my family. They can get a bit loud at times but that's only cause we all think we got sumthin' important to say! I often tell 'em, I may have two ears but trust me, I can only hear one conversation at a time. Anyhow, I'll start introducing the family tomorrow.

PART II
MEET THE FAMILY

'It takes a whole village to raise a child.'

African American Family Prayer

God of Mercy and Love, we place our African American families before you today. May we be proud of our history and never forget those who paid a great price for our liberation. Bless us one by one and keep our hearts and minds fixed on higher ground. Help us to live for you and not just for ourselves. May we cherish and proclaim the gift of life. Bless our parents, guardians and grandparents, relatives and friends. Give us the amazing grace to be the salt of the earth and light of the world. Help us, as your children, to live in such a way that the beauty and greatness of authentic love is reflected in all that we say and do. Give a healing anointing to those less fortunate, especially the motherless, the fatherless, the broken, sick and lonely. Bless our departed family members and friends. May they be led into the light of your dwelling place where we will never grow old, where we will share the fullness of redemption and shout the victory for all eternity. This we ask in the precious name of Jesus, our Savior and Blessed Assurance. Holy Mary, mother of our families, pray for us.

Author Unknown

I really like that prayer. Usually black Catholics say it dure'n November, Black Catholic History Month but I like to say it er'y day. The family that prays together, stays together. *And* chile, let me tell you, my family is more precious to me than any amount of jewels. That's exactly why I named all'a my chil'ren after rare gems. Yes, they's my box of jewels, Diamond, Rubie and Garnet. As with all off springs whether they age two or forty-two, mamas love 'em to death and will do anything for 'em. Sometimes our kids don't make the right choices but we still love 'em.

While we have a lot of relatives in St. Louis, Detroit and Chicago, my sister Tootsie and brother in-law Earl, always been a constant figure in my chil'ren's life. In fact, our kids growd up together, more like brothers and sisters than cousins. Right now I'd like for you to meet my family. I'll start with my sister and her husband, then I'll introduce you to my children.

5

"ANT TOOTSIE"

If Uncle Earl told Ant Tootsie to jump, she would simply reply, "how high?" Yes, I said *Uncle* Earl and *Ant* Tootsie. No, they's not *my* uncle and ant rather my sister and brother in-law but after repeatedly hear'n the children call 'em uncle and antie you begin to use the titles too, initially in fun but ov'a the years unconsciously and deliberately. Ant Tootsie is very attentive and usually anticipates Uncle Earl's er'y want and need before *he* is ev'n aware of the desire. For instance, when he comes home from a hard day's work at the plant, there is a pipe'n hot plate of food wait'n in the microwave, ready to be summon'd at any time, newspaper and slippers by his favorite big green Lay-Z Boy, the 48 inch plasma television on channel 2, *KTVI FOX NEWS* and Ant Tootsie anxiously wait'n to be advised of his beverage of choice for the night. Nine times out of ten, of course, it's a *Budweiser.* Employees are allow'd to purchase a case of beer a month at a significant discount, practically free. Needless to say there's always beer on hand at the Simmons residence. You know what they say about us Catholics, whenev'a there's two or three there's sure to be a fifth, as in liquor.

Tootsie learned early how to keep her weight under control. She always been a pretty girl but dure'n grade school she was as round as she was tall! The boys teased her constantly. But by the time she enter'd the 10th grade she was what the 70's pop group, *The Commodores,* call'd a "brick house." Boys no longer teased but were pleased to gaze upon her 36-24-36 frame. Our parents were strict Christians and we girls were told to nev'a let a boy touch you, only *fast* girls did *that*. Good Christian girls, practiced chastity.

When Tootsie graduated high school she was date'n Earl. We moved to St. Louis not too long afterwards and he follow'd us all the way to St. Louis to keep from loose'n her. Once married, they proceeded to have a child er'y 10 to 14 months for the next nine years. Both Tootsie and Earl are very active and volunteer for the local as well as national Pro-life movement, for years. Majority of folks, black and white, think Pro-life is only about abortions but the truth of the matter is, it addresses life from conception to death, including euthanasia (assisted suicide) and the death penalty.

While most women during the 70's were already liberated and had begun to pursue careers that were traditionally closed to 'em, Ant Tootsie was content to remain a stay-at-home mom for her sev'n children. Lord knows they couldn't afford daycare for the toddlers or catholic grade school for the older children. Be'n at home with the children all day gave Tootsie the opportunity to take in side jobs like iron'n and address'n envelopes to earn extra money for the household.

Earl made *good* money at the brewery but with nine mouths to feed and clothe, money sometimes got short and er'y little bit helped. I used to wonder how come they didn't practice abstinence more frequently so that the money could catch up to the current children's needs before they made another one. Mind you, I ain't too shamed face to say that my faith has come a long way. Some people call it a testimony. Mathew 6:32- 35 says, this is from memory so don't be too hard on me if I don't get it just right but the gist of God's message is, *Don't worry about tomorrow, I will always provide your needs. The birds and fish don't worry how they will eat, take heed, neither should you.* I had'ta learn *that* the hard way. Some say it's easier if we learn lessons from other peoples mistakes but I believe the effects of the lessons is heavier embedded in our memory, if we learn from our own mistakes.

Now that her children are all grown and gone, Ant Tootsie has a lot more spare time on her hands and has decided it would be a good idea to work at the church instead of just sit'n around wait'n for Uncle Earl to come home each ev'nen. She's always at the church anyhow, volunteer'n for sumthin' or another so this way she can also get paid for be'n there. She answers phones, make copies and greet visitors at the parish office four hours, three times a week. This the first and only job Ant Tootsie has had in all her sixty years on this earth.

That's pretty much all she do, go to church and wait hand and foot on Uncle Earl. Chile, that girl know she love herself some church and some Earl. And, in *that* order. I think it's wonderful how much in love they still are! What's that the kids say, "Don't hate, congratulate!"

6

"UNCLE EARL"

You ev'a knowd anybody that just work'd all the time? Ain't satisfy'd unless they work'n. Always sign'n up for volunteer work and they looks forward to mandatory overtime. The golden rule for them is, "They pay'n, I'm stay'n." Earl is sixty-two and has ov'a 30 years seniority at Anheuser-Busch. He could'a retired a long time ago but he prefers to work.

More times than not brothers hav'ta work long hours just to net enuf money to satisfy they monthly living expenses. Yeah, I believe in make'n our sons provide for they children but I also think the formula that the child support system uses to calculate payments is totally unfair and doesn't consider all the absent parents current expenses. That's exactly why many absent fathers try to avoid the court system by come'n to a mutual agreement with they baby's mamas in regards to an acceptable amount of child support payments.

At all costs they try to keep the courts outta they business cause when the Division of Child Support Enforcement gets through with cha', a brother work'n, full-time earn'n a decent wage, with one "outside" child could bring home, after child support payments, as little as $120 a week to provide for his house'n, food and transportation. It's virtually impossible for any individual to be able to survive on such a little income, not to mention if he has other dependants. Well, that wasn't the case with Uncle Earl. He work'd overtime cause he had a lot of children at home not cause he had child support payments. He boasts frequently, "all my chirens got the same mama and I's married to her", mimicking the characters played by Danny Glover and Oprah Winfrey in Alice Walker's, *The Color Purple*.

There's no need for Uncle Earl to continue to work overtime cause the kids are all gone, but he so used to it, he can't stop. He wouldn't know what'ta do with hisself. Earl's idea of a perfect day is to go to work and come home to his wife, whose usually wait'n for him with a meal, beer and the sports page in hand. He's not the type to enjoy a movie, dinner and dance'n on the town. He would much rather stay at home and watch the *St. Louis Rams* on TV. Anyway, he don't ev'n own a suit, to wear out on no town or to a funeral, for that matter. The man lives in his overalls. Truth be told, perhaps, that's all that's in his wardrobe, overalls! A multitude of colors mind you, green, red, blue, black, brown and maybe a checker'd one or two but nonetheless, they still yo' basic overalls. Impossible to dress up!

Tootsie ought to count her bless'ns for marry'n a man that ain't nev'a been interested in another woman. All he's ev'a been interested in was provide'n for his family. He's watcha call a "one woman man." And believe me, theys far and few in between. Especially, if they look anything like Uncle Earl who stands about 6'2" tall and has these big strong arms and shoulders. They the kind that make you wanna grab hold onto and commence to swing'n like you did when you were a toddler and your daddy ask'd if you wanna ride. His face....Lord have mercy! The man's face looks as if it's been chiseled from the finest hunk of dark chocolate by the most'a skill fullest of sculptors. And those eyes, black as coals yet more radiant than the sunshine. Let's not forget his smile. Personally, I think that's his most attractive feature. He could easily make a print ad or TV commercial for *Crest* toothpaste. That boy got the whitest, straightest teeth this side of Mississippi. And ain't nev'a wore no braces! Chile, his whole family got pretty teeth. In a word the man is P-H-I-N-E, fine. But more importantly, he's committed to the Lord *and* his family.

Here's they wed'n picture. This one'a the few times I ev'a seen Uncle Earl in a suit. I remember they got married in my back yard and I ev'n made they wed'n cake. It look like its gon slide off the plate any minute!

7

"DIAMOND"

About five years ago I organized my picture books. This here book is dedicated to my chil'ren. They each got they own section. I wish you could see this cute picture of Diamond, butt naked! I was what you call a late bloomer. I didn't have my first child til I was ov'a thirty years old. But chile, once I got start'd, I had three in a row, pop, pop, pop. Seem like er'ry time I went back to the doctor for my six-week check-up, I was pregnant again. The last time I had a baby, I told my husband, (rest his soul) if he put his hands on me before my six-weeks is up this time, I what'n gon participate. Believe it or not, all three of my children are 11 months apart. I sound like Tootsie, don't I, guess it runs in the family.

Because I spent most'a my early life take'n care of *other* peoples children, I couldn't wait to get my own child. Tootsie had three children before I gave birth to *my* first child. I was always partial to boys and only want'd boys but my first child was a girl, Diamond Michelle, arrived on May 11, 1968. She was so incredibly beautiful. Had a head full of coal black hair and the cutest little dimples you ev'a did see. Neither me nor my late husband was consider'd dark skin'd by any means but Diamond took more after her daddy and is light, bright and damn near white. She darken'd up as she got older but she fairer than any'a my other children.

She was our pride and joy and her daddy spoil'd her to death. If I had'a knowd betta I would'na let him do that. Hind site is always 20/20 ain't it? That's probably why she is such a snob today. I love her dearly but if she wasn't my daughter, I don't think I'd have anything to do with her. She is entirely too self center'd for me and you can't tell her nuth'n, she know it all!

Diamond is married to Duane, a pediatrician and they have one daughter, Jade. They live in a four-story home located in the Central West End, a prestigious neighborhood that caters to yuppies, doctors and lawyers. It's the type of neighborhood that is self sufficient with ice cream and coffee shops, restaurants, boutiques, pubs, a movie theatre, an upscale grocery store, *Straub's* and a public library all within walk'n distance to *Forest Park*, home of the 1904 World's Fair and both major hospitals, *Barnes-Jewish* and *Children's*. Duane works at both them hospitals. That's why they want'd to move there, so he could be close to work cause he puts in a lot of hours. You gotta have money to live or play in the Central West End that's for sure. Personally, I don't like go'n down there cause it's too much of a hassle to find a park'n space. Perhaps it's betta now that they built that new park'n garage above the library but I haven't been down there in a while.

Jade was my third female grandchile, in a row. It's no s'prise she act just like Diamond, she a exact replica of her but whenev'a I'm on the scene she minds her manners and pretends to be as sweet and love'n as they come but she don't fool me none. Too many people done told me how rude and inconsiderate she can be. They ev'n say she real fast too! Like to hang 'round them boys. I say, there must be some truth to the story cause er'ybody don't tell the same lie on you. Alls I know is, she bet not let me catch her do'n' none of that disrespectful stuff. I'll sho' nuff slap her into the middle of next week and think nuth'n 'bout it. Bring that child down a notch or two, embarrass her in front of God and er'ybody! I'll ev'n mess up all them pretty curls in her hair she forev'a frett'n ov'a.

Jade expects er'y thang be hand'd to her on a plate. I tell her all'a the time, just 'cause you was born with a silver spoon in yo' mouth don't mean it's o.k. to look down or speak beneath folks less fortunate than you. She ain't nev'a got nuth'n nice to say 'bout nobody. Jade is a senior in high school and Diamond already talk'n bout how extravagant Jade's prom and graduation gonna be. Get this, she ev'n plan'n on rent'n Jade a car and a hotel room for both events. RI-DIC-U-LOUS, is all I can say cause that ain't my child.

Diamond ain't employed nowhere but she do a lot of volunteer and charity work but the sad thing is, it's all for the wrong reasons. She don't do it to help others but rather to be in the spotlight and be able to brag about all the thangs she done did. She's very materialistic and not happy unless *she* is the center of attention. I constantly tell her, God don't go for no show. He's only interest'd in what's in your heart. She's forev'a talk'n bout how much money they donated to *this or that* charity and how much she paid for *this or that* item but I tell her, God says the right hand should not let the left know what it's do'n cause He sees all.

It makes her mad as hell when I start talk'n bout God and His teach'ns. That don't stop me none! But, sometimes I wonder, is this the same sweet girl I raised? Remember what they say, our children come through us but they are not us and you can't be responsible for they actions once they grown. You can take 'em only so far and the rest is up to them. Chile, I tell you, she ain't nuth'n but the devil in sheep's cloth'n but I ain't give'n up on her though. I pray daily for the Lord to lead her to Him but er'ybody know you can lead a horse to water but you can't make him drink it. God let's you decide for yourself if you wants to be saved. For the life of me, I can't figure out what went wrong with her. I thought I gave her the right amount of love, discipline and care as I did my other children but Diamond is the exact opposite of her brother and sister. It's hard to believe they growd up in the same house. She what'n like that before she went off to college in Savannah, Georgia. That school changed her view on life but that still ain't no excuse for her snobby attitude.

She rides around town in a red convertible 2005 XJ6 Jaguar to the gym to workout with her personal trainer and get'n her nails done or her weave tightened er'y Thursday. These things are very high on her list of priorities. Anyhow, I don't understand why she ev'n wears that weave, she got the best hair outta all my children. It must be a status thang to have long flow'n white people hair. She frowns upon anybody who has natural hair 'cept her best friend, Lorraine. And that's only cause they been friends since the third grade. Otherwise, she probably wouldn't have nuth'n to do with her either. Now Lorraine, that's one nice respectable Christian woman. Why she puts up with Diamond, I don't know, probably the same reason why I do, cause I love her. Lorraine says Diamond is high-spirited and don't mean no harm. I say hogwash! The two of them went through grade school, high school and college together. Actually, it was Lorraine who convinced Diamond that Savannah State was the best place for 'em to go to college. Lorraine was an "A" student and ev'n helped Diamond study for the SAT and the ACT so that they could get some scholarship money, if they scored high enuf. Well, it work'd cause both of them went to school practically free. Also, that's where Diamond met Duane.

I glance at my watch, OMG, look at the time. It's almost sev'n o'clock. I gotta stop this recorder and get in here and try to fix me sumthin' to eat for dinner.....STOP Doctor says it's very important that I eat three square meals a day with frequent healthy snack'n in between to keep my blood sugar in check. You know I gotta check it twice a day. Tonight, I'ma have some broiled fish, steamed broccoli and rice. I'm try'n to stay away from fried foods as much as I can. I like 'em but they don't like me! Give me too much gas.

Oh, I almost forgot to tell y'all about the concert. Chile, it was *sooo* good. That *Yolanda Adams* know she can sang!

8

"RUBIE"

The next ev'nen I come back on the porch with my picture book and recorder to finish introduce'n my chil'ren....RECORD......My favorite photo of Rubie is her third grade year school picture, this one right here with her two front teeth out. Out of all my children, I would hav'ta say Rubie Leigh is the most responsible and level head'd one of the bunch. She my middle child and you know they the ones who usually independent and don't require a lot of attention. People say that's cause they nev'a been the baby of the family. Think about it...., the first child is consider'd the baby and the last child, is the baby forev'a. The middle child is, as Rubie says, ov'a look'd but by far the best! She was born April 1, 1969 at Homer G. Phillip Hospital. Homer G. was the first black teach'n hospital for doctors and nurses and the place where a lot of black babies in St. Louis was born.

Rubie and her family live in St. Charles, Missouri; a community located about twenty miles west of St. Louis. The majority of the population is white but for the last ten or fifteen years or so blacks been steadily move'n out there. The land is plentiful, real estate is affordable and the crime rate is low. The only thing that I don't like about St. Charles is you can't buy nuth'n black there. For instance, one time I went to *Wal-Mart* off Highway 94, mind you this was in 2003 to purchase some hair grease and they didn't sell not one single brand. No *Bergamont*, no *Afro Sheen* or *Royal Crown*. If you really want to know the truth, they didn't have any black hair products but they had at least two isles full of white hair products, permanent waves, shampoos and conditioners, hair color'n and also hair sprays. It's like the retailers simply don't provide African American hair products and plenty'a black folks live in St. Charles. They ain't try'n to cater to us at all.

Get this, they citizens ev'n voted against the St. Louis metropolitan rail system, *Metro Link,* expand'n to St. Charles cause they believe it will bring crime but I say it's cause black folks will infiltrate their community. So, if you live in St. Charles and don't have a car, yo' mobility is very limit'd. Pardon me, but the last time I check'd criminals didn't use public transportation to commit crimes but what do I know, I'm just a black girl from Mississippi. To make a long story short, I think it's a nice place to raise a family (if you don't mind live'n around a bunch of white folks),but personally, I prefer a more diverse neighborhood.

Both Rubie and her husband are educators. Rubie teaches English at *St. Charles High* and Stan, her husband, is at *Duchesne Catholic High School* teaching Algebra. They have three children, all girls, Opal, Amethyst, who we call Amy and Jennifer. Rubie and Stan married right outta high school. She was only sixteen when she got pregnant and Stan was seventeen. Both start'd college while she was carry'n Opal. Chile, I tell you, Rubie and Stan growd up right along side'a they kids.

Rubie decided to break the tradition and not name her youngest child, my youngest grandchild, after a gem as my other children and grandchildren are. At first, I was disappoint'd but quickly came to my senses when I remember'd, *that's her child*. She can name it whatev'a she wants, Lord knows I did. When people used to ask me, "why you name your children after jewelry?" I'd reply, "Cause theys mine."

The other two girls, Opal and Amy are a lot older than Jennifer. In fact, Jenn thinks she's an only child cause she don't recall them ev'a living at home with her. You see, the girls were in high school when Rubie got pregnant and by the time Jenn start'd kindergarten they was gone off to college. Now you can understand why she feels that way. And let me tell you, that Jenn is sumthin' else! She smart as a whip and cute as a button but spoil'd rotten. Luckily she's not bratty spoil'd but rather a very obedient and love'n child. And she talks real proper, wouldn't know Ebonics if it hit her upside her head. One time I ask'd her to speak some Ebonics and she say, Grandma, what's that? Chile, I broke out laugh'n cause she was serious as a heart attack. I don't too much like the fact that she competes in beauty pageants at such a young age but then again, that ain't my child. When she's not model'n or at a beauty pageant, she looks and acts her age which is ten, but once she gets all made up, you would swear she was fifteen or sixteen. Anyway, she must be good, she got so many trophies Stan had to take 'em out her bedroom and move 'em to the display case he built in the garage just to show 'em all off. That man knows he love himself some Jennifer!

They garage ain't like a lot of peoples garages where you can't fit the car inside cause it's cluttered with so much junk. On the contrary, Stan got er'ythang neatly arranged. Bicycles on the wall, water hose in a caddy, and a pegboard to hold stuff like screws, nuts, bolts, and tools. He ev'n built a place for his T.V. out there. (He sits in the garage, watch T.V. and smoke cigarettes while chat'n with his white neighbors. They nice people though, not all snobby and stuff like some white folks.) You can bet Stan got a proper place for er'ythang, it's so neat and clean in there. I often tease him, you sho' you ain't Mother's child from another life? Mother used to say, cleanliness is next to Godliness. I'm sure she would'a just adored Stan for his neatness.

Rubie reminds me of myself, she God fear'n and wise for her age and she make it a point to go to church er'y Sunday with her family, always have. You know how some parents sends they children to church, not Rubie. Ev'n if Stan don't go she always take Jennifer. Ev'n though Opal and Amy done married, moved out and got pregnant they *still* go to church with they mama. Sometimes our chil'ren stop go'n to church when they get to be young adults but after a few hard knocks they usually find they way back to the Lord by the time they thirty or so. Seem like by the time you turn thirty a light goes off in your head and you stop be'n so naïve. You understand the mean'n of life and how to succeed at it. For instance, if you ain't married you know exactly what kind of man you want. You won't stand for no foolishness in a relationship cause you already know you can do bad all by yo' self. Don't need no help from no unemployed man to spend yo' money. You got bills to pay. God says we should be ev'nly yoked. That means my partner needs to bring just as much as me to the table. How I'm gon be work'n two jobs and my mate ain't ev'n got one job, be fo' real now! The relationship is bound to fail.

And if you is married by the time you turn thirty, y'all become more secure in the relationship. Ain't no more this is mine and that is yours, er'ythang is ours. Another thang, you stop change'n jobs so much and become settled in a career or profession.

Last, but certainly not least, if you was raised in the church you will more'n likely come back to the church and if you what'n, you seek guidance from the Lord cause you realize it's too hard out there without God in yo' life.

9

"GARNET"

I got a million pictures of my son. Like I told you befo', I was anxious for his arrival and delight'd when Garnet Charles due March 18, 1970 decided to come early. He arrived February the 29th. He's what you call a leap year baby. Only have a birthday once er'y four years. When he was little, I used to celebrate his birthday on March 1st cause he wasn't here February 28th. But now that he grown, he celebrates his birthday for two days straight cause he say he was already here on March 1st. Chile, I was sooo glad to finally get me a baby boy. In fact, that's what er'ybody call him, "Baby Boy." Most'a my relatives don't ev'n know what his real name is.

I know I was ov'a protective of Baby Boy after his father died but in general, boys tend to be slower than girls when it comes to independence and maturity. I think it's because us mothers teach girls how to be self-sufficient but we baby them boys to death. That's why wives have such a hard time with they mother in-laws, the mama don't think the girl is good enuf for her baby and is usually in they personal business too much. Well, Baby Boy was no exception, took him a little while longer to get it all together. And as far as his wife is concern'd, her name is Yvonne but we all call her "Peaches". I tolerate and love her cause she the mother of my grandchildren but I ain't nev'a really liked any woman he was with. I'd nev'a tell him that though and don't you tell him I said it either. Mind you, I ain't ask'n you to lie for me. If he asks, you can tell him but don't be volunteer'n that information. Thank you very much.

Baby Boy and his family live in the "hood." At 5638 Park Lane, right off West Florissant in a section of St. Louis call'd *Walnut Park*, betta known as the ghetto. To white folks the ghetto is a terrible place but to black folks it's fill'd with family and love. Did you know that the original ghetto was where *Adolf Hitler* kept the Jews before he transfer'd them to concentration camps and ultimately to their final train ride to the gas chamber? See'n as though a high number of blacks live in a small geographic area and are frequently live'n in poverty, the word ghetto is used to describe their live'n conditions but it has nuth'n to do with the love in the community. Know your history children! O.K. I'll get off my soapbox and return to the story.

You know sumthin' I used to love to watch chil'ren play. Remember before video games and DVD's came out, chil'ren used to play outside all the time. They thought it was torture to make 'em stay inside. That's why kids so fat now'a days, they don't get enuf physical exercise. It may be hard to believe but some schools done ev'n cut out recess and they only have gym once a week. All chil'ren do is sit around, eat junk, play video games and listen to rapp music but back in the day, most'a kids, especially Baby Boy, play'd outside from sun up til sun down. He didn't want to stop play'n' long enuf to come in and eat.

The neighborhood kids play'd a variety of games that they made up, *Red Light-Green Light, Mother May I, Dodge Ball* and *Red Rover-Red Rover*. But the girls prefer'd *Double Dutch* and *Jacks* or *Bola Bat* while the boys fancied *Mama Peg* and *Marbles* or *Stick Ball*. I remember play'n *Mama Peg* with my brothers when we lived down south. To play *Mama Peg* you had to use a switchblade or a kitchen knife. (In the country we used an ice pick). The object of the game was to see who had the best skill in throw'n the knife. There was a series of ways to throw the knife, ov'a the hand, under the hand or palm up and hit the butt of the knife with yo' other hand. If the knife lands straight up in the ground, you could proceed to the next level. When you successfully completed all'a the levels you were declared the winner and then you would push'd the knife deep in the dirt. The looser had to "eat the dirt", which meant, pull the knife outta the dirt with they teeth. You talk'n bout big fun, chile we would play that game for hours.

If Baby Boy what'n outside play'n he was somewhere in a corner read'n a book. That boy knowd he loved to read and not just comic books like most kids. He would read all kinds of things from fiction to biography. People used to say he was gon be a writer cause he kept his head in them books all'a the time but that ain't so. My Baby Boy is a po'lice man. And about a year ago he was promoted to homicide detective so he don't wear a uniform no more. Yeah, he the po' po' as the gang bangers say. That's one'a the reasons why he still live in the hood. The City of St. Louis requires that all'a they employees reside within the city limits for a period of time. Once he get eight years under his belt, he can move to the county but I doubt he will cause he loves work'n with inner city youth. When Baby Boy was in the sixth grade he had a drastic change in behavior. Where he had once been studious, docile and easy to get along with he became stubborn, unruly and would fight at school almost er'yday. It's important to note that this was right about the same time that his daddy died. I figured he was mad at the world and want'd to take it out on any and er'ybody he came in contact with.

Chile, I was at that school at least three times a week. I bet he was suspend'd about five or six times. This went on for about a year and then just as quick as it began, it stop'd. To this day I don't know what happen'd to make him straight'n up but I thank God he did. Er'y since then, Baby Boy pretty much been on the straight and narrow. Otherwise, he'd surely be dead or in jail somewhere. Now most'a the time he spends his weekends, whenev'a he off duty, as a Big Brother to under privileged kids in the city. I tell you, that boy got a heart of gold just like his daddy! I purposely made it a point **not** to elaborate about my children's father til now cause it upsets me so but our story wouldn't be complete without me tell'n y'all about Charlie. Unfortunately, I'm not gonna be able to do it today cause I need to prepare myself for this. So let me pray for some strength and guidance tonight and I promise, I'll start with Charlie when I get home tomorrow but quess what?.... I just realized, I ain't tell y'all nuth'n about my grandboys and you know how partial I am to boys! I can stay up a few more minutes.......

Well, I may have want'd all boys but it turn'd out, my Baby Boy had the boys. He had two. In all, I got six beautiful grandchil'ren, the boys come right in the middle, number four and five. Topaz is in the ninth grade and Onyx is in the eleventh grade. Topaz is the football star of the family or at least he think so. Actually he's pretty good for his age. He should be, been play'n er'y since he was a real little boy, about sev'n or eight. If he ain't learnt nuth'n by now, sumthin' must be wrong with him. For real though, I'm so proud of him. He's gon be start'n on the

Jr. Varsity team and this only his first year in high school. He swear he gon be a professional football player and I know he can do it too. Now Onyx, he remind me of Baby Boy the most cause he love to write poems and recently, he been write'n lyrics. There's only two thangs he's passionate about and that's write'n his music and that hair of his. I don't particularly care for the style in general but I must say it look kind'a cute on him. Er'ybody can't wear er'y style, if you know what I mean. When I ask him what they call that hairstyle? He eloquently said, "Granny some folks, particularly those that don't have 'em, say they *dreadlocks* but actually, there's nuth'n dreadful about 'em. Too achieve 'em requires patience and strict discipline. Therefore, it is more acceptable to just call 'em *locks*." Watch out, I say, you learn sumthin' new er'yday!

Topaz and Onyx go to the same Catholic high school in a predominately African American community. Way back in the day, before it was coed, it was a all girl school named *Laboure'* but they changed the name to *Cardinal Ritter College Prepatory* and they now located ov'a there off of Vandeventer and Delmar. A couple of years back the school moved from its original site on Thekla, deep in the hood, to this spank'n brand new location in Midtown St. Louis close to the city's fine arts district. *Powell Symphony Hall,* the *Fox Theatre*, and two black own'd and operated businesses, the *Saint Louis Black Repertory Theatre,* and a art gallery call'd *Portfolio Gallery and Education Center* are all within walking distance of the school.

I remember when the Archdiocese of St. Louis had to uproot a whole neighborhood just to make room for that school. I hated to see those families loose they homes to eminent domain, a government forced buy out, but for the benefit of a greater number of people, young folks at that, I think it was a wise decision. The school is a thrive'n part of that community. It's three times as big as it used to be and they now have a football and a track field but more importantly, enrollment is up. That means they prepare'n more young people for college. They boasts ov'a 90% of they graduates go on to college. And that's a good thing because both Topaz and Onyx plan to go on to college. STOP.....

You know, now that I think about it, all'a my children and grandchildren went to catholic school at one time or another. Ain't that sumthin'! I close the picture album, pick up the recorder and go in the house. Goodnight!

10

"CHARLIE"

I toss'd and turn'd most'a the night and then woke up with a crook in my neck but just as I promised, I'ma introduce Charlie tonight. Charles LeRoy Johnson was my husband and best friend. We was just like that *Natalie Cole* song, *"Inseparable"*, from the day we met 'til the day he died. Though our union was short lived our love proved stronger than the test of time. We met on the Fourth of July 1967, married the first week of August and by the end of the month, I found out I was pregnant. Chile, I knew immediately cause I remember I had this dream about fish and Mother used to say that was a good sign that somebody was pregnant. Well, she was right. Anyway, you heard me talk about people be'n soul mates, right? Well, I truly believe that cause I knowd from the moment I saw Charlie he was my soul mate. In fact, I had religiously pray'd to God to send me a good man, one that He saw fit for me. And He sent Charlie.

Lord knows I didn't know what I was do'n prior to meeting Charlie. The few times that I did call myself have'n a man, it didn't work out cause we what'n compatible, you know, ev'nly yoked, so the relationships merely lasted a couple of months. However, way before I left Sumner, I made a promise to myself that I wouldn't have any more meaningless relationships with men. In fact, for several years, other than my brothers, the only male relationship I had was in the form of write'n letters to my friend boy, from Mississippi. Country folk refer to a female friend of a girl as her girlfriend but if her friend is a male, he is call'd her friend boy and vice versa. If a male has a friend who is a female, she is his friend girl. The title of girlfriend and boyfriend was reserved for people in a romantic relationship not those merely in a friendship. Me and Sam kept our promise to each other and stay'd in touch through letters. He ev'n stops by for a visit whenev'a he in St. Louis, which ain't often but I always look forward to see'n my buddy. Aside from Charlie, I think Sam know me betta than anybody else. We been friends for so long, you know.

Anyhow, I was dateless for eight, close to nine years, before God allow'd me and Charlie's paths to cross. Chile, when you wait on the Lord, you gotta be patient, He not gon send nobody til the both of yous is ready, spiritually, mentally and emotionally. Likewise, you can't get discouraged if you ain't bless'd with a mate. Still, in all you do, put God first. Remember, God don't bless no mess! Trust in the Lord ev'n though you don't know His master plan. Not er'ybody is chosen to live a married life, some of us remain single by His design. No, my marriage didn't last 'til gold nor our silver anniversary for that matter but I thank God He gave me the opportunity to spend fifteen years in pure happiness and bliss with my Charlie. Also, mind you, I'm very comfortable with the fact that I've been a widow for more than twenty-five years now and I certainly don't have any desire to remarry.

Charlie was my sweet, hard work'n man. In the daytime he drove a delivery truck for the *Wonder Bread Company,* up there on Taylor Avenue but his ev'nens and weekends was pretty much reserved for me, our kids and anybody else's kid he could keep off the streets. Charlie used to organize and coach softball, baseball, basketball and volleyball teams for all ages, men, women, boys, girls and coeds. Er'y year he would apply for and receive a grant from the City of St. Louis to purchase equipment, uniforms, sponsor special events and in the summer time, provide lunches for his team players. A lot of times he would take kids who what'n ev'n on a team to the games so that they could cheer for us. And let me tell you, they would come up with some good cheers. Whenev'a one of our teams was win'n, they would break out with, " Look at the score board and what do you see? The Mighty Jaguars are take'n the lead... Ha Ha Ha.... take'n the lead." Chile, the attitude and stomp, clap rhythm they had to go with that cheer was sumthin' else. It was er'ybody's favorite. You couldn't remain seated, you had'ta stand up and participate in that one. I can't believe I still remember it! Funny how you can remember some thangs for the rest of your life but others you forget as soon as you hear 'em.

Twice a year, long before there was a *Six Flags*, Charlie would take the kids to *Chain of Rocks Park*. The park was located directly across from the Water Plant on Riverview Blvd., sat on top'a the bluff and when you rode the trolley lift you could easily see the Chain of Rocks Bridge. Since the weather in St. Louis is usually too cold by the time October rolls around, Chain of Rocks Park was open from late April to the middle of or end of September, weather permit'n. It was your typical carnival, didn't cost nuth'n to get in but you had to purchase tickets to get on the rides or see the sideshows. Each ride and sideshow cost anywhere from two to four tickets a piece but the City would give us a whole big roll of tickets and we would take a bunch of kids on a fun day. Again, anything to keep 'em off the streets! Charlie used to say, "If you keep 'em busy they won't get in trouble". So you can see why all'a the kids want'd to be "in good" with Charlie. That meant they got to do thangs and go places that many black folks couldn't afford for they chil'ren. But cause of them city grants we was able to make a whole lot of chil'ren happy. Anyhow, Chain of Rocks Park closed around 1975-76 and that's when we start'd take'n the kids to *Six Flags*, a big amusement park with sites in Missouri, Georgia, Texas and California. It may be more'n that, but that's all I can think of right now.

My Charlie was a good look'n, short, muscular man. He sport'd a "six pack" way before they start'd call'n it a "six pack". He was only about 5 foot 4 inches, still taller than me but he didn't take no stuff off nobody. Anytime a child got outta hand, didn't matter how big or small they was, Charlie sho' nuff would put them in they place, quick and in a hurry. Most'a the time all he had to do was give 'em that "you betta straighten up" look and they'd get back right. Chile, all the kids respect'd Charlie, they call'd him "Dad", ev'n they parents call'd him that too. Me, they call'd Miss Pearl but er'ybody always refer'd to Charlie as "Dad". It's sad but for some chil'ren, Charlie was the only father role model they ev'a knowd.

I remember in the fall of 1984 our coed softball team went to Cape Girardeau to play in the state championship. Er'ybody came to support us. The cheerleaders, members of all the other teams, family, friends and hundreds of people we didn't ev'n know. The weather was picture perfect, the crowd was full of energy, and we was win'n 16-3, go'n into the bottom of the ninth inn'n. Life is good! Chile, it was highly unlikely that the other team could hit enuf homeruns and take the lead. So, people start'd scream'n, jump'n up and down, give'n high five's, pour'n water on each other and just plain celebrate'n cause they knowd we'd already won.

When I turn'd to face the dug out to blow Charlie our traditional victory kiss, I saw him grab his chest and fall. In the midst of all the commotion, most people didn't know if he was really hurt or simply play'n around like *Fred Sanford*. I knew otherwise cause I saw the fear in his eyes right before he fell to the ground. I immediately cried out for help and ran straight for the dug out. Luckily, by the time I got there, someone was administer'n CPR but it was too late. The paramedics pronounced Charlie dead at the scene. My Charlie was gone! A few days later the Coroner said he had died instantly of a massive heart attack.

11

"THE KNIGHTS OF PETER CLAVER & LADIES AUXILIARY"

Now, this here, is a picture of my church group. Whenev'a we what'n at home, at a game or practice'n you could find me and Charlie at a church or social event sponsor'd by the *Knights of Peter Claver* or *Ladies Auxiliary*. For me, this organization is like family and that's why I've decided to talk about 'em for a couple of minutes. If you don't wanna hear this, I suggest you hit the "forward" button but I also think you'll enjoy and learn sumthin' if you listen. And, we all know that knowledge is power! Remember, that's exactly why the slaves were forbidden to read and write. The white man didn't want us to have any power ov'a him. So, I quess by now you wonder'n, "what in the world is the *Knights of Peter Claver and Ladies Auxiliary?*" Well actually, it's quite complicated but let me see if I can 'splain it to you real simple like the ABC's.

In the Catholic faith we have saints and in order to be named a saint, simply put, three miracles must be confirm' d by the church. We adopt'd our name from *St. Peter Claver*. He was a Spanish Jesuit priest who would go to the docks, meet the slave ships and help the slaves with they needs. He would tend to they wounds, give 'em food or read scripture to 'em. Whatev'a he could do for 'em without the White man killing him, he would do. The only reason why Whites allow'd him to service the slaves was cause he was a priest, a man of the clothe and to some degree they was scared of God. Anyway, he came under a lot of scrutiny but help'n the slaves was his ministry. He ev'n refer'd to hisself as "Slave to the Negro forever". He baptized thousands. Eventually, help'n the slaves and lepers cost him his life cause he caught a plague from be'n exposed to the diseases they brought with 'em. Chile, he was truly a man of God who knew how to love his brother, ev'n at a time when nobody else loved us.

Initially, the Knights of Peter Claver was created to allow blacks the privilege of purchase'n life insurance cause blacks couldn't afford life insurance through any other means. Yet the *Knights of Columbus*, the largest Catholic fraternal organization in the world, offer'd life insurance to its members, blacks were not allow'd to join. Obviously, it's not like that today but back then that's how it was. So, in 1909 three priest and two laymen founded the *Knights of Peter Claver* in Mobile, Alabama, now Council/Court #1. Today there are about 350 councils/courts and approximately 50,000 members with the women out number'n the men by at least 25%. The *Knights of Peter Claver* and *Ladies Auxiliary* is consider'd the second largest Catholic fraternal organization and we focus our efforts on corporal works of mercy. Mind you, we still offer life insurance policies to all our members.

I'm sure you probably already heard of the *Masons* and *Eastern Stars*, most black folks have. If I'm not mistaken, I believe they refer to themselves as a Protestant fraternal organization but don't be quote'n me on that. Anyway, the *Knights of Peter Claver* and *Ladies Auxiliary* have a different mission than the *Masons* and *Eastern Stars* but both theys organizational structure is kind'a similar. Yes, our memb'ship is open to all races but more'n 98% is African American and er'ybody must successfully complete a secret initiation. But, first and foremost, they must be a practice'n Catholic. Which basically means you gotta satisfy your Catholic duty dure'n the Lenten/Easter seasons. Charlie was a **Sir Knight** and I'm a **Lady of Grace**. To this day, I faithfully pay my annual memb'ship dues and I'm also very active in my Court.

Structurally, ladies belong to a Court and the men have a Council. You cannot have a Court unless a Council already exists but your pastor must first give his approval before a Council can be formed at his church. The organization operates on a local, district and national hierarchy. Programs are decided at the national level but Councils and Courts work with they local church community. Some of the thangs that the Court at my church sponsor is, the Aids Ministry, the Annual Scholarship Fund Fashion Show, the Easter Egg Hunt and Breakfast with Santa. In addition, we also have national observance days where all members are required to "turn out", which means the ladies wear they **all** white uniforms, no slacks, no white stock'ns and no jewelry. We have three national "turn out" days, St. Peter Claver Day, September 9th (or the Sunday closest to that date), Low Sunday (the Sunday follow'n Easter) and Mother's Day.

Charlie was the one who got me start'd in the *Ladies Auxiliary* cause he had already been a member of the *Knights* for a couple of years when I joined the *Ladies Auxiliary*. In fact, now I'm Grand Lady of my court, been elected to this position for the last five years. I could be elected one more time but after that, no more, six years is the max. Of course I'll always remain a Claver but I gotta sit out a term in that position before I can run for office again. I've known some'a the ladies in my court for almost 40 years and we have shared a good part of our lives together. In addition to the *Knights* and *Ladies*, we have a *Jr. Knights* and *Jr. Daughters* division that all our children participated in. We also get together for national conventions and various family functions. Together we done watch'd our chil'ren grow up. So you can see why I say, theys my family too.

You know what? In a couple of months, late November, I'ma be a great grandma when Opal and Amy have them babies. I'm so excited, I can hardly wait! When you think about it, my family is begin'n to resemble the *Energizer* bunny. They keep grow'n and grow'n and grow'n! Chile, I'm truly bless'd.

PART III

"MEM'RIES"

'The task ahead of you is nev'a as great as the power within you.'

12

MY ASSIGNMENT

Before we go any further, I gotta make sho' y'all know who er'ybody is and how they fit in our family. If'n you don't I suggest you look in front'a my bible, on the geneology page, it's all written down in there.

I can't remember if I already told you this, if so, now you'll know twice! Anyway, I been keep'n a journal for a long, long time. Well, last night I was make'n an entry about this here challenge to record current family events and past times since the grandkids ask'd me to. Chile, at first they ev'n want'd me to use a video camera but I said no way, I can barley work *this* tape recorder thang. Anyhow, I accept'd they challenge cause I think it's a good way to keep the family alive and start our own legacy. So, I've decided, for Christmas er'y year, I'm gon give er'ybody a copy of the tape I made that year. If'n God will'n and I'm bless'd with longevity, I would like to make a tape a year for at least another ten or fifteen years, betta yet, more'n that. I'm only seventy-five and most'a my peoples live, way past ninety. Shucks, Reverend Daddy gon be a hundred in a few weeks.

Anyhow, while I was write'n in my journal I got to think'n, *what am I gon talk about for that long? Where can I get enuf stories? I don't know if I can remember all of 'em.* Just as I wrote it, the idea popped in my head, *get the stories from your journals.* People always ax'n me, Pearl, you still keep a journal? Sometimes I wanna say, been keep'n one near bout forty years but instead I say, yea and leave it at that cause most'a the time they just be'n nosey, that's all, try'n to pump me for information.

I remember Tootsie joke'nly once said, " I can't wait for you to die so I can read them journals of yours." My response was classic Moms Mabley, whose to say I'll die 'fore you! It may turn out, *you'll* be a journal entry. "*We buried Tootsie today.*" Then you still won't get a chance to read 'em. Chile, we both fell out laugh'n. For those of you who don't know who Moms Mabley is, she was a colored risqué comedian of the 50's and 60's. Although she seem'd old to me, I think it was more costume than her natural age but I maybe wrong. Howe'va, the next time I'm 'round some people older than me, I'ma ax 'em if they knowd how old she really was.

Mind you, it's been a long time but I still pull them journals out er'y couple of years and use 'em as a learn'n tool to examine how much I've matured spiritually and earthly. In addition to write'n about my feel'ns (nuth'n more than, feel'ns ☺), I briefly record family births and deaths, memorable incidents, vacations and notable events. I said all of that to simply say, I already got the *ultimate* family history right here in my journals. All I need to do now is have my brain see a brief written reminder and then, **BAMM!** I'm good to go. You see I'm a visual learner. Once I see it, then write it, I remember it. And I'm pretty sure I can verbally recall many, if not er'y last one of them journal entries, the pictures will help too.

Ummmph....What type of stories shall I tell y'all while I sit up here on this porch? You see, my goal is for each tape to have a different theme. And also, I been wonder'n, *who should I talk about first?* Oooh, I know a good theme, deception. You know, the stuff my family thought they could get away with, without somebody else find'n out. Like lie'n, cheat'n and steal'n. Mother used to say, "Theys two types of people I stay clear of and that's a liar and a thief. Cause if you lie to me, you'll steal from me." Well, I guess you can say I take after Mother in that respect cause to me, lie'n is bad enuf by itself but if you *volunteer* a lie, that's double trouble in my book. When I ask you a question and you answer with a lie that's one thing but if you merely volunteer'n lies for the heck of it and you lived with me that meant double punishment. If my kids told a lie they knew they was gon be in big trouble but luckily that didn't happen too often. They knew betta than to lie to me. God gives parents special gifts when it come to reer'n chil'ren. As a general rule, most'a the time when kids be'n deceitful, as a gift from God, parents often find out the truth without them ev'n have'n to do any investigative work.

Seem like instead, the truth seeks them out and lands right in they lap when they least expect it.

Deception, things ain't always how they appear to be. It's fiercest weapon is the mouth. Yesterday when I was in church the priest ask'd us, "Ever wonder'd why God gave us two eyes and ears and only one mouth? The priest answer'd, "My theory is, He want'd us to do more listening and acting to His word than participating in evil gossip ". I thought 'bout what the priest said throughout the day and night and I kept come'n back to the same thought, obey God's law. They not ten recommendations or suggestions, they His commandments and He expects us to follow all of 'em but if you focus on these two, *Love the Lord God with all your heart* and *Love your neighbor as thyself,* you will automatically suffice all the others cause the first three have to do with love'n the Lord and the rest of the commandments concern your neighbor.

Since there's only one perfect one, Him, don't think for a minute He don't already know you gon make some bad decisions and mistakes. It's call'd life but if you repent your sins, He promises to forgive you. Remember, His son died for our sins! Parents should start teach'n they children right from wrong at an early age and continue teach'n them throughout they formative years. Chil'ren unconsciously learn by example and hopefully by the time they become adults, they got a strong foundation and ultimately will become saints for the Lord and productive citizens for our communities.

13

"BABY BOY"

For Baby Boy's sake and cause he keep complain'n, he's always last when it comes to my children. I tell him, fool, you was born last, that's why you always last. Anyhow, I'ma start the stories with him. Also on this tape, I plan to talk about a current family or worldly event. Whatev'a's going on in the family or in the world when I get to that part, is what I'm gon talk about, no holds barred. Right now, I have no idea what that's gon be but I'm sure we'll find out soon enuf, won't we?

"Mama, can I go play outside?"

"Outside where?" I questioned Baby Boy.

"Just over across the street to play stickball on the empty lot"

"Don't go nowhere else, you hear me? And don' let the sun go down and you ain't in here. You gon be sorry if'n it do." He was out the door before I finish'd my sentence. Baby Boy never miss'd his curfew because he couldn't stand the punishment that went along with the offense. What's that they say, don't do the crime if you can't do the time. Er'y fifteen minutes late was the equivalent to one full hour in the house. You be'n late for thirty minutes meant you was in the house for two hours.

Each day after school we basically had that same conversation. The name of the games that he intend'd to play would change but he would definitely want to go outside. The house rule was nobody could go anywhere or do anything til all they homework and chores was done, and in that order. Baby Boy would do half his homework dure'n lunchtime or class time so he could get to go outside sooner. Chile, that boy know he used to love to play outside er'y chance he got. He play'd so hard I would look forward to bad weather so he could settle down and rest for a minute. He spent most'a ev'nens and rainy days at the desk in his room or off somewhere by himself curl'd up with a book. He didn't enjoy watch'n T.V. as much as the girls did, he much rather prefer'd read'n and write'n.

They daily chores mainly consisted of routine housekeep'n. Sweep, do the dishes, empty the trash, clean up your bedroom *and* the bathrooms. My kids hated clean'n the bathrooms daily but my response was, you use it er'y day, don't you? If you stop using it, we could stop clean'n it so much! Er'y two weeks we rotated chores. Howev'a, there was one chore that was exclusively assign'd to Baby Boy, and that was mop'n. Reverend Daddy nev'a made me and Tootsie mop when we lived down south and I ain't gon make my girls do it either. Mind you, we all know how to mop and if the floor gets too dirty and a man ain't around, the floor will get mop'd cause I can't stand a dirty house.

Saturday was designated the massive clean'n day at my house. We tackled the BIG jobs on that day. If you got up early, didn't get suck'd into the cartoons and completed all your Saturday chores, you could make it out the house by noon or one, at the latest. On the other hand if you slept late, watch'd cartoons for a couple of hours and slow poked around get'n your chores done, you could end up in the house all day. Didn't faze me one way or the other which option you chose as long as the work got done. Since Charlie died, in addition to Sunday be'n church day, we also designated it "share time with yo' family day" and we did whatev'a the majority of the family want'd to do, which meant you could end up indoors all weekend long without any outside playtime. Dut, dut, dummmm!! No way Baby Boy was have'n that happen to him. It would have been torture for him. To avoid such a fate, Baby Boy would rise early on Saturdays, do his chores and head outdoors to play or roam the shop'n malls for the remainder of the day.

My girls didn't want or need to be outside nearly as much as Baby Boy did. That's one of the gender differences between boys and girls. Perhaps young girls stay inside cause subconsciously they be'n initiated into the whole hair thang that we black women go through. Our hair gots to be look'n fly at all times and surely we ain't gon let the weather catch us by s'prise. I don't care what nobody say, black girls gon keep they hair fix'd. And sometimes that's gon get done before anything else gets taken care of. Fly girls know they gotta look good while they stand'n in line at the bank or check cash'n place. They check might not be but a few hundred dollars but that don't mean they gotta look deprived, gw'on feel like a million bucks! And we sho' know how to cord'nate some hairstyles and outfits, don't we? Chile, they soooo creative! Some of them outfits so ridiculous I have' ta to say to myself, *I know they could'na had a mirror in they dress'n room but I'ma pray they get one real soon so next time, they can take a peek in it 'fore they leave home.*

To me, clean'n house always seem to go by faster if you put on a little music while you do'n it. The best kind of music to play is the songs that you *think* you know the words to. You know, the ones you sing along with ev'n if you *are* sing'n the WRONG words. Seem like once you get to sing'n, you automatically get to tap'n your feet, clap'n your hands, pop'n your fingers and before you know it, you dance'n and clean'n up a storm. Chile, me and my broom two-step so good, I forgets it's only a broom. We be just a spin'n and a twirl'n. I know I lose two pounds er'y time I clean my house dance'n to *Denise Williams* sing'n, *There's nuth'n' better that I like to do...*or *Frankie Beverly* croon'n, *Happy feel'n oh yea! Spread it all over the world...* Of course, I like gospel classics too but yo' exercise is limit'd to only your vocal cords when you clean to gospel music 'cause you can't be dance'n to that type of music. At least I can't! I feel like the only dance that you can do and get away with is the "shout dance" where you run up and down the aisle while Sista Bettye wait for you to fall out from pure exhaustion or, the new peaceful, flow'n, grace liturgical dance. Don't matter no way 'cause I ain't got enuf open space in my house to do either one of those dances. I need to move some of this junk outta here! Let me put that on the "to do" list.

We used to keep the chore list on the back of the door in the pantry. Er'ybody always had they chores listed at-a-glance on that big white poster board with the curled up edges. That way, you knew in advance what was expect'd of you ov'a the weekend. Once a month I'd paste a new calendar on the poster board. This weeks' Saturday schedule call'd for Rubie to wash all the comforters, blankets, sheets, towels and rugs. She was also s'pose to dust the furniture and water the plants. Diamond was assign'd to kitchen detail. That meant pull er'ything out the cabinets, wipe down the canned goods and dishes, change the shelf paper, put er'ything back then repeat the same process in the pantry. Don't forget to do the refrigerator and stove too. Baby Boy was just about finish'd with his chores. He had already assembled and emptied all the trash in the house, swept, mop'd, wax'd and buff'd the live'n room, dine'n room, and kitchen floors. He was put'n the final touches on the entryway and I was change'n the curtains in the dine'n room 'cause those other ones need'd a good wash'n.

"Mama, this the last thing I gotta do then I'm done with everything on my list. You mind if I go hang out wit' my boys at *River Roads Mall?* We wanna check out the honeys and that new movie, R*oger Rabbit*. They got real people and cartoons mixed together in the same movie, talk'n to one another and everything. It's 'pose to be really cool."

"How y'all get'n to the mall, what's the movie rated and whose money you gon spend while you at the mall?" I purposely ignored the phrase "check out the honeys" cause just last week, he thought girls were weird and stupid.

"Bobby's mom said she would take us if you could pick us up?" It's noon now and she'll probably drop us off at one-thirty. The movie is over at five and we should be through watch'n for honeys and ready to come home and eat dinner by seven. And yes, I still got some of the birthday money Uncle Bubba gave me. I got like, $15 and the movie is rated PG, anything else you wanna know? "

"Watch yo' self, don't get smart now. I ain't said you could go yet." Again, I let the comment about the honeys go by without me respond'n.

"You know I'm just play'n Mom". He said as he stood up straight, squared his shoulders, adjusted his imaginary shirt collar, brush'd off his fake blazer and with all seriousness, use'n his best Prince William accent says, "Go ahead Mummy, ask me anything."

"Boy shut up. Stop act'n so crazy. O.k. you can go but I need to be somewhere by sev'n, so if you guys could wrap up your "honey watch'n" by six, it's a deal. I'll pick y'all up in front of the movie theatre at six o'clock sharp. Remind your friends that *this here* taxi waits for no one. If they ain't there, they gon get left. Who else go'n wit' y'all?" I decided not to ask questions about his new view on girls, instead I thought it best to table that for a latter discussion. This was not the time and I could tell he was anxious to get wash'd up, changed and on his way to Bobby's house.

Baby Boy holler'd back as he ran upstairs to take his shower. "Meathead and T.K. gon meet us there but they need a ride back home. They live up the street by the YMCA."

The girls had been awake about an hour but they was just begin'n to move about the house. Diamond spent long spells in the bathroom do'n who knows what and Rubie liked to watch T.V. before she got out of bed to start her chores. She still like that today, always watch'n T.V. As a matter of fact, I call'd her Tuesday night at 8:45 and she said, "I can't talk right now. *American Idol* is on."

Me know'n how much she into the T.V. said, "I'm sorry. I thought it came on at 7:00 and it's 8:45. It should be off by now!"

"It do but it stays on for two hours. I'll call you back and don't ever call me again when it's on."

I thought, excuse me, who wants to look at people sing for two hours anyway but before I could respond, she hung up the phone. I don't understand how people get so wrapped up in a T.V. program, especially a musical. I'd rather pull my fingernails out with tweezers than sit through a musical. Mind you, *American Idol* may be the hottest new T.V. show that er'ybody is talk'n about but I think it's just like that other show they used to have. Oh.... What was the name of that show?....... I know, *Star Search* with *Ed McMahanon*. You know, the sweepstakes guy, maybe y'all to young to remember that. Well, the only difference between *Star Search* and *American Idol* is, *American Idol* has a lot more audience participation and the entire view'n audience can s'posedly vote for the *American Idol* but I say it's all rigged plus the networks get'n paid.

It starts off with auditions in selected cites throughout the United States. Hundreds of thousands of people, with various levels of talent and I do mean extremely various, come for try-outs and they gotta sing a capella in front of judges, who I think are BIG characters in themselves, to win a chance to advance on to California where at least fifty contestants compete. Then the number is cut to twenty and the follow'n week to ten. Each week thereafter someone is eliminated til you have your *American Idol*. Meanwhile they got you run'n to the telephone to vote for the person you think should win and its gonna cost you a couple of dollars on your phone bill. Fool, Hollywood already know who gon win whether you vote or not! Bottom line is.......Who cares???? Don't get me start'd 'bout that stupid T.V. show. We could be spend'n our money on a lot mo' productive things, in the world, than pick'n a star for white America. Theys a bunch of unemployed and hungry black folks walk'n round America er'y day. Why not help them instead? Chile, I get soooo carried away when it come to such foolishness.

What was I talk'n bout anyhow? Uhmmm..........., I know. How Rubie would spend most'a of the morn'n watch'n television while Diamond would be in the bathroom or knocked out, sleep. That Diamond know she like to sleep. Girl like *Rip Van Winkle*, can catch 40 winks anywhere. She wouldn't ev'n get up early with the other kids on Christmas to open her toys. When they would try to wake her she would say, "Leave me alone. Them toys ain't go'n nowhere! They still gon be there when I wake up." Chile, Baby Boy would be *long* gone by the time Diamond and Rubie finish'd and sometimes ev'n start'd they Saturday chores.

After I change the curtains, I head for the kitchen to put on a pot of water so I can make my hot tea. I gots to have my hot tea er'yday. Ev'n though we now got microwaves, I still makes my water on the stove cause to me, it stays hotter much longer than microwave water. You see, I can't drink it unless it's real hot, once it cools off, it tastes different and I don't like it. I enjoy sit'n in the kitchen drink'n my tea cause it's so invite'n and it also reminds me of the kitchen we had in our little house in Sumner. Remember the one I tole you that got burnt up by the Klan. Well, in Sumner, our kitchen ran the length of the house and it was the biggest room in the house. Here, my kitchen is not as long as the entire house but it takes up almost all'a the back portion on the house. This kitchen is deep whereas the other one was long but it's still the biggest room in the house.

Ever notice how black folks entertain in the kitchen. Some of us ev'n got T.V.'s in there. Why when relatives and chil'ren come to yo' house, the first place they head for is the kitchen ask'n, "Whatcha got to eat?" And after you fix 'em sumthin' to eat, y'all gon sit right there and chat. Ain't no need move'n to the dine'n room or live'n room cause this room is the most comfortable. If you think back, the kitchen was the only place the field slaves was allow'd in the big house lessen the massa had sent for you. Ev'n if you was sent fo', you always enter'd through the back door and luckily most'a the time it was close to the kitchen. The smell and possibility that you might get a taste of what's smell'n so good is pure delight for anybody but I imagine ev'n more so to a slave. Also, remember the wise cook was required to feed and care for the sick and injured slaves, which was comfort'n to them. Perhaps that's why we consider the kitchen a safe haven today. For generations and generations, black folk have conjugated in the kitchen for food and fellowship. I always knew that was a "black thang" but I nev'a thought about *why* til now… makes a lot of since though, don't it?

Chile, I been live'n in this house for ov'a forty years. It's the only place I ev'a lived since I been in St. Louis. I was finally able to get all the bathrooms and kitchen remodeled about ten years ago but on this particular morn'n, the kitchen was still in it's original condition. When you walk in, the first thing you saw was the back door. It was positioned just so you could make a clean get away through the house. When I first saw the kitchen on my first day in the house, I thought, whoev'a design'd this house must'a want'd a clear shot outta here in case of emergency but over the years I grew to associate that back door with the back door in my old room in Sumner, you know the one er'ybody used as a short cut to go *use it.* In this kitchen you can do about three cartwheels 'fo you get to the back door. I'm not good with precise measurements. Anyhow, you get the picture… it's BIG in here! Back then, half of the room was cover'd in paneling and the other half was all windows. I eventually took the paneling down but I kept all'a them beautiful windows.

My favorite place in the whole house is my think window. It makes me feel closer to God with all that sunshine pour'n in on me. I didn't use to use the window as often as I use it now cause when you have kids in the house you tend not to have much quiet time, you always busy or on the go. The formal name for the window is a "bay" window but I affectionately call it my "think" window. It's decorated with this thick black cushion and a lot of pillows cover'd in various Kente cloth. When I sit in the window with my tea, bible, book, magazine or just me, hours seem to pass by in minutes. Usually, in the ev'nens I sit outside on the front porch but morn'ns are reserved for the think window. This is where I give praises to the Lord and plan out my day, meditate or simply enjoy the view of my flower gardens in the back yard.

"How I look, Mom?"

Was someone speak'n to me or was I in a trance in my think window? If I meditate hard and long enuf I can imagine myself in all sorts of scenarios and sometimes I mix reality with trance. Like when the telephone or doorbell rings, I hear it but then again I don't hear it cause it's incorporated into the trance. It's important to note that this was only my fourth or fifth time sitting in the think window so I what'n as experienced as I am now at stop'n the trance whenev'a interruptions occur.

"Mom, you O.K.? Baby Boy repeated. I ask'd you, how I look?"

This was definitely no trance, I heard Baby Boy's voice for real. I opened my eyes to find my son dress'd in his favorite red outfit but it seem'd as though he had aged a couple of years. I look'd at my watch and s'mised it had only been thirty minutes since he went to take a shower. But sumthin' was definitely different about him. I did a double take... what's different? Think, think….Oh, his hair! How did it change so fast? Or was it that I just noticed him. Yeah, now that I think about it, all morn'n he had this plastic bag on his head but I thought it was to keep the solvents and dust out of his hair while he did the floors. You know, he's always been particular bout his hair, his son Onyx just like him in that respect . I would'a nev'a thought he would change his hair…..

Baby Boy's hair had transform'd from a soft fluffy big afro to this here drippy wet look'n doo that was somewhat curly but had a lot of straight ends. Look'd like somebody set a wet cat on top'a his head. It came close to a Curl but it was not the true replica of the hairstyle that I had seen a few times before. However, I nev'a saw it look quite *this* bad. I initially saw the style a couple of weeks ago when I was at the beauty shop and I had already decided this was not the style for me or mine. Anyhow, guess I should'a took the time to tell my children how I felt 'cause obviously at least one of them didn't share my feel'ns. So you can imagine how shock'd I was to see my thirteen year-old son stand'n in front of me sport'n a Curl. And one I didn't give my money nor my permission fo' him to get.

Actually, I felt as though I was in the *Twilight Zone,* exist'n in another dimension, sumthin' not of this earth. Is this really happen'n? Lord, what has this boy gone and did now! I had to sneak and pinch myself to make sure this was really happen'n. Whowhatwhenandwhere was the questions that came to my mind in one word and obviously my facial expression said the same cause Baby Boy answer'd all of my questions without me ev'n ask'n a single one of 'em.

"I paid for the kit with my own money, Diamond put it in for me and honestly Mom, I didn't think it would matter to you. The only instructions you ev'a gave me about my hair was for me to make sure I look presentable. Most of the time I wear it short but when I started let'n it grow out a few months ago I made sure that I kept it lined-up so I would look "presentable." It's still lined-up but now it's long and I got curls for the girls too. Hold up Mom,.... let me get my camera so you can take a picture of me"

He was so proud of his new hairdo, I didn't have the heart to tell him, his curl was not quite right and it definitely was not presentable. Instead, I suggest'd he get the scissors so that I could ev'n it up a bit on the top, shorten the sides and leave the back long. He was reluctant at first but when he saw I what'n play'n, he got up and fetched them scissors. It took me about fifteen or twenty minutes but I had him look'n pretty descent after I eliminated some of the straight ends and wiped off a lot of that gooey gunk he call'd activator. Me and the girls never wore a curl. We thought it too messy, stain your clothes and your linen! In fact, nobody in my house would let Baby Boy sleep in they bed. I ev'n used to hav'ta make him wash his linen separate from the rest of us cause we didn't want that activator stuff all on our sheets and pillow cases.

While wait'n for Baby Boy to return with the camera, I got to think'n, that explains why when I came home last night, the house smelled faintly of rotten eggs. At the time, I didn't think too much about it then cause I knowd tomorrow was regular Saturday clean'n day and the smell'a be gone after then. Howev'a now I find out, Diamond been do'n hair and this time experiment'n on Baby Boy. Up 'til now she only used the wig headstand I bought at the beauty school flea market for her to practice on. I'm sure Baby Boy didn't hav'ta do too much convince'n to get her to do it though. She was constantly do'n sumthin' or another to somebody's hair all throughout her high school years. Seem like Baby Boy wore a curl for a couple years but he nev'a did let Diamond put it in again. Rather he used to like to go to that place where er'ybody was get'n they curls done at, *Airport Curl Center* on St. Louis Avenue, in between Union and Goodfellow Blvds. Johnny, the owner, was famous for produce'n the best curls in St. Louis.

I would hav'ta say outta all of my children, Baby Boy resembles his daddy the most, particularly in his stance. Both him and Charlie share that stereotypical mean look'n bulldog stature but they also got extra charm'n good looks. Put you in mind of someone with a Mike Tyson body and a Brian McKnight face. Just don't seem like they face s'pose to go with they body. Anyhow, after I finish'd cut'n his hair, Baby Boy hurried up and ran to see how he look'd in the full length mirror that hung on the back of the door of the downstairs bathroom. He didn't hav'ta say nuth'n bout how much he liked it cause when he came out, he was grin'n from ear to ear. I had to admit, that drippy wet hairdo was very become'n on him and it also made him look mature.

When I saw Baby Boy again I thought either my eyes were deceive'n me or was there the faintest resemblance of a mustache? I'm will'n to bet this was first time I saw Baby Boy as a teenager and not my precious little Baby Boy. All at once, I realized, Baby Boy done growd up and reach'd puberty. Now, he desperately wants and needs to be accept'd by his peers. If you think back to when you was a child, the thought of be'n embarrassed at school or in public was and *still* is devastate'n to any teenager and likewise would'a been the same for Baby Boy. Chile, I'm so glad I cut his hair cause if I had'na shaped up his hair, he would'a sho'nuf been the laugh'n stock of the whole school.

I unconsciously went in the house, walk'd over to the mantle and pick'd up the picture I took of him that day in his favorite red outfit with his new "curls for the girls". Oh Jesus, Mary and Joseph, it's hot in here. Im'a hav'ta turn on the air and go back outside til it cool down some. I took the picture back outside with me.

To this day, Baby Boy beg me to take this picture down off the mantle cause can't nobody look at it without laugh'n….. Chile, he had on a pair of red *parachute* pants. Back then we call'd them parachute cause they tend'd to be a bit blousy and the fabric look'd like the same material parachutes was made out of. Who ev'a thought of them pant's, must'a made a whole bunch'a money off black folks. Er'ybody had to have a pair of parachute pants, the mo' zippers on 'em, the betta. Same thang hold true for that red, trimmed in black *Members Only* jacket he was sport'n. And now that his hair was cut into a shag he had the same haircut as that *Michael Jackson* (Off the Wall, pre-cosmetic surgery), T-shirt he had on with them red Chuck Taylor high top Converse All Star tennis shoes. If you glance at the picture, you think he a member of the 1980's pop group *Force M D's*. Chile, my kids love to make fun of this here picture. It's truly a classic family photo that gets funnier and funnier as the years go by. I dare you to look at it and not laugh! They say styles repeat themselves but this is one style I hope nev'a come back.

14

"DIAMOND"

Anyhow, after I snapped the picture, Baby Boy gave me a quick kiss on the cheek and head for the door. "Thanks for the fly haircut Mom. See you at six in front of the movie theatre. And I know, tell my friends you ain't wait'n fo' nobody."

"You got that right! Be good and mind your manners. Love ya." As usual, he was out the door 'fore I finish'd my goodbye. Well, I decided I was gon go back to my think window since he had interrupt'd my much need'd meditation time.

Hold up y'all….wait, is that the phone? Who would be call'n me this late? I gotta stop the story and go inside for a minute. I poked my head in the front do' so I could see the T.V. cause I like how it show on the screen who call'n you. Caller-ID on the T.V. Chile I tell you, technology sho' is sumthin' else, ain't it? I can 'member when we didn't ev'n have no T.V. or electricity when we first got that house in Sumner, Mississippi.

Lawd have mercy, it's Diamond! On account I was rush'n to get to the phone and at the same time try'n not to drop this picture in my hand, I forgot to shut off the tape recorder. I often forget simple things like that and I also sometimes talk to myself, but that don't mean I'm crazy. So, I said "Self, wonder what Diamond wants. She usually only call in the morn'n, sumthin' must be up for her to be call'n me this late in the day."

I answer the phone, "Hey Pooh." That's my affectionate greeting for all girls, whether theys my daughters, nieces or granddaughters. The

boys I call baby but the girls I call pooh. Er'ybody except my daughter
in-law, Peaches. Don't worry, I'm work'n on that…I regularly ask God
to soften my heart when it come to her. Mind you, my heart's not all
the way soft yet but it's a whole lot softer than it used to be.

"Hi, Mommie." Diamond replies in that familiar tone. I like the
fact that both my daughters *still* call me Mommie. It's so sweet. Anyhow,
whenev'a she ain't feel'n well or she depress'd about sumthin' or try'n'
to get folks to donate money, she reverts back to this childlike voice.
Actually, I think the voice is rather annoy'n come'n from a person
her age but what can I say, I'ma be here for my child no matter what,
whiney voice and all. Howev'a on the flipside, she tends to be a bit more
nicer to people when she use'n this voice but that's just 'cause she wants
er'ybody to have pity on her and then, that way they will flourish all
theys attention and money to her. Smart uh? I nev'a said she was stupid,
just selfish. She is queen bee when it comes to manipulate'n people. I tell
y'all, I'm always pray'n fo' her to change them evil ways of hers.

Anyway, I just listened. I decided I was gon play it cool and not let
on how concern'd I was that she was call'n me so late. But believe me, I
knew sumthin" was up.…. call it a mother's intuition if you want.

"How was your day?", she asks. Chile, Diamond didn't give me a
chance to answer fo' she start'd in on the real reason why she call'd. She
continued, "Mine was not that good. Actually Mommie, I haven't been
feel'n like myself for the last couple of weeks. You might think I'm over
reacting but I think something is really wrong with me." This time she
sound sincere, nuth'n at all like her manipulative self but then again,
you gotta remember, Diamond got a tendency to exaggerate, she good
for come'n within inches of flat out lie'n to you.

"Sumthin' like what? And why you say that?" I ask'd as calmly as
possible but I also thought, *don't be beat'n' around the bush with me,
come right out and tell me exactly what you want me to know.* I hate it,
oops, I'm sorry, God. I really dislike, (hate is such a strong word) when
people build up someone's anxiety in a sensitive conversation, especially
when you talk'n bout the well be'n of one'a mine. It makes me so very
uncomfortable and I wanna get the conversation ov'a with as quickly as
possible. For the record, if you ev'a got sumthin' important to tell me,
don't be drag'n thangs out when you come tell me, just tell me, O.K?

She still sound sincere when she say, "I get tired easily so therefore,
I'm tired all the time. Mommie, seem like er'y day I'm loos'n more

energy. I'm constantly moody and also I been losing weight like crazy. I've lost almost 8 pounds in the last month and I ain't ev'n trying to, just don't have an appetite no more." Lately, I have to make myself eat sumthin' cause I know my body needs nourishment in order to survive." I thought, *Pooh, ain't no need to put you on the critical care list just yet.*

Instead, I say, "Sounds to me like perhaps you go'n through the change of life. As you get older you get loss of energy, tired, moody, change in appetite but most women gain weight, you lucky, you losing weight. All these things are signs of menopause but we shouldn't forget, it could also be sumthin'' else, maybe ev'n sumthin'' life threat'n. Oh, *I should'na said that. I don't want to make her more scared than what she already is.* I quickly clean'd it up with, "But the chances of that happen'n is slim to none. How old are you, 36? Well, that is kind'a young to be have'n menopause. Perhaps you need to get that check'd out. I'd rather you be safe than sorry. Have you seen any doctors? And what does that doctor husband of yours hav'ta say about all this?"

"He's a pediatrician and they specialize in children", she told me. "I haven't said anything to him about it. Besides, I wasn't thinking it was anything serious anyway. You probably right, I'm just getting older that's all."

I had to remind her, "Don't use your prefer'd listen'n skills with me Ms. Diamond. I also said that it's betta to be safe than sorry. You need to make a doctor's appointment to be sure ain't nuth'n else go'n on in there." I point'd to my own stomach area as if she could see me through the phone. I hear they already got that type of technology available but I know for a fact that Diamond don't have that kind of equipment at her house, at least not yet. "If you need a good doctor, you can use my internist, Dr. Poepsil. Normally, I go to black doctors but this one is a white man. My black gastroenterologist, Dr. Haithcock, recommend'd him to me. Said he was *his* personal internist and that he was thoroughly pleased with him as his doctor. So, I decided to start go'n to my stomach doctor's doctor. He been my doctor now for the last 20 years or so. I really like him cause he take time with you. Yo' visit ain't all rush'd like at some doctors' offices. Rather, he asks how you been and what's go'n on with cha in general and what bring you here today? He genuinely listens to what you say is wrong, chat about the recent events in your life, examines you and then he tells you what he thinks could be wrong with you as well as discuss a course of action to correct the ailment. You gotta understand *and* be in agreement with his plan befo' he'll proceed. He's my kind'a doctor, we work well as a team, I ask questions and he give me answers that I can comprehend. Also, he got the nicest staff, they always so pleasant yet professional."

"O.K. Mommie, I promise I'll call your doctor tomorrow and make an appointment. Diamond immediately changed the subject. "Don't forget Reverend Daddy's birthday is only three months away? He gon be what, a 100 years old or sumthin' like that? We need to do sumthin' to mark the occasion."

"Chile, what you talk'n bout, that's *my* daddy. You know good and well I'm very much aware of when his birthday is. I was think'n about it just the other day. Instead of us get'n together in St. Louis like we do once a month, I figured in June we could all get together in Atlanta for a big centurion celebration. That way Reverend Daddy won't hav'ta do no travlin' and it also gives er'ybody plenty time to get they dollars together." Since Diamond is good at plan'n stuff and I know she got these health issues, need sumthin' to keep her mind occupied, I ask'd her, "Why don't you find us a hotel and restaurant in Atlanta that can accommodate all of us. It ain't got to be nuth'n real fancy but it's got to be clean and inexpensive. I'll send out a email to er'ybody give'n them the heads up on what we plan'n on do'n for Reverend Daddy's 100th birthday."

You know, I might not be familiar with record'n devices but I am comfortable with computers. Baby Boy bought me a new computer and I been anxious to use it but decided I was gon concentrate on finish'n my legacy tape but this be just the reason I need to fire that puppy up now.

When Diamond spoke next, her voice was back to her normal snobbish tone. "I'll see what I can come up with but I'll tell you right now the hotel is going to cost at least $75-$100 or more a night. Depending on the number of people going, I may be able to get us a cheaper rate at a real nice place. In the email make sure you tell er'y body to RSVP to you. You know, respond if they plan on attending and they should tell us approximately how many people they bring'n with them."

I wanna tell her, *Girl, I know what RSVP mean* but instead I ignored her again. I see she back to her usual Ms. Know It All and er'ybody else stuck on stupid self. Boy, that didn't take long, did it? *Well,* I thought as I end'd the call, *that's enuf for me.* I can't take too much of Diamond in one day but she still my child and like any other mother, I don't won't nuth'n bad to happen to any of my chil'ren. Good or bad, I love 'em all just the same. Remember they come through you, they are not you and you can't be responsible for they actions once they grown.

As soon as I hung up the phone with Diamond, I lock'd up the house and head straight for the computer room. Earlier in the week Baby Boy had put my new computer together but I had yet to use it. I been want'n to play around with it but unfortunately, that won't happen tonight. Once I finish send'n this email, I'ma go get ready fo' bed, didn't realize how tired I really am.

Good night! I'll finish Baby Boy's story tomorrow.

15

"BABY BOY"

I love this weather! It's too hot to sit outside in the daytime but once 7 o'clock rolls around, it's nice and breezy on this porch. Last night while I was lay'n in bed think'n bout where I left off in Baby Boy's story, I thought it might be a good idea to make Reverend Daddy's birthday celebration this year's current event on the legacy tape. Chile, not many people live to be a hundred. A centurion celebration could easily be classified as both a family and a worldly event.

Anyhow, let me get back to Baby Boy's story. When I got to the mall to pick up Baby Boy and his buddies I was delighted to see that er'ybody was where they was s'pose to be. T.K., Bobby and Emanuel aka "Meathead" climb'd in the backseat while Baby Boy got in the front seat and immediately began adjust'n his seat to the prefer'd "thunder cat" lean position.

"Hold up man. My knees right here. You can't be lay'n down like that" Bobby scolded Baby Boy.

"I'm sorry" was all he said in reply.

We rode for over five minutes in silence. Normally the boys would be engross'd in conversation and give'n each other high five's and all but tonight er'ybody was unusually quiet. My motherly instincts kick'd in and suggest'd, *sumthin' happen'd at the mall but ain't nobody say'n nuth'n.* I was gonna hav'ta be clever with my question'n in order to get the information that I want'd. I began gently.

"So, how was the movie?"

"It was a'ight." "I thought it was awesome." "I wanna see it again," were the responses that came from the backseat. But up front, Baby Boy didn't say nuth'n. He was stare'n out the window, obviously deep in thought.

"What about you Baby Boy? You were so hyped up earlier. Didn't you like the movie? I ask'd in hopes of break'n his concentration.

"Yeah Ma, it was cool," Baby Boy answer'd nonchalantly.

"Why the long face? You should be happy. You got to see the movie you want'd to see and you also got to "check out" some honeys. I figured that last line would definitely bring a smile to his face, but no chance, he remained sullen. Baby Boy, you feel'n alright?" I ask concern'd.

When I turn to look at Baby Boy, I noticed sweat beads on his fo'head. He barley spoke above a whisper when he replied, "My stomach don't feel too good right now. I think I ate too much junk today." Instinctly, I put my hand on his fo'head to see if he had a temperature. He was not hot but he was, rather clammy. Using the same tone as I would if I was speak'n to a puppy or a small child I said, "When we get home, you go try and boo boo and I'll fix you a big glass of 7-UP to settle your stomach." The boys in the backseat roar'd with laughter. Oops! I made the parental mistake of embarrass'n my child in front of his friends. I thought, *Oh well, he'll get ov'a it* but I did try to soften the blow for his sake.

"I don't know what y'all laugh'n at. I'm sure y'all mamas give you white soda and make you go the bathroom too when your stomach hurt. Don't be front'n with me!"

It was 6:40 PM by the time I drop'd all'a the boys off and got Baby Boy tucked in his bed. I took his temperature again but this time I used a real thermometer. I had to make sure he didn't need any Tylenol before I left to go to my Claver dinner meet'n. By the time I arrived at the hotel I had less than five minutes to spare. Luckily I had already copied the agenda and related materials and only had to pass er'ything out. Therefore, I was on time and better yet, all was a success. The food was good and the meet'n was productive. When I arrived home about 9:30, I found er'ybody sound asleep in they beds.

The next morn'n I woke up as usual around 6:00 AM, showered, put on my robe and went to fix me a cup of tea. Yeah, a few minutes in the think window with my bible is always relax'n. Mass wasn't til 10:00 AM but I also like to have time to straighten up the house and sometimes ev'n fix us a light breakfast before we leave. Accord'n to Catholic ritual, there should be at least thirty minutes between the time you last ate and the time you take communion. So as long as we finish eat'n by 9:45 AM, we arrive at mass on time and still be in compliance with the food restrictions. After mass we usually did what ev'a we had decided on as a group that morn'n. This week it was Baby Boy's turn to make a suggestion we could vote on. He rarely want'd to do anything other than go out to eat. Which was fine with me cause for the last two Sundays we been at the Cardinal's baseball park, bake'n in the sun and eat'n nasty ballpark food. Mother used to say, "It's not nasty, *you* just don't like it."

Anyway, I had a busy week and was in desperate need of a nutritious Sunday meal complete with air conditioning. Plus, when we go out to eat, we get back home by two, three o'clock at the latest, and then you still got the whole ev'nen free to yourself. Yes, I was definitely gonna vote in favor of us go'n out to eat after mass.

While I was put'n water in the teapot I noticed a message on the kitchen desk. Since I was so tired last night, I didn't ev'n think about check'n the messages. We didn't have no Call Notes or Caller ID back then but we did always keep a pad and pencil, our own message center, next to the desk phone in the kitchen. All that was required was for the person who answer'd the phone was to simply write the message on the note pad and placed it back on the desk. The house rule was to look on the desk for your messages. There was no need for you to go 'round ask'n if anybody call'd you. As soon as I pick'd up the piece of paper, I recognized Diamond's handwriting.

Mommie,
Sam call'd. He'll be in town til Monday. Call him at the Adams Mark Hotel,
432-3000, Room 319.

XOXOXOXO
Diamond

Oh, my God! I hadn't *heard* from Sam in way ov'a a year and the last time I *saw* him was at Charlie's funeral. I'm s'prise'd I ev'n remember see'n him at all that day. Chile, it was so many people there. All the pews was fill'd to capacity. A lot of people had to stand up in the back of the church. Afterwards, I adamantly refused to leave my room or converse with anyone, unless absolutely necessary, for about a month after Charlie's death. I grieved heavily and ultimately turn'd into a recluse. Although Sam respect'd my wishes and stay'd away throughout the whole ordeal, he also made sure his presence was known. No, he didn't come by the house or call but er'y three or four days I would get a greet'n card in the mail from him. The message was always uplift'n and spiritual. Strangely enuf you might find it hard to believe but, Sam and I can go months without any contact and we will still be lifetime friends, no matter what. You know, we been share'n secrets ev'a since that time I patch'd him up in Sumner.

It's already been more than a year, so I'm sure a few more hours won't hurt none. I'll call Sam when we get back from our Sunday outing. If all goes well, we'll be home by three and still have time to visit with Sam. Oddly, for the last couple of days I been have'n a taste for a drink. Perhaps I'll kill two birds with one stone by invite'n him ov'a for dessert and a margarita.

Ohhhhh…..Excuse me, but I just got the weirdest chill and immediately, I thought of Diamond. Uhmmmmm…….that was strange. Maybe I should go inside and get my sweater. It is get'n a little chilly out here and I don't want my ar-tha-ri-tus to start act'n up. Hold on a minute while I go in the house……PAUSE………O.K………RECORD.

As usual, Baby Boy was the first one to come downstairs. We was s'pose to arrive at church a few minutes early that day cause Baby Boy was on the schedule to serve mass. Traditionally, the Catholic Church assigns altar boys to assist the priest with they many preparations throughout the mass. All of Tootsie's boys were altar boys too. Nowadays, both boys and girls can be *altar servers* but back then they only allow'd boys, hence *altar boy*. The minimum requirement to become an *altar server* is to have *received* the Sacrament of Holy Communion and successfully completed altar server train'n. Catholics have a total of sev'n Sacraments/Rites that we strive to receive from the beginning of life til death. They are baptism, reconciliation (commonly known as confession), first communion, confirmation, marriage, holy orders, and the last rite, anointing of the sick. For cradle Catholics, like my children for instance, they received they first four rites by the time they was sixteen. (Obviously, converts can *and* do receive sacraments at different ages). Whereas the first four Sacraments are mandatory, the last three are considered optional. Well, at least two of 'em anyway, marriage and holy orders. Chile, all us gon die but not er'ybody gon get married or become a priest or nun.

"How you feel'n this morn'n, Baby Boy? I ask.

"A whole *lot* better than I did yesterday. As soon as I drank that 7-up you left for me, I went right to sleep and didn't wake up til this morning when I had to go pee," Baby Boy answer'd.

Don't think for a minute I done forgot how strange Baby Boy was act'n in the car last night. I'm not convinced a stomach ache was all he was suffer'n from. I have a feel'n he hide'n sumthin' else. As I start'd formulate'n the sequence of questions that I was gon ask, Diamond and Rubie came in the kitchen and unknowingly interrupted the moment. I look askance at Baby Boy and sit on the edge of the think window. He immediately hunch his shoulders and arch his eyebrows as if to say, "What???" But instead of respond'n, I merely sighed.

"Good morning," Diamond mumbled under her breath, without ev'n look'n in any particular direction. See'n as though she was stand'n in front of the refrigerator with the door wide open, I wasn't sure if she was talk'n to me, Baby Boy or the refrigerator but just the same, I answer, "Morn'n Pooh." I didn't say nuth'n else to her cause I know how irritable Diamond can be. Like most kids and unlike Rubie, she didn't like to talk to people in the morn'n. Howev'a, if she did feel like talk'n, you'd know cause she'd lead the conversation.

"Hi Mommie, how was your meeting last night? Rubie sweetly ask'd as she planted a juicy kiss to my cheek on her way to grab a bagel out the plastic bag on the kitchen counter. I closely watched as she sliced the bagel and drop'd it in the toaster. Afterwards, she stood impatiently behind Diamond who was *still* stand'n in front of the refrigerator. Finally, Diamond decided on the watermelon. Thankful that she had stepped aside, Rubie took the cream cheese and jelly out, put them next to the toaster and sat down at the table for a silent prayer. I waited til she was finish'd befo' I respond'd.

"It was a very good meet'n. Thanks for ask'n and good morn'n to you too Rubie." Anxious for the conversation to move along, I continue, "I don't know bout y'all but I'm kind'a tired and wanna get home early. So, Baby Boy what you got in mind for us to do today?" The aroma of Rubie's bagel was smell'n so good, I decide I'm gon fix me a slice of raisin bread and another cup of tea. It was only 9:30, we still had fifteen minutes before we had to leave. That's plenty of time to munch on some toast and finish dress'n.

"Let's go to *Lee's Family Restaurant*," Baby Boy suggest'd. Much to my delight I might add. You see, *Lee's* (not the fried chicken place) is a All You Can Eat Chinese buffet that got crab legs on it. *And*, we could be back home by three o'clock.

"*Lee's* it is", I declared befo' anybody could object. There was no use pretend'n to be diplomatic and vote cause whether they liked it or not, I was enforce'n dictatorship this week. That's another one of the benefits of be'n a parent **or** president of the United States. You always got veto power ov'a er'ybody. Just ask George W. Bush, cause ain't nobody vote to go to war on Iraq but him.

Right after mass we head straight to *Lee's*. And chile let me tell ya, we ate up some food. I'm talk'n bout fried rice, egg foo yung, sweet and sour chicken, steamed rice, vegetables and of course, crab legs with lots of melted butter. By the time two o'clock rolled around, we was sit'n back, pick'n our teeth and belch'n under our breath as only a good meal can make you do. Fortunately, I was able to persuade the kids to hold off on dessert til this ev'nen since we was invite'n Sam ov'a but I did let 'em get another soda.

When we got back home it was about 2:45 PM. The girls said that they was gone chill out for a minute and Baby Boy said he had some homework to finish ov'a Bobby's house. After change'n my clothes and relax'n for a few minutes, I decided to give Sam a call.

"Adams Mark Hotel. How can I direct your call?," the hotel operator ask'd.

"Room 319 please," I said.

Sam answer'd in his business voice, "Good afternoon. This is Ashley Wilcox"

"Well, well what brings you to this fine city of ours?," I ask without ev'n bother'n to introduce myself cause I knew he recognize my voice. And sure enuf, he did.

"Pearl Ann Johnson, it sure is good to hear your voice. How you been holding up? Are the girls doing o.k? What about Garnet? Have you gone back to work yet? You need anything?" Sam ask'd one question after another befo' I could ev'n answer the first question.

"Which question you want me to answer first," I jokingly said and we both fell out laugh'n. "How 'bout you come ov'a tonight for some dessert and one of my famous margaritas. That way you'll get a chance to see the kids and we can do some catch'n up. I haven't seen you since Charlie died. Anyway, what brings you to town, business or pleasure?"

"Unfortunately neither, but rather a necessity. You see, my father died and I had to make the final arrangements." Sam said it so matter factly. I didn't respond at first cause I was shocked then I thought, *why he making arrangements in St. Louis when his father live in Biloxi, Mississippi?* My silence must'a said it all cause he continued, "Captain Wilcox was in St. Louis when he died but the services will be in Biloxi. I'm here to escort the body home." Sam always refer'd to his father as "Captain Wilcox" and he never show'd any emotion whenev'a he talk'd about his family, which was rare. I know he loved his family cause we talk'd about it once but I also know they was not allow'd to show emotions in the Wilcox household cause it was considered a sign of weakness. "I'm not leaving town til tomorrow night. When would you like for me to come ov'a?", Sam ask'd.

"Oh, Sam I'm so very sorry to hear about your father pass'n. Me and my family will be sure to pray for the repose of his soul. If there is anything I can do to ease your pain, please don't hesitate to ask". Sam was uncomfortable talk'n about his family so after my short condolences, I answer'd his question. "Look, it's almost 3:30, why don't you come ov'a about 7:00. Anything special you want for dessert?"

"Whatever you fix is fine with me. Quite as it's kept, you don't have to prepare anything. It's treat enough just for me to see you and the kids again. I'll see you at 7:00. Bye now", Sam end'd the conversation.

I placed the phone back in the cradle and wonder'd what was I gonna do about dessert. What would go good with margaritas? Ohhhhhhh…I know, a slice of Key Lime pie. I can taste it right now. Once I tell the kids what time Sam'll be here, I'll run down to *Straub's* and get one of they homemade pies.

I found Diamond and Rubie in the living room watch'n T.V.

"Sam will be here at sev'n, please make yourself available and your room presentable", I announced.

When I got to Baby Boy's room I was s'prise'd to see that he was already gone but at least his room was *almost* presentable. He only had a pair of shoes on the floor and a sweater and sweatshirt on the bed. Otherwise, er'ything else was in its proper place.

Baby Boy kept his sports clothes on his closet shelve. So, I folded up the sweater and placed it in his dresser drawer. Then I walk'd ov'a to the closet to put the sweatshirt up. I thought I saw sumthin' different on the closet floor back in the corner but then again I didn't pay it too much attention. Howev'a when I came back in the closet to bring the shoes, I spot'd a new pair of tennis shoes, mind you, that I did not buy. *Question*---Where did they come from? My kids knowd they was not allow'd to bring anythang home or accept gifts that I didn't know bout fo'hand. For instance, don't tell me Jimmy gave you that bike cause I'm gon say, well take it back cause you can't have it unless I talk to Jimmy's parents first. I'm sho' he didn't buy that bike, so how he gon give it away? Also, I nev'a allow'd my children to borrow things from other kids.

16

"BABY BOY'S BLUES"

Since Baby Boy wasn't home, I decide I was gonna ask the girls if they knew how the shoes got here. "I was clean'n up Baby Boy's room and ran across these new blue Nike tennis shoes. Do you girls know how they got there or who they belong to?" I ask Diamond and Rubie.

Both of them act'd like they was so engross'd in the television that they didn't hear me. Sometimes kids make you yell at 'em. So, this time I raised my voice when I ask'd the question.

"WHERE DID THESE SHOES COME FROM?" I demand'd to know.

Diamond look'd away from the television and said, "I don't know Mommie. This the first time I ever saw 'em.

"What about you Rubie. You know where these came from?" I ask. I knew if Rubie knew the answer she would surely tell. Diamond and Baby Boy used to tease her 'bout not be'n able to keep a secret. Telegraph, telephone, tele-Rubie, if she know er'ybody else would know eventually. Rubie wouldn't just volunteer your information but if someone ask'd her, she was sho' nuff gon tell. Ain't no way she was gon get in trouble for sumthin' she didn't do. She still a *Miss Goody Two Shoes* to this day!

"Alls I know is those are the shoes that Baby Boy had on when he came home from the mall last night. I saw him run upstairs and hide 'em before you came up to take his temperature. I also ov'a heard him on the phone with Bobby talking bout how easy it was to get 'em and how he was gon get some more too! He tried them on and walked right outta the store without paying nothing for 'em. Bobby got some too, but at a different store." Rubie rattled off.

"As soon as Baby Boy come through that door, send him to me", I instructed the girls. "And don't tell him what it's about either", I added.

I took the shoes with me back to my room. Fortunately, I was able to find a store tag on the bottom of the shoe. I plan'd on call'n them when I get back from get'n the pie but first I need to talk to Bobby's mother. Martha and I had been friends for a long time. Since we shared similar values and morals, I knew she would wanna know what her boy done been up to. After I told her what Rubie had told me and also what I was plan'n to do, I then ask'd her to wait and send Baby Boy home in about an hour cause I wanna make a quick run before I confront'd him. She agreed and I left for *Straub's*.

When I got back home it was almost 4 o'clock. Stress tends to make me eat and boy did I feel some stress come'n on. So, I bought two pies, a Banana Cream and a Key Lime pie. I put both of them in the refrigerator. Diamond and Rubie had fallen asleep in the live'n room and I didn't want to wake them so I tip-toed up the stairs. I had to do sumthin' in response to Baby Boy's steal'n adventure befo' Sam got here. I call'd the store and ask'd to speak to the manager on duty. I commenced to tell'n her how I had found out my son stole some merchandise from they store and that I was bring'n him back to return it. I also ask'd the manager to be really hard on him. She agreed to be tough but said that she would not press charges. I told her we would be there within the hour. When I hung up, I call'd Bobby's house to make sure Baby Boy was on his way home (to trial).

About five minutes later, he came in all happy and yell'n as usual. "Hey er'ybody, I'm home. What time Sam come'n ov'a?"

"Seven o'clock. Come up here, I got sumthin' to show you", I holler back.

When he walk'd in my room and saw them Nikes on my bed, he knew he was busted. His eyes got as big as half dollars and he start'd fidgeting with his hands. A true indication of one be'n caught red hand'd. "I'ma ask you one time and I want the truth, where did these shoes come from? I questioned Baby Boy through clinched teeth and a pierce'n glare.

"The store", Baby Boy answer'd playfully.

"Look Boy I ain't in no mood to be play'n with you today. I know they came from a sto' but who paid for them? And, why they ov'a here at my house? I suggest you fess up now cause, believe me, if I'm ask'n you about it, I already know the answer. I just wanna see what you gon say." A lot of times, I be bluff'n when I say that but this time I *did* know the answer.

"I stole 'em from the shoe store in the mall cause you never buy me these kinds of shoes. We always have to go to *Payless* or somewhere cheap like that. I wanna wear better looking clothes and shoes", Baby Boy said in between sobs and sniff'n up snot.

I hand'd him a Kleenex. "So, you gotta steal 'em? What's gotten into you boy? How come you can't get a job and contribute to the cost of buy'n 'em. *I* buy what *I* can afford. I'm not gon be spend'n a fortune on tennis shoes when I got other bills to pay. The most I'll contribute to a pair of tennis is $30. If you want some that cost more'n that, then you gotta put in the difference yo' self." I continued, "In any event you definitely ain't gon go around steal'n cause we can't afford sumthin' you want. Chile, your daddy probably roll'n ov'a in his grave behind this fiasco! Baby Boy you should be ashamed of yourself!! Well, I tell ya one thing, you gon take 'em back to that store and tell the manager that you stole 'em, then apologize and hope like hell they don't prosecute and have your butt lock'd up", I scolded Baby Boy. Thank God he didn't try to lie about it, cause then I would'a probably beat all'a the black off'a him.

"What you mean, take 'em back?" Baby Boy ask look'n all confused. "Mama, please don't embarrass me like that".

"Pardon me. Which word you need more clarification on, *take, back or shoes?* You should'a thought about that fo' you decided you had to have 'em. Also when we come home, I want you to write a two-page essay befo' you go to bed tonight. Topic: Why I should not steal. In addition, young man, you are grounded for two weeks. That means no television, no outside and no allowance for you, brother man. You can only go to school and then back home. Now tell me, was those blue Nike's worth all these blues? HA…HA…HA…. I suggest you get them shoes and let's head for the mall. And, hurry up, Sam'll be here in a couple of hours."

Baby Boy was quiet all the way to the mall and I was concentrate'n on how well I handled the situation. Charlie would'a been proud of me.

You see, he was the disciplinarian in our household, not me but I soon took ov'a that title after his death.

When I pull'd in front of the shoe store, I noticed a policeman park'n a few spaces ov'a to my left. Ummmph, *perfect time'n* I thought. Once Baby Boy got out of the car, I could see in the store that he was about the fourth person in line at the cash register. I had enuf time.....Meanwhile, I casually walk'd ov'a to the cop to ask for his assistance. I told him I was a recent widow raise'n three children and that my teenage son had start'd act'n delinquent. In fact, the reason why we are here now is cause he stole sumthin' and I'm make'n him bring it back. I also ask'd if he would talk to Baby Boy. Perhaps he could tell him sumthin' to scare him straight. He said he would be more'n happy to help me. Come to find out, he say his kids used to play on one'a Charlie's baseball teams but I couldn't place 'em in my memory at all.

I got back in the car to watch the scene unfold. Too bad we didn't have no portable video camera back then cause I could'a won $10,000 for *Americas Funniest Home Video*. The cop walk'd up behind Baby Boy and tap'd him on the shoulder. Chile, if that what'n a Kodak moment I don't know what is. He was sooooo scared, eyes bout popped right outta his head. The cop motion'd for him to step out of line and follow him. They came outside and the cop put Baby Boy in the back seat of the patrol car. When they took off, Baby Boy was cry'n and look'n absolutely terrified.

It seem like a long time but when I look at my watch, I see they only been gone 'bout fifteen minutes before they came back. Baby Boy was no longer in the backseat but rather he sat up front with the cop. He got out and went in the store to return the shoes. While he was in the store, the cop came ov'a to my car and said that I shouldn't have any more trouble out of Baby Boy. He offer'd me his card and tip'd his hat as he got in his car and drove off. It was as if no words could escape from my mouth and my eyes was transfixed dead on him til his car was outta sight. When I finally look'd at the card, an instant smile came to my face. This couldn't be true. His name was Lieutenant Guardian Angel.

The next day I call'd the police station and ask'd to speak to the officer so that I could properly thank him. S'pris'nly, I was told, "Nobody works here by that name and *Lady* I think you're too old to be play'n on the phone."

I apologized and told the policeman I had dial'd the wrong number. When I hung up the phone I was baffled but in the same instant I realized, God must'a had sumthin' to do with this. Me and Baby Boy ain't nev'a talk'd about that day and I nev'a told any body about that phone call… til just now. All these years I done kept that inside'a me. This legacy tape is a good reason to let it all out. Chile, I don't know who that man was but he sho' nuff turn'd my son's life around.

You might find this hard to believe but I've been search'n for that business card for ov'a twenty-five years. It's like the card nor the cop ev'a existed. And I know, I put that card on the dresser in my bedroom… right next to my bible. Stranger things have been known to happen.

All I can say is, don't under estimate the power of GOD!!!

17

"WHO ALL GO'N?"

I'm not gon sit on the porch this ev'nen and start another picture book story. Instead, I need to work on the centurion celebration but I've decided to keep the recorder on while I do it. You know, I haven't talk'd to Diamond in almost a week and I've received numerous *RSVP*'s that I need to respond to. Let me call Diamond right now while it's fresh on my mind, then I'll answer those emails.

Duane answer'd the phone, "Good ev'ning, this is the Roberts' residence."

"Hey Baby. How's thangs going with you? I ask Duane.

Duane mimicked Soul Broth'a #1. "E'ry thang is er'y thang ov'a here, Mama Pearl." Normally Duane is real serious, he seldom let the lighter side of him show but when he do, it's funnier than all get out!

After I regain my composure, I ask, "Is Diamond available?"

"Sure Ma. Hold on." I heard Duane yell in the background "Diamond, telephone. It's yo' Mama." Diamond must'a been sit'n right next to the phone cause she pick'd it up immediately.

"Hi Mommie. What's up wit'cha?" I thought, *I should be ask'n y'all the same thing. Why you talk'n like that?*

"Well," I start off, "looks like both y'all in a good mood tonight." Did you make any progress on get'n us a hotel and restaurant for Reverend Daddy's birthday bash?"

"Of course I did. Nothing is final yet but I contact'd two hotels. The Omni International on Marietta Street near downtown Atlanta and the

84

Sheraton-Airport. There's a significant difference in pricing and services. Did you receive any RSVP's?"

"Yeah! In fact, I got back about 25 emails but I haven't had the time to open any of 'em cause I been work'n on my legacy tape but when I finish talk'n to you I plan on tackle'n that job. I was try'n to wait and see if you had any more information that I could pass along in my responses. So tell me, which hotel do you think we should use? Betta yet, give me a run down on each one and we'll let the family decide."

"Personally, I like the Omni but I'm sure they'll vote for the cheaper Sheraton. Anyway, you got a pencil?

"Yes I do. Go right ahead."

"The Omni is $189 a night and some of their amenities include, cable, internet, sauna, pool, laundry, fitness center, 24-hour room service and three four-star restaurants located in the hotel. The Sheraton cost $99 a night and you get a pool, laundry, limit'd cable and limited room service." Diamond continued, "If we let the Omni cater the meal, it's gonna be about $30 a person. I was thinking perhaps we should rent a hall and get a soul food restaurant to cater it for us. You know they got the famous Paschal's Soul Food place on Metroplitan. Maybe we can even rent a room and after we eat the family could visit the M L King Memorial and Ebenezer Baptist Church cause it's only a few blocks away. We could make a day of it and also go to Underground Atlanta to walk off some of them calories while we do a little tourist shopping. And, for those who don't want to shop, we can arrange for the bus to take them to the hotel and come back and get the rest of us in a couple of hours".

Diamond's nev'a been a fan of family functions but this time I could hear the excitement in her voice. Perhaps plan'n this event is affect'n her personality. Lord knows it could use some adjust'n.

I respond, " Well, I'ma tell ya right now, I wanna stay at the Sheraton, eat at Paschal's, visit the M L King Memorial and the church and then shop at Underground Atlanta. Cause if we stay at the Omni and let them cater the food, it ain't gon be as good as Paschal's and the children won't be able to see the historical sites. Also, since you say we got a bus, how bout on Sunday we take the teenagers on a tour of the HBCU"S, Historical Black Colleges and Universities in Atlanta while the little kids have a pool party at the hotel? Anyway, where you get the bus from?"

"I called Reverend Daddy earlier this week to see what day was good for him. You know what he said? "Any day I wake up is a good day for me."

We both laf'd at that. Diamond went on, "During the conversation Reverend Daddy asked me how I was gon get everybody from one point to the other? I told him I hadn't thought about that yet.

He said, " Don't worry, my buddy Big Mike got a fancy coach line that he leases out and I'll make sho' it's available for y'all…What date did you say?"

"On your birthday, Reverend Daddy and also we gonna celebrate on the day after it. So that's June 29th and 30th."

Chile, my daddy know he get'n old. Shucks, me too for that matter. Anyway, after I hung up with Diamond, I respond to all the emails and ask that they vote on the itinerary. Howev'a, I changed the order cause it make more since to visit the M L King Memorial and the church before we eat. Diamond call'd back as soon as I finish'd them emails. She wants to know what I thought about us have'n entertainment at the dinner and suggest'd a talent show, some live music or both. I thought she was get'n a little bit exorbitant and said as much. But, after she volunteer'd to pay for any expenses related to entertainment. I said, "Go for it!" Then she ask'd me to request people sign up for talent once I receive they itinerary vote. Sounds like this gon be a fabulous celebration, and rightfully so. Diamond was get'n ready to hang up when I stop'd her, "Hey, did you call the doctor and make that appointment?"

"Yes, I did but since I'm a new patient, I can't get in for ov'a a month. Actually, my appointment is the week before we go to Atlanta. Anyway, I 've been feel'n better but I plan on keeping the appointment just the same."

I end the conversation, "That's good to hear. O.K. Pooh. I'll talk to you tomorrow, love ya!"

"Love you too. Bye Mommie."

18

"RUBIE LEIGH"

Since I got all those emails sent out and I'm just wait'n to see who gon be do'n what in the talent show, I think I'll go sit on the porch and work on my legacy tape. In fact, I can probably work on it for the next few days befo' I gotta go back to be'n the family event communicator. Ohhh, it feels so good out here tonight. Let's see. Look here at this picture of Rubie when she was in the march'n band in high school. She work'd so hard to save up the money to buy that uniform. High school was very eventful for Rubie Leigh.

RECORD.....Hope y'all enjoy'd Baby Boy's story. I thought it would be nice to continue with the reverse birth order, so now I'ma talk about Rubie for a spell.

All my chil'ren's got very different personalities. I imagine that's true 'bout er'ybody else too but it still amazes me how siblings can grow up in the same household and be as different as night and day. While Baby Boy craved to be outdoors, Rubie could care less about ev'a going outside to play. She much rather be in the house play'n a game or peeking ov'a my shoulder. No matter what I did, cook, sew, wash, iron or clean, Rubie want'd to do it too. Unlike Diamond, she was the one who want'd to help me out around the house. Well that is, 'til she got to smell'n herself, if you know what I mean. Then she didn't wanna have nuth'n to do with me. Look! There I go get'n ahead of myself again. Let me slow down and tell y'all the whole story. Ain't no use rush'n thangs, we got plenty-a-time left on this tape.

Rubie Leigh, Rubie Leigh, Rubie Leigh! From the very begin'n she was destined to be different. I chose the name Rubie cause I want'd to use the name of a gem. And Lee sounded betta than anything else I could think of to go with it but I didn't particularly care for the Oswald reference. You see, I didn't want people to look at my child's name and associate the name with Dr. King's assassination in any way, form or fashion. So, I had to pick another name but I liked the sound of *that* name.

Then one day when I was about sev'n months pregnant, I was ride'n down the street in St. Charles and I saw a billboard advertise'n this brand new subdivision that was still under construction. Guess what the name of it was?....."*The Prestigious Leigh Estates*". **BAMM!** Who'da thunk? I nev'a knowd nor had I ev'a seen the name Lee spell'd any other way. Chile, I was so fascinated, right then and there, I decided that was gon be my child's name. I was on'a roll so I ev'n changed her first name from its traditional spell'n too. You couldn't tell me nuth'n! I was sooo proud of my baby's new classy name. Look'd like sumthin' right off'a the soap opera credits.

You gotta remember this was pre-*Roots* era. Howev'a once *Alex Haley's Roots* air'd in 1977, a lot of black folks start'd come'n up with all kinds of exotic titles and unique spell'ns for they chil'ren's names. But befo' then, it was virtually unheard of. Also, don't forget, I'm from a country town call'd Sumner, Mississippi and er'ybody down there spell'd it, L-E-E, whether they's Betty Lee, Robby Lee or General Lee, we spell it all the same, L-E-E.

Most'a the time you not gon be able to use the same set of parent'n skills on all your children. Some kids require more love, attention and rules than others. Rubie Leigh didn't require much of either. She remind me of *Ceiley* from the movie *The Color Purple*, not that they look alike at all but rather cause they both so accommodate'n and loyal. Ev'n as a little girl Rubie did and said thangs you'd expect come from someone much older than her. And, her teachers simply adored her. On her report cards they wrote she was courteous, obedient, intelligent, inspire'n and a good influence on other students. She only received one "B" and the rest was all "A's" throughout the whole time she was in school. I mean all the way from kindergarten to college. Rubie was a very smart, compassionate, independent, grown-up like child. Frequently and naturally, younger kids flock'd to her side. She welcomed er'y last one of 'em and made 'em feel special too. As I said befo' she didn't like to go outside as much as my Diamond and Baby Boy but she used to want Tootsie's younger kids or them little girls from down the street, to come play with her in the house. It's no s'prise her favorite house game was "*School*" and of course she was gon be the teacher.

You think that might have sumthin' to do with why she chose teach'n as her profession today? Maybe, but I think it's in her blood. You see, we come from a long line of educators. Legend has it *my* great grandparents, Papa Milton and Mama Carrie were ex-slaves who used to secretly teach other slaves how to read and write. They daughter was my grandmother, Ouida and she was a school teacher from a all black town in Florida. I think it was call'd, Rosewood. As God would have it, my Mother (who is also named Ouida) received the finest school'n but along the way she fell in love with a farm'n preacher from Mississippi and they had a bunch of chil'ren. Yeah, my parents were simple people who work'd the land but they constantly show'd us how important the bible and a good education was to our benefit.

When we was kids often times Reverend Daddy had to rotate who went to school depend'n on the time of the year and the farm'n work that had to be done. Usually the older kids stay'd home at the begin'n of the school year cause that was corn and wheat harvest time and we need'd all the brute strength we could muster up for a successful harvest. The middle-aged children stay'd home to pick fruits and berries and also to plant vegetables when it was time for that. Er'ybody stay'd home when Mother said it was spring clean'n time. While each of us had mandatory seasonal and daily chores, Mother insist'd the babies start learn'n thangs long fo' they was ev'n big enuf to go to school. And, she said, who ev'a went to school had to come back and share what they learnt with the ones who stay'd home. Many'a night we had both bible study and school study in that old multi-purpose room. Home school'n ain't no new concept, black folks been do'n it for generations! It may have taken me the longest but in keep'n with the family tradition, I made sho' my sister and er'y last one of my brothers graduated from school. Back then, all the grades was in the same one or two-room schoolhouse. Umph.... What'n no separate build'n for high school students. Just think, we didn't have no high school in Sumner but in St. Louis they had and *still* got a school call'd *Charles Sumner High School*, ain't that ironic?

Anyhow, above all, Mother made sho' we received a fine education, had respect for our elders and that we went to church er'y Sunday.

My children received they primary education in Catholic schools from nuns (most of the religious communities had already stop'd wear'n habits by then), but when it was time for 'em to go to high school they had the option of going to a public school on the condition that they would keep a 3.0 average or it was right back to Catholic school for 'em. Rubie was the only one who transfer'd to public school and that was mainly cause of Tootsie's daughter, Joyce Ann who was about the same age as Rubie, went to Vashon High School. Diamond graduated from an all girl Catholic high school and Baby Boy went to a coed Catholic high school. In fact, it's the same one his kids go to today. Throughout high school, Rubie kept her part of the bargain and maintained a G.P.A. well above the required "B" but she went from little *Ms. Helper* to little *Ms. Sneaky*. I remember the last time I saw her as my little helper was when she was in the 8th grade and a finalist in the National Annual Catholic Spelling Bee Tournament.

Sniff…Sniff….I smell some bar-b-que and it sho' smell good. Chile, the way my stomach growl'n, I need to be concentrate'n on what I'm gon eat fo' dinner. I took some chicken out but if I eat one mo' piece'a chicken this week, I'm li'ble to grow wings and fly away. Instead, I think I'ma make me an omelet and some home-style potatoes with onions. Er'ybody know breakfast food always good, no matter what time of day you eat it. If I hurry, I can cook, eat, change my clothes and be back out here in an hour, which would still give me at least anuth'a hour's worth of time to talk to y'all befo' my bedtime. Yeah…..that's what I'll do. Be back in a few minutes. PAUSE…

\#   \#   \#   \#   \#

RECORD….Ain't nuth'n like take'n a bath . Submerg'n yo' self in water is one'a the most rejuvinate'n physical and spiritual feel'ns that I've ev'a experienced. You know water cleans physically *and* spiritually. Let me just say, I have empathy for the homeless, cause if I was homeless, me not be'n able to bathe whenev'a I want'd to, would be really difficult to endure. Have'n said that, I immediately send a prayer up for all those without………. *Whatev'a* theys without, bless 'em, Lord………

Halleluiah.......Thank you, Jesus...... Well, now that I'm clean, stomach full, and spirit uplifted, let's get on with the story.

The National Annual Catholic Spelling Bee was highly anticipated and attend'd by Catholic students all ov'a the United States. Students practiced for months prepare'n for the competition. Rubie was no exception; she start'd study'n six months in advance. The first round was held at the local level and then the winner advanced to the state, regional and possibly the national level if they could spell good enuf. Rubie's school, Blessed Sacrament, usually host'd fund-raisers to help pay for travel'n expenses to the National's. Didn't matter if the win'n student was from they school or not but they had already won the National title three years run'n and the pressure was on to take the title again... Rubie was determined to win *this* year. She figured this was her last chance cause she was start'n high school in the fall.

The winner would receive save'n bonds and an array of gifts, mostly educational ones but gifts nonetheless. Actually, the kids could care less about the bonds, calculators, books, backpacks and paper. Alls they was interested in was the all expense paid trip to Disney World in Orlando, Florida. I guess you know, Rubie won the National Annual Catholic Spelling Bee Tournament that year. In fact, she's the first African American to ev'a hold the title. All'a us, include'n Joyce Ann, went to Florida and had big fun for a whole week. Not only did we go to Disney World but we also went to Universal Studios. I was so proud of my little *Ms. Helper,* what'n no way I could tell her she couldn't go to Vashon High School. Especially, after she proved she was the best speller outta all the Catholic grade schools in the U.S. Chile, she could have gone *anywhere* her little heart desired! And, that's exactly what she did.

19

"VASHON HIGH SCHOOL"

Public school is a world away from Catholic school. First and foremost, Catholic schools do not tolerate any disciplinary problems from they students. If you can't sit down, shut up and learn, you outta there! Period. Unfortunately, the Public schools don't have that same privilege. They gotta deal with whomev'a is a dependant of a tax pay'n citizen in they community. It don't matter if all the child do is act the fool, they gon still be assign'd to that school, regardless. I take that back, some Public school districts have schools specifically design'd and staff'd for students with behavior problems/disorders which more times than not also leads to learn'n disabilities.

Dress codes are strictly enforced in Catholic schools. All students wear the same outfit which in turn, eliminates a good deal of argue'n and fight'n ov'a who got on what. From Pre-K to fourth grade, the girls wore jumpers with white Peter Pan collar shirts, white or navy socks and black rubber sole shoes. Tennis shoes and shorts were NEVER allow'd but by the 5th grade and continue'n through 6th the uniform upgraded to a skirt and vest or sweater. No more jumpers. Usually 7th and 8th grade girls wore khaki pants and a collar polo-type shirt, school blazers were optional. So I guess you could say, they really don't all look exactly alike but rather er'ybody in the same age group dress the same, therefore, no cloth'n disagreements amongst peers.

Another good thing about students wear'n uniforms is they parents can purchase practically all they clothes from one or two stores but when they gotta annually buy *back to school clothes,* that's easily five to six stores and about three times as much money. Chile, these merchandise buyer's today need to be ashame of theyself for some'a the outfits they buy to be sold in department and specialty stores. Come on now, they know *they* didn't wear that kind'a mess when they was in school. Let's be realistic, how you gon go to school with yo' stomach and thighs hang'n out and expect the boys and teachers to concentrate on learn'n and teach'n?

I always said cloth'n is too much of'a distraction in the Public schools and now more and more school districts mandate uniforms for they students. I guarantee you, not have'n to wear a uniform was probably the number one reason why Rubie just *had* to go to Vashon. Also, that was right about that same time that she got really obsessed with *her* perceived outward appearance. Luckily it only lasted a couple, three years and that's normal but some folks who are extremely unhappy and insecure, *Michael Jackson*, for instance, get too hung up about they looks and they start have'n all types of plastic surgery. I ain't with that! I'ma keep the same face and body God gave me. I heard a joke one time about plastic surgery. Bear with me now cause you know I ain't no *Richard Pryor* when it come to tell'n jokes but let me see if I can get this one right....

A middle-aged woman had a heart attack and was taken to the hospital. While on the operate'n table, she had a near death experience.

See'n God, she ask'd Him, "Is my time up, Lord?"

God said, "No child, you have another 43 years, 2 months and 8 days to live.

Upon recovery, the woman decided to remain in the hospital and have a face-lift, brow-lift, lip enhancement, boob job, liposuction and a tummy tuck. After her last operation, she was finally released from the hospital. While cross'n the street on her way home, she was hit and kilt by an ambulance.

Arrive'n in front'a of God again, she demand'd, "I thought you said I had another 40 years. Why didn't you pull me out of the path of that ambulance?"

God step'd forward to get a betta look and replied, "Girrllll....., I didn't ev'n recognize you." ....HA...HA....HA.....HA....

\# \# \# \# \#

Nah, Rubie didn't wanna have an operation to change how she look'd but she did wanna wear her hair down and not wear uniforms to school anymore. You see, when Diamond and Rubie was little girls they wore braids most'a the time. The braids were neat and convenient. Also, they would last a long time if I made sho' the girls tied they heads up er'y night. I didn't have time to be do'n no hair er'y morn'n. I had to go to work!

Anyhow, Rubie graduated grade school a few weeks befo' we went to Florida and then in the fall she transfer'd to Vashon High School, home of the Wolverines. Mind you, Rubie went to the Vashon on Grand Avenue but they done since built a new one not too far from there. I believe the original, "for coloreds only" Vashon was located somewhere on Laclede. Sumner "Bull Dogs" and the Vashon "Wolverines" were (and still are) public school rivals in sports and most'a the time Vashon came out on top. The curriculum at both schools, I'm afraid, is less than to be desired. That's not to say public high schools don't have good teachers but rather they teachers have to work with the limit'd resources available and the curriculum has not been design'd to encourage students to "think outside the box" or prepare them for college, they just gotta graduate, that's all. It's sad to think how many students today graduate high school but only can read and comprehend on a 6th grade level. There was an unwritten rule that er'ybody in my household was expected to do sumthin' post high school. After primary school was secondary school and after secondary school was hopefully college. Howev'a they didn't have to go to a four-year college but they did have to do sumthin' productive, junior college, trade school, military, anything but lay up in *my* house all day.

Initially, I was concern'd that Vashon would not fully prepare Rubie for college but I also knew she received an excellent primary education and that she was a very intelligent, responsible individual who could succeed at anything she want'd to. Rubie would frequently say that the assignments the teachers gave at Vashon was stuff she had already learnt and mastered at Blessed Sacrament a few years prior. Academically, high school was a breeze for her. In fact, after the 10th grade she was skipped to the 12th grade and actually graduated a whole year earlier than she was s'pose to. Her and Diamond graduated high school the same year but she was pregnant.

As I said earlier, I nev'a had to worry about Rubie complete'n her homework assignments nor get'n good grades but by the end of the 10th grade she start'd stay'n gone all the time but she continued to bring home all "A's". I didn't know who she was with or where she was at and I had heard somewhere, ain't but two thangs make a woman change they normal routine and not come home. That's drugs or a man. I knew she what'n do'n no drugs but I wasn't too sure about the man. Me and Rubie went round and round bout her not let'n me know her whereabouts. Chile, she thought she was grown way befo' her time but I sho' nuff put her in her place.

Since, Rubie went to Vashon, she had to catch a Public school bus and it came heck'a early in the morn'n. Diamond had her own car by then and I usually drop'd Baby Boy off on my way to work. I didn't hav'ta leave til 7:30 AM but I'm a morn'n person so by 6:00 AM I'm up and about, drink'n my tea and sit'n in my think window. Rubie's bus pick'd her up at six, thirty-three so when I came downstairs a little after six she was still have'n breakfast.

"Good morn'n Pooh", I softly said as I got to the bottom of the staircase land'n cause I didn't wanna wake-up Diamond and Baby Boy. Howev'a, I also didn't wanna startle Rubie, so I said it again as I enter'd the kitchen, this time a little louder, "Good morn'n, Pooh."

"Oh, Hi Mommie, you want me to put some water on for you?"

"Yes, that would be nice. Then hav'a seat cause we need to talk."

"But my bus comes in a few minutes."

"You got plenty-a-time. What I gotta say won't take that long, sit down."

After Rubie put some fresh water in the teapot and placed it on the stove, she came to the table and sat in the chair face'n me. I thought it best for me *and* Rubie that I put some distance in between us so I moved to my think window about three feet away cause I didn't wanna spontaneously knock her teeth out when I punch'd her in the face for talk'n smart, which was highly likely to happen. You see, this was the *second* time she had stay'd gone and not call'd home but I'll give her some credit, she *was* in the house by curfew.

"So, what did you do when you got outta school yesterday? I ask very calmly.

"After majorette practice, I hung out with some of my friends, that's all."

"And you couldn't call me to say where you was or who you was with? I didn't wait for a response but instead I continued, "This ain't the first time you done done this either, remember last week? Why all'a sudden you gotta be gone all the time? Rubie, I'm not ask'n you to check in with me er'y time you go pee but I do expect to know your general whereabouts. If you came up miss'n, I wouldn't ev'n know where to tell the police to start look'n for you at. Now tell me specifically, where were you and why didn't you call home?"

"Well, about a month ago, Mr. Phillips who is my music teacher and band director told our class how we could get some free tickets for the *New Edition* concert that's coming to town in three weeks. Seems the Special School District is sponsoring this musical workshop design'd for slightly mentally and physically challenged children, grades K- 4. The thought is, each kid will receive one on one basic coach'n from people that they can relate to and emulate, like students in a marching band. By the end of the workshop, which is scheduled for the next two weekends, the challenged students, depending on the severity of their disability, will learn how to play a simple instrument, twirl a flag, maneuver a large ball and/or march in formation. They ev'n gon participate in a parade at their school with real band members at their side. This' the first time the district's ever had a workshop like this but from what Mr. Phillips say, all the children they selected have shown some sort of interest in music. Also, in exchange for donating our time and talents, we the real band members, will get tickets to the *New Edition* concert or the *Cardinals* football game."

"Did you *not* hear me say "specifically"? Stop stall'n, Rubie. What does Mr. Phillips and the band hav'ta do with yesterday? I suggest you just stick to *my* questions."

"I'm getting to that part but you gotta let me tell the whole story in order for you to fully understand and appreciate *my* answers to *your* questions."

Y'all see what I'm talking about, if I had'a been a little closer, she be pick'n her teeth up right about now. It ain't so much what she said but rather how she said it. As my kids got older, I refrain'd from actually hitting 'em cause when you take away they privileges the effects lasts a lot longer than a whup'n do.

"Watch your tone, young lady. I'm not your friend, I'm yo' mama. Remember, we ain't got all day. Yo' ride be here shortly and you bet not miss that bus, so I suggest you move yo' story along a little faster cause if you miss yo' bus, you walk'n to school." I thought, "*Ummmph...Just cause she gon be do'n a good deed don't excuse the fact that she **still** didn't call home.*

She realized I what'n in no playful mood so she quickly answer'd the questions I had previously ask'd. "After practice some of the band members went to *Kentucky Fried Chicken* for a bite to eat, then we decided to go to the mall and try on the clothes that we wanna wear to the concert. Since most of the girls on the majorette squad are seniors and they what'n call'n home, I didn't wanna embarrass the squad in front of all those boys by be'n the only girl who had to call home."

With my pointer digit, you know, the finger next to my thumb, I motion'd for her to come closer to me and she did. When my lips were about two inches from her ear, which by the way, I was squeez'n, I whispered, "Let me let you in on a little secret, I don't care what them *other* girls do. I ain't but only *one* girl mama on that squad and the next time *you* don't call or let me know where you at, you might as well stay where ev'a you are cause I ain't let'n you back in here. It's gon be like the game of baseball ov'a here. One, two and three strikes, you're outta here! Is that perfectly clear, do we have an understand'n, young lady?" I released her ear and she stood up.

"Yes, Ma'am. Can I please go now Mommie?"

"Yeah, get on outta here but don't forget what I said. Then I motion'd for her to come close to me again but this time I gave her a kiss *and* some advice, "You betta believe, I mean what I say." She turn'd around, put her dishes in the sink, grabbed her books and hurried out the door.

For the next two weeks Rubie follow'd the rule and call'd home whenev'a she was s'pose to and on the weekends she coached the challenged kids at the music workshop. I ev'n fixed a big picnic and me and Tootsie and our families went to the parade. It was such a wonderful sight to see the happy faces of the young children as they march'd side by side with the band members. I was amazed at how precise and synchronized they routines were. After the parade we all went out for pizza and Mr. Phillips pass'd out the concert and football tickets to the band members. Chile, them kids was holler'n and scream'n, jump'n up and down, just simply elated to get them tickets.

If you ask me, I believe Rubie Leigh was *New Edition's* most loyal fan cause she had posters of the pop group plaster'd all ov'a her bedroom walls. In addition to group shots, she had individual poses of the members too.

20

'I CAN SHO' YOU BETTA THAN I CAN TELL YA'

On the way home from the pizza party I got to think'n, *I should do sumthin' nice for Rubie Leigh too.*

"I know you told me before but I forgot. When's the concert again?" I ask'd Rubie who was sit'n up front with me. Baby Boy and his friend Bobby was in the backseat with they headphones on listen'n to they kind'a music.

"It's this Saturday and I don't know what I'm gon wear. I ain't got nothing cute in my closet for a big occasion like this. Just think Mommie, this my first real concert and it's *New Edition*!" She yell'd as she repeatedly stomp'd the car floor and waved her arms in the air. If she *this* excited now, I pity the people who gon be sit'n next to her at the concert. She'll probably loose her mind. I hope she don't faint like I've seen some fans do and miss the whole show.

"I thought you said you already tried on the outfit you wanna wear to the concert when you was at the mall a few weeks ago?"

"I did and it look real good on me. But it ain't free and I ain't got no money. Maybe I could ask my uncles to give me some. What you think Mommie?"

"I think you gotta ev'n betta chance if you offer some services in exchange for that money. You know like, clean'n they house, wash'n they car, rake'n the yard or sumthin' like that. I tell you what, I'll pay for the outfit and you work on get'n you some spend'n money. How 'bout that!"

"Oh, thank you so much Mommie. When can we go to the store?"

"Definitely, not tonight. I'll take you after mass tomorrow. Nah, that's not gon work cause I'm s'pose to go somewhere with Tootsie. Let's go Monday at 6pm. Then we can have dinner afterwards." Rubie was constantly on the phone for the next couple of days let'n er'ybody know she was gon get that hot outfit she had tried on. I hoped she realized, me buy'n the outfit greatly depend'd on *how* hott the outtfit actually is. I what'n buy'n and she what'n wear'n no sleazy clothes. Period. I don't care how special the occasion is. Howev'a, the outtfit was teenage hot not sexy, sleazy adult hott. I'm glad my definition of hott was not the same as her definition. Anyway, I bought the outfit, some shoes and ev'n a purse to match. Chile, I spent way mo' money than I had originally intend'd but schucks, this was a special occasion, right up there with the prom. Speak'n of which, I think Jade, Diamond's daughter prom is next weekend. I'ma hav'ta call and see.

As fate would have it, Rubie's anticipation swell'd as Saturday grew nearer but the Friday before the concert, all hell broke loose. For the life of me I can't remember what Rubie did but I knowd I was furious with her and we had a really big pow wow. Of course, I came out on top and the result was Rubie was grounded and forbidden to go the concert the next day. Oh, I know what it was…I came home unexpectedly dure'n the day and caught her at home with a boy in her room. It was Stan! Mind you, they what'n do'n nuth'n sexual but rather Rubie was sit'n on the bed read'n a magazine and Stan was slump'd down in the bean bag chair play'n a video game. They had remnants of food sprawl'd out all around 'em. I guess they had plan'd on clean'n up and leave'n before anybody came home but they was busted cause it was one o'clock in the afternoon and they was s'pose to be at school *not* at my house pig'n out. I immediately excused Mr. Stan from my house, express'd my disappointment in Rubie Leigh and ground'd her in her room with no television, no radio, no telephone and definitely no *New Edition* concert for her. Ev'n though I knew how bad she want'd to go to that concert, this was a serious infraction of school and house rules. I couldn't believe it! Instead of go'n to school she was bring'n people ov'a my house to play hooky.

Aahhhhh........Well, I'ma hav'ta stop right about here. I'm get'n so sleepy, can hardly keep my eyes open. Since tomorrow is Sunday and I go to 7:30 AM mass, I should be back home by 9:45 AM and I plan on devote'n the betta part of my day to the legacy tape. In tribute to one'a my favorite vaudeville comedians, Redd Skelton, as he would say er'y week at the close of his variety show, "Good night and God bless." ...STOP

# # # # #

RECORD.......Strangely, I woke up with Jade on my mind this morn'n and I call'd her as soon as I got back from church. She said her prom is next weekend and her graduation is two weeks after that. I ask'd if she need'd anything but I already knew Diamond had taken care of the slightest of details but Jade did request one'a my famous homemade pound cakes with lemon glaze for her graduation party. I told her, say no mo' it'll be there.

Normally I don't sit outside til after the sun goes down but today there's a cool breeze out here *and* I'm anxious to finish Rubie's story cause I got over thirty emails in my IN Box I need to look at, so let's get on with it.

Needless to say the house was unusually quiet the next day. After Baby Boy finish'd his chores he went to the skate'n rink with Bobby and Meathead. Diamond was thrill'd *"Miss Goody Too Shoes"* and not herself was in the hot seat for a change. She left as soon as her chores were done. On account Rubie didn't have no television or radio privileges she completed her chores and went back to her bedroom long before noon. To give Rubie a break from be'n lock'd up in her room, at about 3:00 PM I made her go to the grocery store with me but my conversation to her was very limit'd all while we was gone. Then when we got back home, she brought the groceries in and I put 'em up in silence. Afterwards I began preparations for dinner. It must'a been about 5:00 PM.

"You mind if I help you fix dinner? Rubie ask'd test'n the waters, unsure whether I was back on speak'n terms to her yet or not.

"Of course I don't mind. That'll be nice. Just like old times. You used to always help me in the kitchen, the laundry room, or whatev'a I was do'n but all that changed a few months ago and I don't know who this new Rubie is. Chile, if someone had'a told me last week you would be play'n hooky, this week, I would 'a call'd them a liar and quickly defend'd your honor."

Rubie held her head down for a few seconds and when she raised her head up she look'd me straight in the eye and said, "I'm sorry Mommie. I know I should'a been at school and I know you don't allow us to have boys in our room. Why I did it, I don't know....I just don't feel like staying at school no more. The kids are so immature and the teachers are bore'n. I'm sick of the whole scene. I'm ready to move on with my life."

I told ya' that Rubie Leigh could catch you off guard with some'a the thangs she would say and be so sincere about it too. At first I thought, *Wow* but instead I said, "Obviously you don't know a thang about "move'n on with your life" if you skip'n school. How you gon be a teacher or any other profession for that matter without a college degree? Just cause you think you gon get skipped to the 12th grade don't mean you can start skip'n school or disobey'n my house rules either. I suggest you slow your roll young lady, follow my rules and try to finish high school before you "move on with your life" or you gon frequently find yo'self on punishment. Be'n able to endure thangs that we prefer not to do is a big part of move'n on with your life. All through life you gon hav'ta do *this* in order to be able to do *that,* I reiterate'd with hand gestures. You gon hav'ta make sacrifices all'a the time."

As I head toward the cabinet to retrieve the herbs and spices that I need'd for the corn'd beef I was gon cook, Rubie responds, "I understand all'a that Mommie and I will *never* play hooky again. I'll even stay in my room a whole week longer if you just let me go to the *New Edition* concert tonight."

"Nope, but I will grant you one hour on the phone to find someone else to take your place." I could feel her dagger stares in my back but when I turn'd around she was also turn'n around and all I saw was tears stream'n down her face then she huff'd and walk'd away.

About thirty minutes later Rubie came back in the kitchen all red eyed to see if I need'd any help and to tell me that Stan was gonna take his little sister to the concert instead and he'd be ov'a in an hour to get the ticket. She ask'd me if I would give it to him cause she couldn't bear for him to see her look'n like this. I thought, *Whatev'a*. Stan arrived as expected and I gave him the ticket. When I look'd in on Rubie she was lay'n in the bed in her robe with her back to the door. I told her I'd make sure to wake her up when dinner was ready but she didn't respond so I shut the door and went on about my business.

At 8:00 I call'd out, "Dinner ready. Rubie, come eat." I lost track of time cause Diamond and Baby Boy came home tell'n me what they had did that day. We talk'd while they ate and then they ask to go back out. This time they was go'n to the bowl'n alley. Saturday is Family Night and it only cost a dollar a game so I gave 'em ten dollars and told 'em to be back home before elev'n.

By the time 9:00 PM roll'd around, Rubie still hadn't come downstairs to eat. Concern'd, I go see what's take'n her so long. She probably still sleep but it's time for her to get up cause she need to eat sumthin'. I knock on the door a couple of times but didn't get a response. As I open the door, the first thing I see is the curtain blow'n out the window that was open and Miss Rubie was gone. OMG!!!! Initially I thought, *my child been kidnap'd* but I look'd to my right and saw that her new outfit what'n hang'n on the closet door. I didn't need to be no rocket scientist to figure out what had happen'd to her. It was plain to see that Rubie had jump'd outta the window and gone to that concert anyway! LOL..LOL. . It may seem funny now, but it what'n then.

Chile, I was so mad I start'd shake'n and then I remember'd what I told her would happen the next time she didn't tell me where she was go'n. Without give'n it a second thought, I commenced to gather'n all'a her things. You would'a thought I was *Angela Bassett* in the movie *Waiting to Exhale* when she was put'n her husband's stuff outta the house. The only difference was, I what'n gon burn Rubie's thangs but they was sho' nuff get'n outta this house. I paused just long enuf to call Tootsie and let her in on my plan then I got busy remove'n Rubie's stuff outta her room. Within thirty minutes I had haul'd er'ythang of hers in the house out onto the front porch. First, I laid a tarp down to keep er'ything from get'n too dirty. Next, I took the dresser drawers and dump'd the contents on the ground all on top'a one another. I also put in the clothes that was hang'n in her closet, *just* to make the pile bigger. Then I threw all'a the rest'a her stuff inside her sheets after I stripped the bed. Out went books, trophies, shoes, cosmetics, toiletries and her *New Edition* posters and I didn't ev'n use a single box or bag.

Once I had finish'd throw'n er'y thing outta the room, I put anuth'a tarp on top'a all'a her stuff, (in case it rain'd) lock'd all the windows, reinforced the basement and backdoors and then went to bed. About an hour later, Diamond and Baby Boy came home from the bowl'n alley rush'd upstairs. They didn't ev'n bother to knock on the door but rather rudely busted in my room. They ask'd, "What's all that stuff on the porch for?"

I poke my head from up under the covers and said, "Did you forget to knock? Ya'll know betta than that. I continued, "All'a that stuff on the porch belongs to Rubie and it's stay'n out there with her. AND, ya'll betta not let her in this house unless you wanna be out there too."

"Oooooohhhh.....What she do, *now*?" they ask'd in unison.

"She snuck out the window and went to the *New Edition* concert after I told her she couldn't go. Ya'll make sure that dead bolt lock'd good and tight on the front door." Normally we didn't put the dead bolt on til the last person came in the house but as far as I was concern'd, the last person was already in the house. Plus, I knew nobody else had'a key to that lock except me.

"Ooooohhhhh", was all I heard 'em say and then they closed my bedroom door. I roll'd ov'a and went back to sleep. A couple of hours later, I heard the doorbell so I got up to make sure nobody was gon let Rubie in. I ignor'd the persistent knocks at the door and secretly watched as she finally gave up and just lay'd down and start'd cry'n right ontop'a all'a her stuff. I call'd Tootsie and told her it was time to execute the plan. She agreed and said she'd be right ov'a. Tootsie and 'nem only lived a few blocks away on Maple Avenue so she was at my house within ten minutes of me call'n her. She approach'd Rubie, bent down and touched her on the arm to try to arouse her. When Rubie got up, Tootsie led her to the wait'n car with the passenger door already open. I could tell Rubie was still cry'n as they got in and left. I then went back to bed hope'n this would be my final attempt at get'n a restful night's sleep.

Of course I what'n gon kick my child out the house foev'a but I had'ta put the fear in her. This here *my* house and I'm the only one who make or break the rules up'n here. Rubie be a lot betta off remember'n that *she* live with me, I don't live with *her*. I had already arranged for her to stay at Ant Tootsie's house for a week but Rubie sweet- talk'd Tootsie into bring'n her ov'a my house right after we got back from our regular Sunday out'n. Tootsie made Rubie wait in the car while she beg'd me to go outside and talk to her.

"Pearl, I think Rubie done learnt her lesson. I agree you should keep her on punishment but at least let her come back home. Why you act'n so mean? You shouldn't be so *hard* on her."

Unconsciously, I thought back to the homily my pastor gave at mass that morn'n, entitled, "If today you hear His voice, *harden* not your heart.".........God sho' nuff got His own way of get'n your attention, don't He? Needless to say, without hesitation, I went outside to get my child. When I open'd the door she was sit'n on the porch with her back to me and all'a her stuff was still on the porch. She slowly turn'd around when she heard the screen door open. As I step'd beyond the door frame, I held out my arms for her to come to me. When we embraced, it was as if she had just return'd from a year-long furlough overseas. Both of us was cry'n, kiss'n and wipe'n tears off each other's face for about a minute before either one'a us could speak.

"I'm so sorry Mommie. I ain't gon nev'a break anuth'a one'a your rules again. Please let me come back home."

"I'm sorry too Pooh, for put'n you out *but* don't think this all ov'a. You still gon be on punishment. Now get this mess clean'd up before the neighbors start gawk'n and talk'n." I gave her one last kiss on the fo'head and then I went back in the house. It took Rubie almost four hours to refold all'a those clothes and get her room back in order.

Well, I nev'a did have anymore problems with Rubie break'n the rules but I guess you could say she *did* "move on with her life" cause she graduated high school, married and became a mother all within thirteen months. Chile, I'll hav'ta bring ya'll up to date on that story some other time. That's a whole nuth'a tape in itself! HA...HA...HA... Maybe next year.

21

LAST CALL!

It's been ov'a a week since I last check'd my emails. I thought it best to wait til after our RSVP deadline. That way I could have a good *guesstamation* of how many people go'n to Atlanta. With almost fifty emails, it's gon take me a while to get threw 'em all. So, I guess I betta get start'd or I'ma be up all night.

The first one I open is from Joyce Ann, Tootsie's daughter.
****

From:	Joyce Ann Simmons_Smith@purina.com
To:	PAJohnson @aol.com
Date:	6/1/06 1:02 PM
Subject:	Centurion Celebration

Hi Ant Pearl,

I hope everything is good with you. Just wanted to let you know my family will definitely be in Atlanta for Rev. Daddy's birthday party. Jamal says sign him up to play a saxophone solo in the talent show. Me and Larry just watch'n. We ain't got no talent.

Let me know where and who to send the money to.

Love Ya'
Joyce Ann

P.S. In regards to the hotel, I vote for whatever one you vote for.

Joyce Ann Simmons-Smith
Regional Sales Manager
Purina Foods
1111 Purina Drive
St. Louis, MO 63101
314-792-8000 Office
314-792-8050 Fax
****

Chile, I sho' am proud of that girl. She my favorite niece but don't tell my other nieces I said so. I'm glad she finally got herself back on the right track and turn'd her life around. She was a college graduate strung out on crack for almost ten years before she check'd herself into a rehab, start'd go'n back to church and got herself a real good job. She been clean now bout eight or nine years, er'y since she got that job at Purina and start'd date'n Jamal's daddy. Thank you Jesus....for by the grace of God, that child done come a *long* way!

The next email I open is from my brother Bubba.
****

From:	bubbainsumner@aol.com
To:	PAJohnson@aol.com
Date:	6/1/06 2:06 PM
Subject:	Centurion Celebration

Hey Sis,

I'm responding for my entire family. I had a meeting with my children and grandchildren and just about everybody is coming. We don't care where you decide to have it. We will be there. So let me see, that's two seniors, me and the little woman, four of my children and about 10 grandkids and one great grand baby. Everybody still deciding on who and how they will participate in the talent show but I told them they had to let me know by the end of the week. Hope that ain't too late.

When you need the money?

Love,
Bubba

****

There was one common question throughout all the emails… when we gotta pay? By the time I answer'd all'a those emails it was almost elev'n o'clock. I decided to make a tally before I go to bed. Ummmmmmmph……The numbers are look'n real good and *my* choice hotel, the Sheraton Airport, got the most'a votes. Let's see how many people come'n….20 Seniors, 85 Adults, 32 Teens, 15 Toddlers and 5 infants.

I'll call Diamond first thing in the morn'n with the count. Maybe now she can get a solid commitment from the hotel and restaurant. Oh by the way…I need to get a good nights sleep tonight, tomorrow is Jade's graduation.

#   #   #   #   #

I was sleep'n sooo good, I didn't wanna get up this morn'n. My bed was feel'n too good but I knew I had to get'a move'n with the centurion celebration cause it's less than a month way. Last night I know I told ya'll I was go'n to bed but before I got in the bed I took it upon myself to send a group email to er'ybody tell'n them to send me a $100 deposit immediately and the balance, once we let them know, within two weeks. This morn'n instead of sit'n in my think window with my tea, I call Diamond.

"Gut morning, Vobert vesidenz." Chile, they maid's accent so thick I hav'ta to look at the phone display just to make sure I dial'd the right number but I ask her to repeat herself anyway.

"Pardon me, what did you say?"

"Vobert vesidenz. Who vould you like to speak to?"

"My daughter, is Diamond home?"

"One moment, please." I tell ya' seem like er'y other month or so Diamond get'n a new clean'n lady and each one got a different accent. Maybe that's why she can't keep a maid, perhaps a break down in communication.

"Hi, Mommie."

"Hi, Pooh. How you feel'n this morn'n?"

"Like there's a musician inside my head pretending it's a drum. We went to one of Duane's doctor friends house for dinner last night and I had one too many glasses of wine. My head is really throbbing this morning. I just took some *alka-seltzer,* so I'll be fine in a few minutes. But til then, I'd appreciate if you would keep your voice down. Did you read your emails yet?"

"Sure did. All fifty-three of 'em".

"Wow! Do you know how many people are come'n?"

"One hundred and fifty-sev'n. About a hundred of those people need rooms and plus they unanimously voted for the Sheraton. I ev'n broke it down into age categories so that we can better plan activities accord'n to the number of participants."

"That'll also be helpful when we determine the fee. I'm pretty sure I can get a lower hotel rate than what was originally quoted since so many family members will be staying at the hotel. I'll get busy making calls as soon as this headache subsides. Also, the hotel will want a deposit."

But before she could start that next sentence, I cut her off...."That's already taken care of. Monies should start arrive'n in the next day or two. I told er'ybody to send a hundred dollars for now".

"Well, I'm sure it's going to cost more than a hundred dollars but I won't know how much more til I make those calls and do a few calculations. Can I get a break down of the age groups?" Diamond ask'd.

"OMG, not now! I gotta get my cakes out the oven 'fo they burn up. I'll send you an email. Bye!!"

Good thing I gotta keen nose cause I had done forgot about them cakes. As soon as I came downstairs this morn'n, I start'd make'n the pound cakes for Jade's graduation party. I put two homemade cakes in the oven a hour and a half ago. Now I gotta give 'em plenty'a time to cool off before I can glaze 'em up and then wrap 'em in cellophane. Since I'm ride'n with Diamond tonight, I'll give her the cakes when they bring me home. That way they'll be perfect in time for the party tomorrow. Howev'a if I know Jade like I know Jade, only one'a them cakes gon make it to the party. The other one gon stay at home and become her private stash. Jade say pound cake with lemon glaze is *absolutely* her all time favorite dessert in the whole wide world and I make it betta than anybody else.

So I put the cakes on the cool'n rack and go into my office to send Diamond that email so she could get start'd on her assignment. We don't have any time to waste, the big day is less than a month away and we got a million thangs to do.

Two Weeks Later

RECORD.......I been so busy with all the preparations, I ain't had no time to work on my legacy tape but now that er'ything is finalized I can get back to my tape. I finish'd side A a few weeks ago. Side B will include a current event and I think Reverend Daddy's Centurion Celebration is the perfect event.

Almost er'ybody sent they money as anticipated and we book'd the hotel, caterer, D.J., and bought the snacks for the bus ride and the swim party. Rev. Daddy's friend Big Mike donated the buses and half the gas to go along with it. Hold on, let me go get the flyer that was sent out to all'a the households. I wanna make sure I tell ya'll er'ythang we got plan'd. PAUSE..... O.K.....Here we go.

Happy Birthday To Ya'.......Happy Birthday to Ya'……

HAPPY BIRTHDAY!

Reverend Daddy

THE CENTURION CELEBRATION OF A LIFETIME

For: John Bishop Gooch **When: June 28th – 30th**
Where: Atlanta, Georgia **Fee: Individual $250**
Sheraton Gateway **Couple $500, Family $600**

- **Meet & Greet 6/28**
- **Underground Atlanta 6/29**
- **ML King Center & Home**

- **Ebenezer Baptist Church**
- **Six Flags**
- **Centurion Celebration**
- **Talent Show**
- **Church Services 6/30**
- **Tour of the HBCU's**
- **Swim party**
- **Return to St. Louis 6/31/06**

Package Also Includes:
Hotel Room with free breakfast
Round trip transportation to
    Atlanta
Transportation to tours & parks
Hospitality Suite
Baby Sitting (Tips not included)

Send Payments to:
Pearl A. Johnson
4620 Bessie Ave, STL, MO 63115
$100 due 6/10/06
Balance due 6/21/06

CASH OR MONEY ORDERS ONLY!
CHECKS NOT ACCEPTED AND YOU KNOW WHY!!!!

PART IV

LA

LOVELY ATLANTA

'The will of God will never take you where the
Grace of God will not protect you.'

22

YA'LL GOT ER'YTHANG?

RECORD......I was so anxious last night, I hardly got any sleep. Today is the day we leave for Atlanta. Oh, excuse me, my grandkids told me I'm s'pose to say Hot'lanta. I don't know nuth'n bout all that but I do know I'm more familiar with the old LA, lovely Atlanta. When Reverend Daddy moved there in 1965, me and Faye used to go party down there all'a the time but now that the city done got so big and I'm so old, I only visit once or twice the year. Er'ything done changed so much. Atlanta used to have that down home hospitality feel'n but now, to me, it's just like San Francisco, Chicago, New York and all those other big metropolises, impersonal, over crowd'd and too expensive.

Back before Atlanta host'd the 1996 Olympic games, I used to know my way round the city pretty good but they went and built a lot'a new stuff and made so many streets one-way to accommodate the traffic flow for Olympics, I'm not sure I could find my way from downtown to Reverend Daddy's house anymore. But I do remember when not so long ago Stone Mountain was nuth'n but Klan country and black folks had to get outta there before the sun went down or risk be'n lynch'd. Also back then, to me it seem'd, Decatur, GA was sparsely populated and a lot further from Atlanta but now that the population done exploded, er'ything seem closer or is it simply cause the increase in population done stretch'd the metropolitan boundaries outward? I hear some folks commute from as far as Lithonia, GA, which is about thirty minutes outside'a the city limits. But with all the traffic they got, on a busy workday it'll probably take longer that that to get home to Lithonia.

I imagine a lot'a commuter's park they cars and take the MARTA train. MARTA stands for Metropolitan Atlanta Rapid Transit Authority, they rail system. I remember one time when I was in Atlanta, I ask'd this lady for directions to ..... Shucks, I can't ev'n think of the place right now but anyhow she respond'd with the heaviest southern accent that I have ev'a heard and I'm from Mississippi, so you know, I done heard some country talk'n people in my day but this lady is definitely the winner, hands down.

When I ask her for directions, she says, "You know it'z sma'da to take ma'da."

"@#**@! *What did you say?*" I ask her a total of three more times to repeat herself and then finally I just gave up and ask'd someone else. It took about two days later for me to get a translation of what she had really said. I was ride'n the train and saw a advertisement that read **"It's smarter to take MARTA!"** People on the train must'a thought I what'n play'n with a full deck cause I read that sign and I immediately thought back to what that lady was try'n to tell me. I laf'd so hard it brought tears to my eyes. Mind you, I hadn't open'd my mouth prior to my break'n out in hysterics. Chile, them passengers on the train didn't have the slightest clue what was go'n on with me. LOL...LOL

Well anyhow, whenev'a my family get together you can expect a good ol' laugh'n time and it's my hope to get as much of they laughter as possible on this Centurion Celebration on this tape this weeknd. I'm ev'n gon ask some'a my family members to take pictures and carry small tape recorders around with 'em while they at the plan'd activities. That way I'll get first hand knowledge of what really happen'd and then I can pick out the best incidents to include on my legacy tape. Ya'll should'a knowd I was gon come up with a plan cause I can't be er'ywhere at the same time. Especially, consider'n we got two buses and several cars caravan'n to Atlanta. A whole lot'a stuff gon be go'n on and I wanna know 'bout it all. You probably say'n, why not just use a video camera instead? That way you get picture and sound. Well, I prefer the audio and still shots cause it requires a more in depth thought process, which in turn nourishes the imagination. Also, don't nobody hav'ta walk around hold'n and operate'n that recorder thang and ultimately end up not be'n in the activity. These pocket cameras and audio recorders attach to the belt loop for easy access so you can participate *in* the activity, not just on the outside videotape'n it.

Anyway, we all s'pose to meet at 7:00 AM this morn'n on the Northland Shop'n Center park'n lot. We'll probably be the onlyest people out there cause most'a the stores done already went outta bizness. About a year ago St. Louis County executives decided to tear it all down and put up a new shop'n mall named *Buzz Westfall on the Boulevard*. They will probably start rebuild'n in the next month or so.

As I predict'd, the park'n lot was dessert'd when Diamond and I arrived an hour earlier than the others. We need'd the extra time to finalize the hotel room assignments, prepare the sign-in sheets for the buses, separate the T-shirts and mark the door prizes. Each family gon get a gift bag that got they commemorative T-shirts and ink pens, room assignments, discount Six Flags coupons, info'mation about the shuttle service, baby sit'n hours, dinner tickets and plastic champagne glasses for the birthday toast.

Just as we finish'd mark'n the door prizes people start'd come'n. Diamond put the stuff for the gift bags on our fold up make shift table and s'pris'nly by 7:15 er'ybody was accounted for. Of course you know we had some last minute stragglers show up who neither emailed nor call'd to say they was actually go'n but nonetheless they had dollars . Plus we can make extra gift bags and there is space available so, welcome aboard. This here's a family affair, how we gon be turn'n people away?

My brother Clyde from Chicago stop'd and bought a bunch'a donuts to go with the juice, hot coffee and tea Clarice and 'nem was pass'n out to er'ybody. Chile, it look like we was have'n a tailgate party at the *St. Louis Rams* game. Once er'ybody got they donut and beverage, Diamond pull'd out a bullhorn. "May I have er'yone's attention? It's time for us to board the buses. Please listen for your name then place your luggage in the compartment on the bottom, board the bus and quickly find a seat. Remember, your seat is not a life-time commitment but rather only yours for a few hours so don't linger too long choose'n a seat. We *would* like to be on our way before 8 AM."

Clarice, Bubba's wife yell out, "I got a weak bladda so I'ma need a aisle seat."

"Me too", Clyde said.

I took the bullhorn from Diamond. "Hold on! We gon take care'a er'ybody's request but before we get start'd I'd like for ya'll to take the hand of the person next to you and let's pray the prayer our Father taught us." When I reach'd for Baby Boy's hand, I had to remind myself to say it the way Black Protestants say it and not the way Catholics say it cause the majority of my family here, other than my off springs, is Baptist.

In unison, we began, "Our Father which art in heaven, hallow'd be thy name; thy kingdom come; thy will be done on earth as it is in heaven. Give us this day our daily bread; and forgive us our trespasses as we forgive those who trespass against us; and lead us not into temptation, but deliver us from evil." We then stretched our arms upward to the sky and said, "For thyne is the kingdom, and the power and the glory forever, Amen..."

For those of us of the Catholics faith, dure'n mass when we recite the Lord's Prayer, right after we say "...deliver us from evil," the priest recites a short prayer and the congregation responds, "For the kingdom, the power and the glory are yours, now and forever." Then we exchange a sign of peace to our family and fellow parishioners. Generally white Catholics don't hold hands while they pray unless they in African American parishes. So it's safe to say when Black Catholics hold hands dure'n the Lord's Prayer it's a cultural gesture not a Catholic religious ritual. Likewise Black Catholic parishes allow about two or three minutes to shake hands with the congregation while White Catholics *only* exchange a sign of peace with the person on either side'a him. That's all! Chile, they sign'a peace lasts all'a ten seconds, again, merely a cultural difference.

On account we got two buses we gon separate the kids and the old folks. I'm the bus monitor for the older bus with people ages twenty-six to seventy-six and some case-by-case exceptions. Rubie's in charge of the young peoples bus, ages zero to twenty-five.

Since Diamond suffers from motion sickness and can't stomach long car rides she fly'n to Atlanta later this afternoon. She'll be there by the time we make it to Chattanooga, which is about two hours north of Atlanta. The entire ride shouldn't take more'n elev'n hours and that's allow'n for several gas, restroom and eat'n stops.

Rubie rang this old fashion schoolhouse bell to get er'ybody's attention. I thought it both clever and effective. She didn't need no bullhorn cause er'ybody got quiet and all eyes were on her. Leave it to a teacher to quickly quiet a crowd down.

"Can we all get together to take a picture. You know how mama is about her "picture book", as she calls it. Afterwards, listen up for your name so you'll know which bus to get on."

I had ask'd the bus driver to take a picture of us with my disposable camera. Several other relatives also want'd to capture the picture on their camera, so, it took about another 20 minutes for us to finish taking pictures.

Once we was finish'd, Rubie pull'd out her list and began call'n names and people proceeded to get on they assign'd bus. Immediately the teenagers start'd help'n load the luggage in the bus' bottom compartment while the men situated the beverage coolers contain'n water, fruit juices, soda, beer and wine onto the appropriate bus. There was to be absolutely no drink'n of spirits take'n place on the young peoples bus instead Rubie brought plenty'a snacks, games and DVD's to keep 'em entertained. We had already told people to bring they portable media players with 'em but we had a couple extras just in case somebody forgot theirs.

23

WHAT WE WAIT'N ON? LET'S GO!

When we pull'd off the park'n lot at eight o'clock sharp, I stood up in the aisle to make some announcements. Be'n as though this the older folk bus there's some stuff I'm not gonna ev'n touch on cause I assume adults know how to act. Howev'a I do have some general housepkeep'n notes.

"First, I'd like to send a special prayer up for all'a us on this bus to arrive in Atlanta without harm, have a marvelous, joyful time while we there and then return home safely, in Jesus' name."

As if on cue we all replied, "Amen."

I continued, "Welcome aboard, er'ybody. And for those of you who don't know me, my name is Pearl Johnson. I'm Reverend Daddy's oldest child. Please make note'a where you sit'n cause we won't be play'n no musical seats on this trip. Print your name and cell phone number on this seat'n chart that Jade's gon pass around. Listen, if you don't already know the person sit'n next to you, I suggest you introduce yo' self cause ya'll gon be sit'n next to each other for a long time. Remember, that's your seat til we get to Atlanta, then yo' turn's up. For all fairness, I would ask that you choose a different seat for the time we're in Atlanta and for the ride back home."

"Also there's an emergency bathroom in the back of the bus but we'll be stop'n er'y couple'a hours so that we can gas up, use the bathroom, grab a bite to eat and stretch our legs so we can to keep the blood flow'n in our butts. Plus we got free snacks and beverages in the back of the bus and the ice cold water is right here," I kick'd the cooler next to me up front. "About er'y three or four rows there's a trash bag tied to the back of the seat. Please make use of these trash bags and whenev'a we stop let's take it upon ourselves to see if any of 'em need empty'n. Did er'ybody get they T-shirt? If not, see me cause we want ya'll to wear 'em tomorrow morn'n at breakfast and then all dure'n the day whether you go the King sites, Underground Atlanta or Six Flags, wear your T-shirts. Likewise, you should already have your room assignment but we'll pass out the keys when we get to the hotel."

Before wind'n up the announcements, I look at my watch," Since it's still early for some'a us, I figure we need to get comfortable, go back to sleep or entertain ourselves for the first couple of hours. Then perhaps we can look at a movie after our first stop. Oh, and another thing, the admission to Six Flags is **NOT** included in your all-inclusive rate. Howev'a we did put some half off coupons in your bags to help defray the cost. Don't' forget to see me for your T-shirts and room assignments." I put the mic back in its holder.

Our bus was the lead bus and my cousins Noony and June Bug was follow'n the other bus in they SUV's cause a few folks said they want'd to come but they couldn't sit with they knees cramp'd up on a bus for that long so my cousins offer'd to drive 'em. What'n that nice of them? Anyhow, Jade's ride'n on this bus with me so that she can help me with the snacks and anything else we might need. Right after I sat down two or three people came up to me to exchange they T-shirt for a different size and one person said they didn't get one at all. I made the necessary exchanges while Jade got er'ybody to sign the seat'n chart.

"O.K. Grandma Pearl, er'ybody has signed the chart and is accounted for. If you need anything else I'll be stretched out in my seat over there", Jade point'd across from my two seats. I had saved the first row of seats on either side of the aisle for me and Jade and all'a the stuff we need'd for the ride. You know like water, the first aid kit, cards, dominoes, DVD's, tissue, blankets and media players. Earlier Jade had arranged a self-service approach to the snacks in the back of the bus on the last row of seats.

"Thanks Pooh. I really appreciate you help'n me out like this. I'm pretty tired myself, got up way 'fore the sun this morn'n *and* I been on my feet the whole time. Think I'ma take'a load off for a little while too." I sat down to untie'n my shoes. Once I slid my feet outta them shoes, took off my socks and wiggled my toes I felt a lot better cause my feet what'n cramped up in them hot tennis shoes no more, they could breathe again. I brought a pair of black leather slides for the ride so I put them on and sat back to enjoy the view. Look'n out the window at all'a the roll'n hills, trees, grass, picture perfect sky and graze'n animals puts me at peace. Nature has a way of do'n that, it's very relax'n and I especially like ride'n and look'n out the window.

When me and Faye used to drive to Atlanta, she would do most'a the drive'n cause I just like to ride. It work'd out perfectly for us, her drive'n and me ride'n. That girl used to love to drive er'ywhere. In fact, she died drive'n. I remember I was s'pose to go with her the night that she was kilt but I got sick unexpectedly and stay home instead. For a long time I used to wonder why God took her and left me but with time I changed my way of think'n. Chile, you gotta believe and have faith in His master plan cause I guarantee you, if He bring it to you, He'll see you through it!

Now that the bus done quieted down my eyelids get'n kinda heavy, so I'ma turn off the recorder for spell. Its 8:45 AM, ov'a and out!

"Ouch!" I must'a fell asleep with the recorder on my lap cause when it fell and hit my foot I immediately sat straight up, pick'd up the recorder, turn'd it back on and placed it on the seat next to me. Then I grabbed my foot. RECORD… "Jesus, Mary and Joseph!" Chile, my foot is hurt'n real bad. Er'y since I had foot surgery a few years back, my feet very sensitive to pain and believe me, right now my foot's throb'n big time but I'll be o.k. in a couple of minutes once the initial pain subsides. Just then the driver told me it was time for our first stop. The noise from the recorder fall'n on the floor with all'a my other stuff woke er'ybody up so it was a good thing we was stop'n before they start'd get'n restless. I look'd at my watch; it was elev'n o'clock, we right on schedule. I stretch and lean forward.

"Mr. Richard, I ask the bus driver, where are we?"

"We barely in Kentucky but if we don't stop now, the next service stop is fifty-seven miles away in Paducah. I figure we betta stop while we can. I know it's about two or three eating places and several restrooms right ov'a there in the same area. Let everybody know we'll be stopped here for about thirty minutes."

I stood up so er'ybody could see me. "Ya'll listen up, we gon stop at this *BP* gas station/convenient mart and there's a *Burger King, Kentucky Fried Chicken* and *Taco Bell* right next door. Please take the trash out with you and" ….. before I could finish, someone in the back of the bus interrupts with a question, "How long we got?"

"Just long enuf to use the bathroom and stretch yo' legs. Mr. Richard, our bus driver, has ask'd that we be back on the bus in thirty minutes. Don't forget to take your cell phones in case I need to contact you."

After I gave all'a the instructions, I move outta the aisle so that they could get by cause I what'n leave'n the bus til Jade came back. She had left dure'n the announcements. Ev'n though we's amongst family, I ain't gon leave our thangs unattend'd. Especially since I got a few things I borrow'd from other people that I'm responsible for. Much to my delight, Jade was back on the bus in ten minutes with a *Taco Bell* bag in tow.

She asks me, "You want some, Grandma Pearl?"

"Oh, no thank you. Chile, I can't eat that kinda food out in public. If I eat that, I'm liable to blow this whole bus apart. No, my stomach too sensitive, I gotta eat that kind'a food at home, behind closed doors with plenty of air fresh'ner. HA..HA… But I got some fried chicken wings and potato salad in my bag that I'm gon eat when I get back. You welcome to have some. "

"Nah, I'm good with this Mexican pizza. Thanks anyway."

With that, I depart'd the bus, I need'd to stretch my legs a bit. Mind you, I attached my other recorder to my belt loop. When I step off the bus the humidity hit me dead in the face and I gasp'd for air. Thank God for the cool-air conditioned store.

I betcha the towns people could tell I what'n no regular cause my face express'd a sight of amazement, I couldn't believe my eyes, they got er'ything in here. In addition to the usual convenient items, snacks and beverages, they also got homemade pizza, bar-b-que and submarine sandwiches served on fresh baked bread. I what'n interest'd in eat'n cause my food was on the bus but I did need to go to the bathroom and as usual, there was a line. How come men don't hav'ta wait? Answer: Cause they stand up like the Chinese do when they use *it*. China's got billions of people and they say it take too long to sit down and use *it*. Stand up, more people can go in a shorter period of time.

Last spring I was fortunate enuf to go to China for a ten-day visit with a tour group and let me tell ya', the public restroom situation ov'a there was absolutely deplorable. I mean it was downright nasty! First of all, they don't have toilets but rather porcelain troths in the floor that you gotta straddle while at the same time try and hold your panties and hope you rolled your pants legs up far enuf not to get wet. And to make a bad situation ev'n worse, usually they don't provide tissue, so, now in addition to all'a that you gotta search for some tissue in your purse. Needless to say, not er'ybody got the best aim, which means waste ia all ov'a the floor and the stench is way pass foul, it'll make you wanna puke. The hotels have the same type of troth system in they lobbies but they a lot cleaner, got toilet tissue and they don't stink. Thankfully though, in your hotel room, both toilets and tissue are the norm.

But this here bathroom facility is a lot nicer than some of the ones you normally find when travel'n the nation's highways. I close the door and the hourly check-list taped to the back of the door immediately catches my attention. I look at my watch to see if it is current and s'pris'nly, it was. Whoev'a built this bathroom think like a woman and design'd it for maximum comfort and cleanliness with such amenities as baby change'n stations, automatic flush'n toilets, motion sensory water faucets, electric hand dryers and deep sink wells with a contour to keep the water from get'n on your clothes or on the floor when you wash'n your hands. Women, especially mothers, appreciate when management require that they bathrooms be check'd and clean'd regularly. And by do'n so, they can pretty much guarantee a repeat customer. - Lord knows I'd hate to be the one who had to clean them bathrooms but I sho' am glad somebody do'n it.

I use the bathroom, wash my hands and go back out to the bus. "Is er'ybody back on the bus", I ask Jade as I sit my *Icee* down in my seat. I'm like a magnet when it come to *Icees*, er'y time I see one, I gotta get one. Lemonade's my favorite flavor.

"No, we still wait'n for Uncle Chuck and Randy ov'a there smoke'n a cigarette but they on they way back now. I wonder if er'ybody on the other bus yet? I'ma go ask Ant Rubie." She was gone before I could say, "How bout we call her on her cell phone".

While she was gone I sat down to watch Noony and June Bug clean off they windshields and wipe down they headlights as to help keep the bug splatter to a minimum. My little brother Chuck and his son Randy got on the bus but stop'd at the front cooler to get some water as they made they way to their seats. Sniff..Sniff.. Yuk, they reek of smoke. I sho' am glad they ain't sit'n next to me smell'n like some old ashtray. I'd hav'ta pull out my can'a *Lysol* and spray they butts. Jade came back on the bus and gave the thumbs up signal, which means we ready to go. And off we went! It was 11:45 AM.

Let me tell ya, these buses that Big Mike sent down here for us to use ain't no shabby buses, by no means. They got state of the art décor and technology. They both spank'n new with plush cushions, overhead lights, air vents, foot rests as well as headrests, headphone outlets in the armrests and an intercom system. We ev'n got the option of listen'n to five or six different radio stations or you can switch it to T.V. and hear whatev'as play'n on one of the four monitors strategically placed to benefit er'ybody's perfect view without somebody's head block'n your picture. I don't think there's a bad seat on the whole bus.

Be'n as though we gon be visit'n the King memorial and other historical sites, I thought it'll be nice to look at the documentary, *Four Little Girls* by *Spike Lee*. It's about the bomb'n of the Sixteenth Street Baptist Church in Birmingham, Alabama and the lives of the four little black girls that was kilt. In response to the tragedy, Dr. King came to the community to provide hope, strength and determination, which further enhanced the other freedom marches that was go'n on at the time. The bomb'n incident was bitter with the sweet cause it also spearhead'd the successful voter registration movement. Anyhow, before I can put the movie in, I need to pass out one'a my recorders and it can't be to just anybody, I gotta find the *right* person. So, I began comb'n the aisle in search of the best possible will'n participant and my eyes focused on Ant Hattie Pearl, Mother's youngest sister. She's my namesake, I'm named after her.

When I was a kid, Ant Hattie was (and still is) my favorite aunt. I was fascinated with the thangs she said, the way she dress'd and the money she had, or so I thought she had. She used to sometimes slip up and cuss when we kids would be in the room and chile, we thought that was so funny cause adults didn't usually cuss around children. Plus, the general rule back then was chil'ren were to be seen and not heard but Ant Hattie would make sho' she include us kids in all'a the festivities whenev'a she had holiday parties or bar-b-ques at her house in Detroit. No matter what time'a day I saw her, she was always dress'd up and look'n good. I used to wish I could dress just like her! Her shoes, purse, belt, hat and ev'n nail polish match the color of her outfitts. You know, she used to make all'a her own clothes; ev'n had'a bizness call'd *Stitch N Time* where she design'd and sew'd clothes and draperies for wealthy white folks. Not many black folks, especially black women, owned they own bizness back in the 60's but she did. *And* was quite successful too!

Er'y summer Mother and some of us kids would pile in the car and head for Detroit or Florida. We would alternate our visits between my grandmother in Florida and Ant Hattie in Detroit. I remember one summer Mother let me spend two weeks in Detroit with my Ant Hattie Pearl. It was one'a the best times of my childhood. But after Mother died, I nev'a did see my maternal grandmother again nor did I see Ant Hattie again til the summer of '65 when I moved to St. Louis.

#   #   #   #   #

I got this picture of Ant Hattie all dress'd up with a apron, on top'a her fancy clothes. I remember that day as though it were yesterday!

We had just finish'd plant'n some new roses in the back yard when I heard this horn honk'n and'a honk'n out front. I lay'd the spade down, took off my gloves and proceeded to the fence to see if I knew who was make'n all'a that racket. I thought, *why blow the horn when people got do'bells?* I still what'n used to the noises of the city yet, especially all'a them sirens dure'n the night. Well anyway, when I walk outta the gate I see the back of this lady get'n in a blue Cadillac that was parked in front'a my house.

"Excuse me, you look'n for us?" By this time Tootsie is stand'n next to me at the bottom of the front porch steps.

The mystery lady turns around in her seat and say, "Is this where Pearl Ann Johnson live?"

"That depends on who wants to know?" Her voice was familiar but I couldn't get a good look at her cause the sun was shine'n in my eyes and all I could make out was her sit'n in the car wear'n a big hat that cover'd most'a her face and she had on sunglasses. I see her motion to the driver and he gets out, come around the car and open the door for her. He's also wear'n a hat so I couldn't get a good look at him either.

I thought *what they want with me?* Just then, out step'd the most graceful woman I ev'a seen in my life. You could tell from the way she walk that she was someone important *and* to top it all off, she was impeccably dress'd. She had on this big white floppy hat, which perfectly match'd her black silk pants suit trim'd in white along the collar and bell sleeves. Her kitten heel shoes and purse were of the same black and white color but with small polka dots plus, she carried a pair of black lace gloves in her hand. Her whole demeanor scream'd stylish yet classy. She look'd like a movie star and I only knew one person who could look like that.

I yell out, "**ANT HATTIE PEARL!**"

"Yes, it's me. Girl, come give me'a kiss. Sorry we was franticly blow'n the horn like that but we had been knock'n on the door for about five minutes and didn't nobody answer. Reverend Daddy already told us you was at home."

I made a mental note to see about move'n that doorbell to a better location cause several people had told me they didn't see it. Tootsie stay'd at the bottom of the steps cause she really didn't know Ant Hattie, she'd only heard tale of her. When I ran to give Ant Hattie a hug, I stop'd dead in my tracks and look'd down and saw how dirty I was. You see, when I was plant'n I wiped dirt all ov'a the front'a my shirt.

"Me and Tootsie was out back plant'n flowers, that's why we didn't hear you knock'n at the front door. Ooooh, you look so pretty but I don't wanna get you dirty, so I'ma hold off on the kiss'n. Ya'll come in and have a cool drink. Make yourself at home while we change our clothes."

They follow'd us back in the house. I go and take a quick shower, towel dry my hair and was back downstairs within a few minutes. To my s'prise, I found Ant Hattie in the kitchen with my apron on pour'n lemonade into iced glasses. Next to the glasses is a platter of sandwiches, a bowl of potato chips and a fruit plate with sliced orange quarters and grapes. Tootsie didn't make it downstairs for at least twenty more minutes after me. You know how teenagers are about meet'n new people, especially old folks, they rather be do'n chores cause it's just as unpleasant to 'em.

"Hope you don't mind me fix'n a few sandwiches. You said for us to make ourselves at home and if we was at home we'd be eat'n lunch right about now, so I decided to fix a little sumthin' for er'ybody. You hungry?" I shook my head yes. Ant Hattie wiped her hands on the apron and moitioned for me to come closer. "Come here girl, let me get a good look at you. I ain't seen't you since you was a little girl. Chile, you know you look just like your mother did when she was your age."

"Yes Ma'am, people always tell'n me I look like Mother. Thanks for do'n all'a this but ya'll s'pose to be my guest, sit down, relax, and at least let me do the serve'n."

"That'll be nice but first let's go in the living room, I want you to meet my husband. He in there, watch'n the baseball game. We been married for about ten years but I don't think you ev'a met him." I gave Ant Hattie Pearl a big hug and kiss and we head for the live'n room arm n' arm as if we's best girlfriends walk'n home from school.

"Alex, turn that T.V. down a minute, I want you to meet someone, she my favorite niece. This is my sister Ouida's oldest child, Pearl. And Pearl, this my husband and subsequently, your uncle, Mr. Alex Wash'nton."

"Nice to meet you, sir." I nod my head as I extend my hand.

"Why ya'll be'n all formal like that? We's family, come on give your Uncle Alex a hug. If you Hattie's favorite niece I sho' gotta make sure I do right by you then, don't I?"

Either I'm mistaken or that's Harry Bellefonte stand'n in my live'n room cause this man look exactly like 'em but older, could be his daddy! I couldn't say a word, I was trap'd in a spell. Now I see why Ant Hattie pick'd him to be her husband, he was dress'd just as smooth and debonair as she is. *And* he good look'n too! He put you in the mind of the kind'a man that after you look at him, you need to go to confession cause you probably done committed the sin of lust. Chile, that man what'n just handsome, he also smells *real* good. I found that out when he hug'd me. Reverend Daddy used to say, "You can tell' a lot about what a man does for a live'n by his fingernails and his cologne or lack thereof." As a graduate of the school of *hard knocks,* I'm here to tell ya', it's a big difference in the type of man that wears *Old Spice, Grey Flannel* and *Cool Water* fragrances.

I brought the lunch that Ant Hattie prepared into the dine'n room and we all sat down to eat. Once we finish'd, Tootsie excused herself from the table and Uncle Alex went back in the live'n room to watch the rest of the game. Meanwhile, I gave Ant Hattie a tour'a my new place. I had only been in the house for about three weeks so in one'a the spare bedrooms, there was still some boxes wait'n to be unpacked. But for the most part, er'ything else is where it s'pose to be.

After the tour of my house, me and Ant Hattie Pearl sat in the back yard and talk'd for hours about Mother and the different things that done happen'd to our family since her death. I was inspired by her visit and vow'd to nev'a loose contact with her again and I'm proud to say that I have kept in contact with her ev'a since.

# # # # #

Ev'n though Ant Hattie is just a few years older than me, ten to be exact, she has had way mo' life experiences than I have and I'm sure she'll jump at the chance to be a part of anything positive that could possibly empower our young people. Traditionally in black families, whenev'a family members gather, they all make it a point to go ov'a and personally acknowledge, give respect to, the elders of they family. So I patiently wait my turn, til the seat next to Ant Hattie was empty, then I sat down.

Before speak'n, we kiss. "How you do'n Ant Hattie?"

"I can't complain, the Lord still bless'n me. How you and your family come'n along, Pearl?"

"Rubie, Baby Boy and Diamond all just fine, they kids too. Ant Hattie, I got sumthin' to ask you…. Will you do me a favor?"

"I don't know, depends on what the favor is?"

"Well, a few months ago I promised some'a the young folks in the family that I would make a audio tape about our family. I'm call'n it my legacy tape and it'll include pictures, childhood stories, ancestral tales, current events and words of knowledge for the young and old folk alike. I plan on give'n 'em as Christmas gifts to our family members. So far, I've been the only one provide'n the stories and such but I thought it would be a good idea to maybe get some other relatives' input as well, especially someone from Mother's side'a the family. Which brings me to the favor, will you please wear this mini tape recorder for me this weekend?"

"And say what in it?"

"Nuth'n if you don't wanna but you're welcome to say whatev'a you like. All I ask is that you make sure that the recorder's on dure'n the celebration activities that you go to. I wanna get a true record'n of all'a the events. Other than that, it's up to you to decide what you wanna share on your tape with us. I plan on ask'n one or two other folks to participate too cause er'ybody might not go to all'a the events. But this way, I'll have most'a my bases cover'd. Outta four people, I'm pretty sure at least one'a us gon be at each of the activities."

"Yeah, I guess I can do that for you. And you say you don't care what else I talk about, right?"

"That's correct but I can't guarantee you it's gon end up on the final legacy tape cause it might end up on the cut'n floor but I'm the only one's gon be edit'n the tape for content. If I wind up with too much material for a tape but I think it should be shared with er'ybody, then… perhaps I can have it put on a CD, they got a whole lot more space on 'em and I can combine audio and photos. Thanks for the idea Ant Hattie."

"Uh, I don't ev'n know what I said. Do you want me to let people know they be'n taped?

"Not necessarily, you be the judge of that. Look, here's mine, I'll show you how it work. I've had mine on and off ev'a since we left St. Louis. I forgot to tell you I was tape'n our conversation just now but we what'n say'n nuth'n private either, otherwise I would' a told you right up front I was tape'n. That's exactly what I mean about use'n your own judgment."

I remember I don't have an updated picture of her. "Will somebody please take a picture of me and Ant Hattie with my camera?"

Jade said, "I'll do it Grandma Pearl."

I told myself, *this gon be a good picture of us.* Jade snapped the photo and hurried back to her seat. I began to show Ant Hattie how to use the recorder.

Amazingly, Ant Hattie didn't have nearly as much trouble as I did the first time I used the recorder. I only had to show her one time. But come to find out, she no stranger to mini recorders; before she retired, she used to use 'em during fit'n sessions. I return to my seat'n area to get the movie. Since it was bright inside'a the bus, I ask er'ybody to close they shade and use the overhead light'n so that we can get the glare off the monitors.

I put the DVD in and immediately I hear the song *Cry Sunday* that Joan Baez wrote in tribute to the four little girls kilt in the Birmingham bomb'n. By the time I get situated with my chicken wings and potato salad the song ends and the movie begins. I turn around and am glad to see, er'ybody look'n at they monitor. I'm sure most'a the people on this bus more'n likely actually remember live'n with segregation and Jim

Crow laws, especially if they growd up in the south but there are quite a few people under age fifty on here who don't remember and need to know the history of the civil rights movement cause a lotta black people was jailed or died unjustly fight'n for equality.

The documentary captured er'ybody's attention. It was so quiet on that bus you could hear a pin drop. Just as the movie was end'n, Mr. Richard tells me it was a quarter to three, time to make another stop. We ride for anuth'a twenty minutes or so and then turn'd into this huge truck stop about 20 miles outside'a Nashville, by the way, that's the half way point o Atlanta.

"Listen up er'ybody. We gon be here for about an hour or so. That should be plenty'a time to stretch yo' legs, get sumthin' to eat, smoke a cigarette or whatev'a you fancy. The bus will be serviced for the first half hour but after that you can come back on the bus whenev'a you ready. We'll be leave'n at four-thirty. Oh and don't forget to take your cell phones with you." I had plan'd on be'n the last one off the bus so I step aside and let er'ybody else leave. When I got off, Mr. Richard closed the door behind me and drove ov'a to the bus and truck area. The other bus is already ov'a there; both need'd gas and clean'n up.

This truck stop is call'd *Huck's* and it's twice as big as the place we stop'd at in Paducah. *Huck's* has a motel, gift shop, newsstand, internet Café, two restaurants, a video game room and a homemade bakery that sells the best mile high pecan pie I ev'a tasted. After I ate my pie and drank a cup of tea, I decide to go browse around in the gift shop for a bit. As I was walk'n down the aisle towards the gift shop, I happen to glance out the window and see several police cars parked out front. I figure somebody must'a done stole sumthin' and I hoped to God it what'n none'a my people but I had to know for sure, so I go ask the person behind the sales counter.

"What's go'n on? Why all'a them cops," I ask?

The attendant replies, "They look'n for a prisoner who escaped early yesterday. He's believed to be head'n in the other direction but they check'n this area out just to be safe. They assured us there's nuth'n to worry about."

"Do you know what prison he come from?"

"I know it's not Kentucky State but I can't think of the name of it right now. It's the one right outside of Paducah", he says.

"Well, thanks for the info anyway." I continue on to the gift shop and guess who I run into; Jennifer, Rubie's youngest daughter. She look'n at the souvenirs when I walk up behind her. I tap her on the shoulder and she jumps.

"What you do'n in here by yo' self", I demand to know.

"You scared me, Grandma and I'm not really by myself, Mom just went to the bathroom a second ago and told me to wait right here. Why you going around scaring people?"

"I'm sorry baby, Grandma didn't mean to scare you but it's time for us to start head'n to the bus. Let's go get your mama." We look at a few more items and by the time we make it back to the entrance; we see Rubie come'n outta the bathroom. I gave Jennifer five dollars and told her to go get me a lemonade *Icee* while I make a stop in the bathroom. When we meet up, I show Rubie where Jennifer is so she wouldn't be look'n for her. I didn't waste no time dolly'n in the bathroom cause I still had to give out the other tape recorder and some disposable cameras.

Jade and mostly er'ybody else was already on the bus, so when I got back on the bus I hurriedly retrieve the recorder and go take it to the other bus. Chile, the noise on that bus is sumthin' else. I sho' am glad I'm on the old peoples bus, I can't take all'a that racket! Just like Jade and me, Rubie and Jennifer reserved the first row of seats for they self and all'a they stuff too. Jennifer was sit'n in the seat next to the window drink'n a *Icee*, which I presume is mine.

"How come you didn't get yo' self one," I ask, point'n to the *Icee* in her hand.

"I did. Yours is ov'a there with Mom. Can I have your change?"

"Only if you do sumthin' for me, I'll ev'n throw in anuth'a ten dollars to go with it, if you do a good job."

"Ok. What I gotta do?" I sit down in the seat next to her and lower my voice.

"I need you to wear this here tape recorder and carry this camera whenev'a you go to the activities we got plan'd this weekend. The only thing is, you gotta keep the recorder a secret. That means you *can't* let the other kids know you got it. You think you can do that for me?"

"Grandma, does this have anything to do with these legacy tapes my mama say you making for er'ybody?"

"Yes, it does and I would appreciate you help'n me out."

"Of course, I'll do it and you don't ev'n hav'ta pay me. I think it's a great idea what you doing and I'm glad to help out. But, I gotta confession to make. I did sort'a like, already spend your change."

"That's ok Pooh. Here's the recorder and camera. Do you know how to work 'em"? She look at me like I ask'd the obvious but in any event, she shook her head yes. *I should'a knowd she did. How many teenagers today can't operate electronics?* "We'll talk more later on. For now, just put it with your stuff and remember shshshsh......mums the word," I say and press my fingers to my lips. Then I turn around, get my *Icee* from Rubie and head back to my bus.

"Is er'ybody on the bus," I ask Jade as I get on.

"Yep, everyone's accounted for. We can go as soon as we hear from Antie Rubie.

Just then, my cell phone rang.

It's Rubie, "June Bug and Noony say they're ready and we're ready too. How 'bout ya'll?"

I shout, **"LET'S Gooo!"** and hang up the phone. It's 4:30 PM and I forgot to call Diamond back.

24

DIAMOND

Diamond was relaxing in her sunken bathtub when she began to feel light-head again. Was it the alcohol? She surmised, this time, it was from her increased body temperature so she turned on the cold water to regulate the bath water temperature. As the water ran out of the faucet, she placed her face towel underneath it. Then she held her arms above her head and squeezed the towel to allow the cool refreshing water to flow over her face. Unconsciously, she contemplated taking a later flight if she didn't feel better but she did. Within seconds, her wooziness subsided and she felt like herself again. Her non-stop flight to Atlanta was scheduled for a 4:30 PM departure but she could easily change it to the red-eye flight and travel with her husband Duane, if need be. She glances at the clock on the wall to gage how much longer she can relax but instead she realizes it has been almost five hours since her family left for Atlanta, more than enough time to check to see where they were. She immediately picks up her cell and dials her mother's phone number.

Pearl answers on the first ring. "Hello."

"Hi Mommie, where are you guys?"

Pearl whispers. "We're about a hour away from Kentucky but I can't talk right now cause we watch'n *Spike Lee's* documentary about the Birmingham bomb'n and I don't wanna be rude and talk on the phone when er'ybody else try'n to listen to the movie. I'll call you back just as soon as it go off. Bye now." She didn't wait for a response but instead disconnected the call.

Diamond looked askew at the phone because she didn't even get a chance to say bye and thought, *I hate it when people end a conversation before I say goodbye. Civilized people refer to that as hanging up on somebody but I guess that's not the case when it's your mother on the other end of the line. But,* she *did* say bye.

Diamond had about two hours before she was due to arrive at the airport so she decided to soak up some more relaxation and comfort. Soaking in the tub not only clears her mind but it also relaxes and calms her nerves and her nerves need extra calming today because she seems a bit agitated, anxious and on edge. Not to mention the unusual fatigue and dizzy spells she has been experiencing all week. Before getting in the tub she decides to put on some music to help get her in the right mood. She puts on her favorite *Jill Scott* CD, undress and get in the tub. Duane has a passion for music and he insisted speakers be wired and placed in every room of the house. This elaborate sound system is as clear in the bathroom on the second floor as if you are standing right next to it in the great room where all the media and entertainment equipments is kept. *Jill Scott's* neo-soul sound equally permeates the house just as much as the rose scented pillar candles Diamond strategically placed in the powder room and the bathroom to achieve maximum ambiance.

The bathroom suite is Diamond's favorite room in the entire house. In fact, this bathroom layout is what actually sold her on the property. It's enormous compared to the average person's house bathroom and by far, even larger than most of her own relative's bedrooms. Upon entering one might think of a spread in a home décor magazine like, *Better Homes and Garden* or somthing off one of those popular home remodeling shows on the cable network. It's very lavish.

The dominate color of the walls in the powder room is of the palest lavender with white gardenias lining the border. In addition to the twin porcelain pedestals accented with sterling silver faucets and handles, the silver-plated matching diamond shaped mirrors are surrounded with theatrical lighting similar to that often seen in dressing rooms of movie stars. The towels, rugs and curtains are all different but complimentary shades of lavender to enhance the orchid paintings displayed on the wall opposite of the mirrors, just above the vanity where she keeps her make-up, perfume, oils, nail polish and such. It is at this very table, a few years earlier, that Jade would spend numerous hours playing dress-up. The thought of the familiar scene brought a smile to Diamond's face. Lord knows she could use some happiness because for the last week she has been harboring a horrible incident that she's trying to convince herself is not true but deep down, she know what she saw is for real.

On the way to the bathroom she got foliage and candid nude black & white baby photos of Jade (in the bathtub and on the toilet) line the massive hallway from the powder room to the master bedroom. In the bathroom, the color of the tile on the floor and the base of the walls is a deep purple that gradually ascends into lighter shades of lavender with an iridescent radiance as you reach the ceiling. The hot tub, shower stall and lavender sunken vintage bear claw tub are all included in the room but fashionably separated. The shower stalls on a wall by itself, shaped like an octagon and the outside is incased in mirrors from the floor to the edge of the ceiling. Keep in mind, the same sterling silver faucets, handles, towel racks and mirrors displayed in the powder room also accessorize the bathroom. About two feet left of the shower is the hot tub and then another three feet to the right of that, smack dab in the middle of the bathroom , is a huge sunken tub that requires three steps up before submerging deep down into the tub.

Diamond eased her head back onto the mini pillows and closed her eyes. When she picked up her wine glass and saw that it was empty, she became irritated, pushed the intercom button and told the maid to bring her some more wine. A couple of minutes later, Hilda arrives with the bottle of wine. After refilling the glass, she rearranges the ice in the bucket to ensure the wine stays cold.

"Vill you be need'n anything else, Madame?"

"No thank you, Hilda. That will be all. Oh! I almost forgot, I will need some assistance with my luggage but that'll be in about an hour. Will you please inform the chauffer?"

"Sure. I'll let Fletcher know. Is that all, Mrs. Vorberts?"

"Yes and thank you," Diamond replies with closed eyes.

The combination of rose scent, soft music, warm water and alcohol eased her tensions and she began to relax. Lately, it was become'n increasingly harder for her to ward off the episodes of depression, fear and anxiety that she had secretly battled with for most of her adult life. Rubie and Duane are the only ones privy to her mental challenges merely because they each have shared a bedroom with her and personally witnessed her in action. To er'ybody else, the outside world, she appears to be confident, stable and very assertive.

Actually, she's far from stable now that her suspicions have been confirmed but she can't decide how to proceed. *Should I confront him or just leave?* Duane is unaware that she knows about his infidelity and likewise she is unsure if she wants to let him know and consequently take the steps necessary to end her marriage. Or perhaps they should try counseling first? *How long has this been going on? Does he love her? If we divorce, who will pay the bills? What will people say? Can Jade still go to college?* Diamond asks herself these questions repeatedly in her mind over the previous week. As always, she manages to keep up a good front, not even Duane suspects anything is wrong with her but truthfully, the whole ordeal is mentally weighing her down fast!

She has to do something soon, make a decision. Another week of silence is out of the question, but with all the festivities going on this weekend, today is definitely not a good time. After finishing her fourth glass of wine, she made a promise to herself that as soon as they return from Atlanta she will confront Duane with the evidence the private detective gave her the last time they met. But for now, all of that will have to be put on hold because she needs to concentrate on catching her flight on time and hosting the family celebration all weekend long. In her world, appearances are everything and since she refers to herself as an acclaimed organizer and fundraiser, her family will naturally expect her to show them the best weekend of their country bumpkin lives.

I hope they remember the fee is only five hundred dollars. She pours herself another glass of wine. Diamond is having serious doubts that she can muster up the energy required to be the gracious host while at the same time pretend her life is *still* loving, spectacular and meaningful. Little does everybody know, she is living a BIG lie. But she has to! *How am I going to get through all of this? More wine? Prayer? (OMG! Where did that come from.)* Besides, prayer is not somthing she regularly practices, that's her mother's thing, not hers. But desperate situations require desperate measures. Plus as Diamond got out of the tub she paused to say a quick prayer to God asking for His strength and guidance to make it through this weekend without incident, be it marital or otherwise.

Since Diamond travels frequently, she's an expert when it comes to packing light, only bringing the essentials, no extra stuff. Two of the eight pieces of her Louis Vutton luggage ensemble sat open on her bed. Closing the suitcases is the very last thing she usually does before leaving home, in case she forget anything, which is highly unlikely given her extensive organizational skills but the suitcases remain open just the same. While sitting next to the luggage the phone rings and instead of letting Hilda answer it after the customary third ring, Diamond quickly picks up the phone on the first ring, expecting her mother to be on the other end. So sure of who is on the line, she skipped the usual greeting formality and said, "I'm glad you called, I was hoping I could talk to Jade before my flight left. Where are you guys now?"

The voice on the other end startled her because it wasn't Pearl's voice but rather a man's deep voice. "Pardon me, obviously you were expecting someone else. Is this the Roberts residence?"

"Oh, I'm sorry. Yes, this is the Roberts residence. Who would you like to speak to?" His voice was familiar but Diamond couldn't identify the caller, she needed a little more conversation before she could accurately guess his identity. Her anticipation was short lived when the caller spoke again.

He said, "My name is Ashley Wilcox and I'm looking for Mrs. Diamond Roberts. Is she available?"

"Yes she is. Sam, it's me, Diamond. How are you?"

"I'm fine. I thought I recognized your voice but I wasn't absolutely sure. How's everybody else doing?"

"They're all on their way to Atlanta as we speak. We chartered a bus but I'm flying. As a matter of fact, I'll be leaving for the airport in the next thirty minutes. Are you going to be able to make the festivities?"

"Yes, that's exactly why I'm calling. I forgot to rsvp but wanted to let you know that I *will* be there. I'm in Dallas right now and have a two-hour layover in Phoenix. I'll be in Atlanta tonight at nine and should arrive at the hotel no later than ten o'clock. When is your mother due to arrive?"

"They should be there by sev'n or eight o'clock. We'll all probably be in the hospitality suite for the meet and greet cocktails. Unfortunately, I don't know the room number yet but ask at the hotel desk when you check in. How long will you be staying?"

"The entire weekend! I gotta go, my flight's boarding. See you tonight. Good-bye."

"Good-bye," Diamond said and released the call. She began to dial her mother's number to let her know that Sam would be in Atlanta but then she remembers their last conversation and decides to wait until Pearl calls her back. Anyway, Diamond didn't have any time to waste.

She needs to leave in twenty minutes and she wasn't even through dressing nor had she put on her make-up.

There was no need for Diamond to do her hair because earlier that day she persuaded her hairdresser to squeeze her in for a last minute appointment. Even though she had kept her regular appointment at the salon two days ago, she wanted, better yet, needed a drastic change to help her deal with the stress she was having from the information the hired detective had given her. Exercising, shopping, eating and getting a new hairdo are all excellent ways to release stress but due to time restraints, she opts for the new hair do. A new care free look, no more weave. After reviewing several hair magazines she decides on a not so trendy haircut and hopes for the best while the stylist goes to work. She could see the hair falling in her lap and onto the floor. Too late to turn back now! Initially, she cried when the stylist turned the chair around revealing her new look, but the more she stared at herself in the mirror, the more she liked her new hairdo. When it is all done, she leaves the salon sporting a new short pixy hairdo with golden highlights. Diamond can't remember her hair ever being this short, except maybe when she was a toddler.

She put lotion on her body, then took off her scarf, fingered the top of her hair a bit and turns to the right to capture her profile in the full-length mirror. Yes, this hairstyle definitely compliments her high cheekbones and thin neck. But what I like even more is I look ten years younger and ten pounds lighter, a double stress releaser. *You go girl!* Diamond dresses quickly, applies some light make-up and calls for Fletcher to come get her bags.

When she came downstairs five minutes later, she went in the kitchen to let Hilda know she was leaving and instructed her to remind Duane that his flight leaves tonight at 11:30 PM. Fletcher had already opened the car door before he began loading the luggage just in case Diamond came out while he was loading, and she did. She paused to inhale the cool refreshing air. The sun was awfully bright so she reached in her handbag to retrieve her favorite sunglasses. By the time she approaches the car, Fletcher is at her side, ready to assist her but she shooed him away. If Duane wasn't with her, she much rather preferred driving but whenever occasions or convenience dictated, Fletcher drove her in the limousine.

She hated how riding alone in a limo all by yourself made you feel but she also enjoyed sitting back, soaking up the scenery and watching people. In most instances, the driver doesn't get to people watch often, that's a spectator's sport. So every time Diamond is alone in the limo, she playes a game where she creates a name or career for the people she sees on the street, based solely on their appearance. The game is both thought provoking and hilarious. Not to mention it occupies empty time. Some people, she sees every time she's in the limo, but most folks are having their debut. The regulars kept the same identity and in a way, she feels as though she knows them. One regular in particular, Billy Baton, is sure to be on the corner of *Lindell Boulevard* and *Euclid Avenue* in the afternoon on most weekdays. And today is no different. On the northeast corner there is a very skinny man who stands over six feet tall in a light blue cat suit with a matching boa. He twirls a baton while reciting pleasantries to anyone who might listen. Residents and other people familiar with the *Central West End* district anticipate seeing Billie in action and are not shocked nor offended by his outlandish performances. Visitors on the other hand, are absolutely amazed at the reality of it all.

The evening rush hour hasn't begun so Fletcher is able to get to the airport in twenty minutes. The skycap opened Diamond's door while Fletcher gets the bags out of the trunk. She gathers her carry-on items and head for the terminal. When she reaches the first-class check-in counter, two people are ahead of her in line. She motions for the skycap to leave her bags at the counter so she won't have to drag them through the line.

"Ma'am, they'll probably ask you to take your luggage over there to be x-rayed after you check them in. Would you like for me to wait and help you," the skycap ask.

"Yes, that would be nice," she replies. The line is moving fast, it's already her turn and she doesn't have her identification ready. The agent is patient as she digs for her wallet and ticket. She answers the customary questions about packing your own luggage and if it's been in your possession the whole time? Then she gets her boarding pass, tips the skycap ten dollars and walks to security, which by the way, always has a long line. *You would think by now that erverybody knows the airline security routine but no, people still try to bring scissors, nail clippers and fluids in excess of three ounces through security. Also, don't wait til it's your turn to pass through the metal detector before you begin removing your shoes. As a general rule, if you're not wearing flat sandals or flip flops, take them off while you're standing in line and don't forget to empty your pockets. All of these things hold up the line, cause delays and missed flights.*

Traveling is totally different than before the September 11ᵗʰ bombing of the World Trade Center in Manhattan. Back then, arriving at the airport an hour before the flight was scheduled to leave was plenty of time to check-in and walk to the gate. Today, the chances of boarding that same flight are slim to none. Actually, for the last twenty-five years the FAA has gradually changed the whole flying experience. It started with discontinuing youth fares, then skyways were added, luggage specifications enforced, smoking banned, designated areas assigned for non-passengers and now it's x-rays, metal detectors, DEA/ATF dogs and random searches. These mandatory measures are necessary to alleviate and deter future terrorist attacks.

Diamond simply doesn't understand why some people get so upset about the impact and inconveniences security has on traveling. *It's all about their safety.* She kept her thoughts to herself and waited patiently as the line snailed along. By the time she maneuvered through security, she has less than thirty minutes to spare and a twelve-gate walk ahead of her. Luckily, when she arrives at the gate the agent is making the initial announcement for first class passengers to board. Relieved that she was going to make the flight, she slows her pace and then gets in line to board the plane.

C-8 is an aisle seat with plenty of leg room. Diamond couldn't remember the last time, if at all, she traveled in coach. She puts her hand bag in the overhead compartment and decided to keep and place her briefcase underneath the seat in front of her. Perhaps she should use this time to make some strategic notes about what should be her next steps with Duane and his infidelity. *Not another headache, I should get a glass of wine while we taxi.*

"Oh excuse me, will you please bring me a glass of Merlot?" Diamond asks the flight attendant passing out magazines to first class passengers.

"Sure, sit back, prop your feet up and I'll be right back with your wine."

"Care for a magazine to go with that glass of wine?"

"No thank you. I have plenty of things to work on to keep my mind busy."

25

JIM DANDY TO THE RESCUE!

"*Wow, I forgot to call Diamond back,*" Pearl thought for a second time.

"Jade, what time is it?"

"It's almost five o'clock, Grandma."

I pick up the phone and push the number one for speed dial to Diamond's phone. It went straight to her voicemail which mean, she probably already on the plane and done turn'd her phone off. What'n no sense in me leave'n no message cause she hardly ev'a check messages, at least from me anyway. *I'm sure she'll call me once she lands in Atlanta.* Often times, I put my cell phone in my bra when I'm busy do'n chores or shop'n so I can keep up with it, especially if I'm expect'n a call and right now, I need to talk to Diamond to make sho' er'ythang's in order at that hotel. *I bet I won't miss the call now!* I put my phone under my left breast, that way I can feel it vibrate and it won't fall out if'n I need to bend ov'a.

"Jade, did you check and make sure er'ybody back on the bus?"

"Yes ma'am, everyone's here."

We been back on the bus for only a few minutes and I'm still contemplate'n how I'm gon spend the next couple of hours entertain'n myself. I look at all'a the stuff in the seat next to me, activity books, cards, and music but I feel like talk'n so I grab the recorder and prop my head up against the window. This a good time to catch up.

RECORD...... "Well ya'll already know we on our way to Atlanta, for Rev. Daddy's birthday celebration, and guess what....we just pass'd a sign say'n we now in, Nashville. They call this, land of the Ole Opry, country music capital, U-S-A. Personally, I don't like country music, too much twang in they sang'n, but I loves me some blues. Chile, I could sit and listen to a good blues band play all night long.

Look'a here, Atlanta 218 miles! We should be there in about 4 hours. Perfect. The Meet and Greet is scheduled from 9 to 11pm in the hospitality suite. We s'pose to have some drinks and light refreshments, folks expect'n Pepsi and chicken wings but Diamond prob'ly order'd sumthin' our relatives can't ev'n pronounce, know'n her.

Oh, did I tell y'all Ant Hattie and Jade agreed to carry the extra recorder and cameras while we at the celebration events? You know, they prob'ly gon go to different things and I'm sho' they'll be a variety of relatives around, should make for some interest'n stories." STOP.....

Sumthin' in the sky just caught my attention. The way that God shapes the sky can take your breath away or cause you to break out in a big toothy grin. Like when the sun is kind'a peek'n from behind a cloud and you see sparkles or you imagine the clouds as silhouettes of black folks with big afros. The sky is so pretty this time of day. The sun has begun its four hour descent, on its way down and I'm really enjoy'n this eve'n sun on my face. It's not hot but rather calming and relax'n. A few people in the back of the bus, play'n dominoes but most'a the folks in the front of the bus, is either read'n, play'n solitaire or take'n a snooze. I don't feel like play'n no games or read'n a book , I gaze out the window and unconscieneously start read'n the road signs. One by one, mile after mile, I read signs for hotels, Rubie Falls, gas stations, Lookout Mountain, restaurants and the Chattanooga Choo Choo. *Is that a real place?*

Atlanta, 215 miles. Watch'n all these signs make me think of that time we took the whole family on a trip to Florida. RECORD...... Our first real family vacation!

# # # # #

Tootsie and I usually do er'ythang together. See, ain't no other girls amongst our siblings, just me and her. We was (and still is) so close, ev'n our *own* families do er'ythang together. After we move'd to St. Louis and she got married, we nev'a lived more'n five or ten blocks between us. Our children grow'd up like brothers and sisters instead of cousins. Er'y holiday and most'a the weekends we celebrated "whatev'a the occasion", either at Tootsie's or ov'a to my house. Mind you, we didn't have a whole lotta money but what we lack'd in money, we made up for in love, spirit and of course, all'a the food we shared. Not to mention the creativity, (y'all know how we black folks can rig up thangs) well, each party had to have its own theme and color scheme to match. Chile, we used to use them ol' homemade decorations ov'a and ov'a again!

This time, we was celebrate'n for Rubie cause she had won the National Spelling Bee Tournament. The color scheme was yellow and black for "Bee". Baby Boy had intertwined yellow and black crepe paper in the chain link fence all around the yard. The card tables had either a yellow or black table cloth on them with the opposite color decorated plastic top hat as the centerpiece. You know, like a yellow table cloth with a black center piece or vice versa. The kids made some big paper mache bumble bees and stuck them on sticks of different lengths so that it look'd like bees was fly'n all around the yard. It went great with the BIG pastel flowers that we had originally made last Easter. To further accent the theme, large cut-out alphabets swung from the tree limbs and spell'd out words.

Close your eyes, imagine the decorations and all'a the guest dress'd in they yellow or white outfits (we requested that on they invitation). It was so pretty and for dessert, Tootsie made a white cake shaped like a bumble bee with yellow and black frosting. That Tootsie, she know she can make any kind'a cake you could ev'a dream of. She got a lot of practice bake'n for her chil'ren and each one of 'em want'n sumthin' different for they birthday. *Superman, Cats/Dogs, Mermaids, Mickey Mouse, Voltron* and ev'n one time, Earl her husband, requested a can of *Budweiser* beer! It look'd exactly like the actual beer can, too. Quiet as it's kept, shhhhh......, she could open up her own bakery store if she want'd to, she just that good.

Tootsie saw Rubie seated at a table with Uncle Earl and her brother Bubba. She need'd to ask her a question and there was an empty chair next to Rubie, so she sat in it and waited for the opportunity to interrupt the conversation.

"Somebody ask'd me and I can't remember if it's Disneyland or Disney World. Where is it you go'n?" Tootsie asks Rubie.

"On a five day trip to Disney World in Orlando, Florida. Disneyland is in California and I'm going to **Flo-ri-da**, so it's Disney **World**".

144

Tootsie was s'prise'd by her curt tone. All of this new attention was make'n her nervous and a bit on edge but it's no excuse to use this tone with her aunt. "I'm sorry Ant Tootsie, I didn't mean no disrespect but people keep ask'n me that question." Tootsie gave Rubie the "evil eye" then blew her a kiss and head back to the table of bid whist players. If it what'n for the two margaritas Tootsie had already drank, she'd of prob'ly slap'd the s-h-i-t outta Rubie.

"Have you decided who you gon take with you?" Uncle Earl ask'd Rubie, "It's just a question, now don't go get'n upset." In a playful gesture, he start'd move'n things off the table, outta her reach.

"Stop play'n Uncle Earl, you know I ain't gon get upset. I love my family. Honestly, I wish er'ybody could go. Both of our families, all'a us."

"How many FREE tickets they give you? I'm sho' it what'n enuf for all'a us."

"It's for four people and it includes admission, airfare, hotel AND food. So we only gotta pay for about five people, that is, if the little ones stay home. I guess then, I really *don't* want all'a us to go but most'a us or at least, some of us. How can I choose and still be fair?" Rubie left the table unsure who she was gonna take with her. Of course a grown up had'ta go, someone over 21 but that would leave space for only two other people.

Later that eve'n after er'yone had gone home, Uncle Earl came back ov'a to the house, said he need'd to talk to Charlie. They went into the family room, closed the door and stay'd in there for ov'a an hour. I put my ear up to the door but all I could hear was the television. They was obviously whisper'n. I didn't know what they was in there talk'n about but I knew it was sumthin' important so I call'd Tootsie and told her to come ov'a. Generally, Charlie didn't allow closed doors in the house, he used tell us "Open that door, what'cha hide'n in there?" I was so tempt'd , I nearly bust'd in the room to ask him the same thang but I didn't. Anyway, when they came outta that room, all'a us was waiting (as if the Massa had summoned us) to hear what was go'n on. We knew it was sumthin' good cause they was smile'n from ear to ear, put you in the mind of Cheshire cats.

They announced that they was take'n our families to Orlando with Rubie, the entire house exploded with screams and holler'n. We was kiss'n and hug'n each other. Over the next few days, there was more talk about who would go, who would stay at home and how we was gonna pay for it but when it was all said and done, we all went to Orlando. Charlie was able to work out a deal with the promoters and we only had to pay the airfare for additional family members. The admission, hotel and food was FREE for er'ybody if we sign'd a release for our pictures to be taken and used in upcome'n promotions. *Hertz* included two complimentary mini vans. Chile, you couldn't tell us nuth'n, we all was go'n to Florida AND in style!

I remember when I was a little girl, Reverend Daddy and Mother used to take us down south to Florida er'y summer to visit my grandmother but this was different, we what'n gon be stay'n at somebody's house, we stay'n at the *Walt Disney* hotel and we got tickets to *Universal Studios* for all'a us, too. At the time, Tootsie had five children and a husband and I had three children and a husband. The airfare for eight people was $2,000. S'prisngly, it might not sound like much today but in 1982 that was a whole lotta money to spend on a vacation, especially when we didn't have two wooden nickels to rub together for a vacation. Our family always managed to barely float above the poverty line, we what'n nev'a on public assistance but likewise we had nev'a been fortunate enuf to go on a real vacation with airplanes, hotels, restaurants and amusement parks.

To God be the glory! Good bye ole' *Chain of Rocks Park*, hello *Disney World.*

Er'ybody pitch'd in to meet ends, the adults had two or three car washes, a couple of bake sales and a 70's kind'a party to help raise the money. Our kids baby sat, cut grass, took out trash and clean'd dirty garages for neighbors to support the effort. The church and local businesses ev'n donated money in exchange for services. Within three weeks, we had all'a the money and then some. The extra money was used to get the boys' hair cut and we bought all'a the kids a new outfit with flip flops or tennis shoes and the younger girls also got swim'n caps. The older girls, Diamond and Rubie and Tootsie's girls, Lonnie and Joyce Ann didn't need no swim cap cause they what'n about to put they head under the water and get they hair wet.

The airline tickets arrived in the mail the same day as did the promo package from *Disney World,* about two weeks before we was s'pose to leave. I look'd er'ything ov'a carefully to make sure our names were spell'd correctly and that we had hotel rooms and enuf meal and admission tickets to last us throughout the vacation. Then, for safe keep'n, I shoved the entire package in my bible case with other books, crayons and magazines that I was gonna to take on the plane with us. I zip'd up the leather carry-on bag and placed it on the floor in the hall closet, right by the front door.

During the two weeks lead'n up to us leave'n, both houses was busy with they preparations, shop'n , clean'n , do'n laundry, fix'n hair and a whole lotta pack'n. We had two suitcases full of nuth'n but snacks. Yeah we was gon get three free meals a day but we still need'd to stay within a budget and buy'n high priced snacks at amusement parks was definitely NOT in the budget. We agreed when it was time for snacks, for the most part, we would return to the vans or go back to our hotel rooms where the snacks and ice chest with cool drinks would be stored.

On Saturday, the day before the flight, Charlie and Uncle Earl told er'ybody to put all'a they stuff by the front door no later than 9 pm cause they was gonna load up the luggage tonight. The flight what'n due to leave til 2 o'clock Sunday afternoon which gave us time to go to church first and then go to the airport. Back then, our families usually ate breakfast together er'y Sunday morn'n before go'n to mass. Most'a the times breakfast was at Tootsie's house. Chile, she make the best biscuits you ev'a taste'd. Anyway, after we ate, we left for mass at St. Englebert Catholic church. We had to take three cars because of all'a the luggage.

Remember how when, in preparation for Y2K, er'y body was plan'n for the computers all ov'a the world to malfunction and loose important data but s'prisingly none'a that nev'a happen'd. We had all'a them back-up plans for nuth'n. Too bad we didn't have equal anticipation and regard for our church communities. You see, also at the turn of the century, a lotta of Christian churches experienced a drastic decline in they attendance, which made it difficult or virtually impossible for them to meet ministry expectations and church expenses. In response, it seem'd like churches er'ywhere was close'n, Catholic and Protestant. This was also the time that victims of sex crimes began to speak out about the church's participation and shameful denial. Whole communities was in jeopardy of loose'n they physical house of worship. This caused for much concern in the St. Louis Catholic community and in an effort to continue to provide spiritual leadership to the Catholic community the Archdiocese of St. Louis came up with a plan for strugglin' parishes to merge with other parishes. Initially, St. Englebert's merged with Holy Rosary and then a few years later, with Blessed Sacrament. Now the name has change' d to St. Elizabeth, Mother of John the Baptist, affectionately known as SEMOJB but back then it was St. Englebert.

That's the same church that all'a us, the adults as well as the chil'ren, received our sacraments of baptism, reconciliation, holy Eucharist, confirmation and holy matrimony. I'll prob'ly be laid out right there for my funeral! Yeah, I've been in there many'a time, home to me. Like most'a folk that regularly go to church, I got my favorite seat and I make sho' I get there early enuf to get it too. I hate it when people want to save seats, this ain't the theatre, this church, you can't be save'n no seats. Anyway, we arrived with several minutes to spare, so we immediately began fill'n up our usual two pews. For two reasons, I'll nev'a forget the homily we heard on this particular Sunday. First, cause it was the same day we left for our *Disney* vacation. Second and most important, because of the powerful message the visiting pastor delivered that day. His tone is inherently low, soft and spiritual yet his thick African accent is a constant challenge for North American listeners but if you focus on the words and NOT the accent, God will make sho you hear the message clearly.

Compared to whites, few black Protestants (for whatev'a reasons) seek a lifetime of vocations. It's no different amongst Catholics either. So whene'va one'a our *own* is a guest homilist or a keynote speaker at a church event, local black Catholics usually turn out in record numbers to listen and support 'em. This was Fr. Paul's second or third time come'n to our church. He was well liked in the community and needless to say, the church was pack'd.

After read'n the scripture, the priest raised the bible and said, "The Gospel of the Lord."

The church respond' "Praise to you, Lord Jesus Christ".

You could hear folks, sit'n down, move'n papers, pull'n out fans, get'n they self ready to listen to Fr. Paul. He wait for movement to quiet down, for about a minute or so he stood there look'n out at the congregation, from person to person, check'n to see if they was ready to receive the message. Once he deemed us ready, he said, "Are you working on your treasures?" He paused again, search'n the eyes of the congregation, give'n us an opportunity to come up with some kind'a answer. He walk'd down from the altar and stood in the center of the aisle. He continued, "I want to share a story with you today, church."

Y'all, this ain't word for word how he said it, but you'll understand. The story is about two people, a rich man and a poor woman.

The rich man what'n born with a silver spoon in his mouth but rather he work'd hard and was able to rise above poverty, eventually own'n his own business. He was a successful retailer who provided low income residents with affordable small appliances, refrigrators, TV's, washers, dryers and furniture for rent. While his interest rates were generally higher than what the bank charged, lending institutions and other small businesses were not in the habit of serving this neighborhood. Over time the man became rich and richer. Within a short period of time, he had over a dozen stores serving low income families. His businesses continued to prosper and he regularly made donations to charity to satisfy federal tax regulations. On most Sundays you could find him and his family in church services."

And the man's house was absolutely fabulous! Look'd like sumthin' you might see in an interior decorate'n magazine. He lived in a gated community and his house sat on a couple of acres with one'a them circular driveways out front, windows as tall as they is wide, allow'n all'a the warm mid day sun to come in, nourishing the plants and the soul. Rooms expensively decorated and large enuf to have two sets of furniture in 'em but it didn't look like nobody live there, er'ything was sooo....organized. Ev'n though he made all'a his money off 'a poor folks he was a good man, he went to church and was considered a respectable citizen of the community. And, so was his entrepreneur and investment banker friends with all'a they money.

The woman, on the other hand was poor, a descendant of slaves, had been poor all'a her life but she what'n poor in spirit. She was a single mother who held down a job and self support'd her family. She pray'd daily to God for those less fortunate than her, often times she took chil'ren in off the street, shared her money, food, clothe'n and sometimes ev'n the roof ov'a her head, with whomev'a was in need. Though her house was small her heart was BIG! She didn't make much money but she was always faithful with whatev'a she had. She was obedient, follow'd the commandments and loved the Lord our God with all her heart and soul. She taught her chil'ren the same values.

Well, life goes on for these two people and then one day, they finds themselves together, at the gates of heaven ,with none other than St. Peter. It's St. Peter's job to show 'em around heaven a bit. Point out some'a the sights and also take 'em to they new home in heaven. Just like on earth, heaven got neighborhoods too, some nicer than others but just the same, they in heaven. He also tell 'em they life in heaven gonna be based on how they lived on earth but without bills. In heaven, er'ything is free. The ransom has already been paid. God done made a way for all'a us.

Anyway they walk'n down streets paved of gold and silver, just'a oohh'n and awwww'n at *this* and *that* as St. Peter was guide'n 'em through heaven. They smile'n from ear to ear, what more could anyone ask for, bless'd and in God's favor. Chile, both of 'em was soooo happy, to finally be here. Heaven, the very place Christians on earth, try'n to get to! They kept walk'n and when they got to this particular section of town they noticed right away that it look'd and felt different than the other places they had seen so far. They admired the diversity in the neighborhood, the extra wide streets lined with jewels, plush gardens, manicured lawns, massive mansions and children freely play'n outside. Love was all around you and you could feel it, ev'n by just stand'n there.

St. Peter turn'd to the woman and said, "S'prise! This is where you will live."

She wiped her eyes for tears of joy had begun to cascade down her face. Overcome with emotion and unable to speak, she repeatedly mouth'd, "Thank you Jesus… thank you Jesus……thank you Jesus!"

St. Peter held out his arm, motion'n for the rich man to continue walk'n. They walk'd in silence. The man was truly happy for the woman and couldn't help but start think'n 'bout his own fate. *Well, if you get that type of house for be'n poor and good to people, I can only imagine where I'll be living. I was rich and good to poor people, like I was s'posed to do. Otherwise, I wouldn't be here, right? God knows I'm use to living in luxury. I can't wait to see the place He pick'd out for me.* They walk'd on for a few more minutes, all'a the while the man was picture'n what his house was gonna look like. He was sure it would be twice as big as back home, with all'a the perks. And of course, he would be a successful businessman in the community. They were approach'n another neighborhood. He could tell cause each one had a band of angels at its entrance and the man could see angels suspend'd in air about a block up the road. There was twice as many angels at this entrance than at the other ones.

Pleased with the images and anxious, he ask'd St. Peter, "So, how long before we arrive at my new home?"

"Not too far now. Ushers will be meet'n us."

Did he say, "ushers?" The woman didn't have an escort. Ummmmph, I must be special. "Can I ask you another question?"

"Sure, go right ahead."

"How come the woman didn't have an escort?"

"These ushers are a safety precaution, similar to the ushers at church, they guide and assist. All new residents in *this* neighborhood are blind fold'd and usher'd to they new home, to add to the element of s'prise."

The rich man thought, *must be a whole lotta shout'n and faint'n go'n on here!* Just as they reach'd the band of angels, three of 'em flew down, two land'd on either side of him and the other in front'a him. The third angel, the one in front'a him, tied a scarf over his eyes and they immediately start'd walk'n again. Seemingly, for a long distance but actually it was only a few steps and then they stop'd. The man was fill'd with anticipation and excitement. He could hardly contain hisself.

"Don't open your eyes til I tell you to," the angel said while slowly untie'n the scarf.

The man held his eyes tightly shut but his heart was beat'n a mile a minute and his palms began to sweat, he wobbled briefly. The alert ushers was right by his side.

"Breathe deeply." The angel encouraged the man. "You're gonna hyperventilate. Slow down….. take deep breaths. This is exactly why we have ushers. Relax…... We can't go on 'til you control yourself……. You o.k.? That's right, breeeeathe slowwwwwly. Once you get your wings, breath'n will be a thing of the past. We don't need breath in heaven but til then, you need to breathe…..breathe……breathe. On the count of three, you can open your eyes. One…. Two….. and… Three…. S'prise!"

The man open'd his eyes and couldn't believe what he was see'n. He faint'd. The ushers kept him from fall'n to the ground and gently woke him up. He rub'd his eyes to focus better but the image didn't change, it was clear, his eyes was not play'n tricks on him. He was stand'n in front of a small structure without windows or doors, just a shell of a house on a small patch of dirt. "There must be some kind'a mix up. I'm sure this is NOT the house Jesus pick'd out for me", said the confused man. "I did all'a the things I was s'pose to do. You need to call the manager or sumthin'."

St. Peter replied, "That won't be necessary, I have my instructions and I'm sorry sir, but this is all'a the raw material you sent up here for us to build your house. You see, it's the unconditional love in your heart, plus your actions and God's grace that provides the materials." Looks like you were more interest'd in build'n treasures on earth than in heaven.

The priest end'd the homily with a question, "Where are you build'n your treasures?" Hear'n that homily changed my life. Previously, I was go'n through motions like the rich man in the story but since then, faith, love, peace and give'n has become a big part of me and my life. I taught my children the same and I hope you teach yours! The passage, *for to whom much that is given, much is required* has equal mean'n in heaven and on earth.

When we arrived at the airport Charlie was not there yet. He had left church right after communion to go back home to check to make sure the kid's turn'd off the iron. Earl went with him cause he couldn't remember if he had unplug'd their coffee pot. Tootsie and I had the kids with us. We park'd the cars and er'ybody grab'd sumthin' to put on one'a those luggage carts that you rent at the airport. It took us about 30 minutes to unload the cars, balance the luggage, inspect the children, walk to the terminal and get in line. I was expect'n to see our husbands already in line because they left the church twenty minutes before us and we didn't live that far from the airport but they were nowhere in sight.

"I wonder what's take'n them so long? Hand me that black shoulder bag with my bible case in it. I need to get the tickets out so we can start check'n in some'a this luggage while we wait'n on 'em."

"Here come Earl now", Tootsie said. I turn'd around and saw Earl come'n through the automatic doors with anutha cart full'a luggage. He navigated the cart to where we was stand'n. I assumed Charlie was park'n the other car.

Diamond said, "Mama, your bible case ain't on this cart."

"Y'all look on that other cart then. You sho' we got er'y thing outta that car?"

"Yeah, I look'd in the windows of both of 'em before we left," Baby Boy replied.

"Well, we definitely need to find that bag cause all'a our tickets are in it and we ain't go'n nowhere without 'em. I definitely remember put'n the bag in the hall closet but I thought Charlie got it out when y'all load'd up the car yesterday."

"I don't remember see'n it but that don't mean nuth'n, Earl said.

"Ma'am, I'm gonna have to ask you to step aside while you locate your tickets. I need to assist other customers. Once you find your tickets, just let me know, there's no need for you to go back through the line," the ticket agent said.

Needless to say, by this time er'ybody was get'n antsy and I was extremely nervous. *Did I leave the tickets at home? There's no way we can go back home again and make it back to the airport in time for this flight….. the next flight isn't til late tonight.* Rubie start'd cry'n first and that start'd a chain reaction. In a matter of seconds, all'a the chil'ren was out right cry'n or either get'n real teary eyed. I ax'd the kids to help me take er'ything off'a the carts, secretly hope'n that they had overlook'd the bag but when we finish'd, the tickets was still miss'n. Disappoint'd, we load'd up the carts and head for the park'n lot. Our only alternative was to go back home and get the tickets. As we was walk'n through the terminal, I kept apologize'n and say'n that we gon definitely make the next flight. I felt so bad that we had to delay'd our trip because of me. We had park'd the cars on the third floor of the garage so we had to wait for the elevator. When the elevator arrived, the doors open'd and there stood Charlie, to our s'prise, with the miss'n black bag on his shoulder. Er'ybody scream'd out loud with joy. Chile, we was soooo happy to see Charlie with that bag!

Charlie later told us that when he went to the house to turn off the iron, sumthin' told him to check the closet by the front door, that's when he saw the bag with my bible case in it and he knew I wouldn't want to leave town without my bible, so he grab'd the whole bag. And by do'n so, he saved our vacation. We had a blast in Florida and have had numerous vacations ev'a since then but Charlie hasn't gone on none of 'em. You see, he died that same summer. Now, er'y time I take a trip, I usually, at some point or another, reminisce on the fond mem'ries of how Charlie saved our first real vacation. I smile and thank God for those happy times….STOP. *I sho' do miss my Charlie!*

#   #   #   #   #

The next sign read, Chattanooga, 5 miles, Atlanta 125. Richard, our bus driver, rear'd back in his seat then lean'd his head back towards me without take'n his eyes off the road and said, "This will be the last stop before we get to Atlanta. Tell everybody we'll be stopping in a couple of minutes."

I tap'd the microphone with my finger to make sure it was still on, "Listen up er'ybody. We come'n up on our last stop, so make sure you take all'a the trash off the bus when you leave and remember, we only gonna be here for a few minutes. So, please do whatev'a it is you gotta do and be quick about it. We s'pose to be in Atlanta by nine o'clock and it's already sev'n!"

Most'a all'a the people got off the bus but some of 'em didn't go inside the store. I, for one, didn't have to use the bathroom but I did need to stretch my legs. We been on *that* bus for almost eight hours. I stay'd outside to walk around and get the blood flow'n in my legs again. This place is much smaller than the other two we stop'd at. In fact, this ain't ev'n no truck stop, this only one'a them mini mart type gas stations.

I hear sirens, look up and see blue and red lights flash'n in a distance, move'n fast and head'n this way. I didn't ev'n have time to speculate on where they was go'n, cause they sped right into the gas station where we had stop'd. And instantly, the entire park'n lot was surround'd with a bunch of cops that look'd to me like a SWAT unit or sumthin'. I'm scared! There are some blue uniform cops here but most'a the police got on black clothes with yellow write'n across the back, wear'n boots and helmets plus they carry'n guns, batons and shields. I don't know if I should run in the store to get Jade or dash back on the bus and hide but as soon as I saw guns point'd at me and heard a voice from a mega phone say, "Don't move stay right where you are", the decision was made for me. Immediately, without think'n, er'ybody (at least all'a the black folks) who was stand'n outside, drop'd to they knees and raised our hands up above our heads. Signaling, surrender, **DON'T SHOOT!**

Of course, we gonna cooperate with the police. I'm too old to be go'n to jail and I definitely don't plan on be'n shot by the po po. Several uniform'd police began search'n us and ask'n our name. The folks that was outside as well as the people in the store and my relatives on the bus, was escort'd more'n 500ft away from the bus. Once that was done, we were allow'd to bring our arms down by our side and they told us older folks that we could sit on the curb if we want to. I noticed a plain clothes tall obese man with sunburn'd face and unkept hair who seem to be the one in charge. I watch him talk'n to the police dress'd in SWAT gear and the uniform'd police but it's the sheriff's department that's guard'n the bus and rope'n off entrances. *Where's Jade?* My eyes rapidly scan the park'n lot and I see that she is safe, near the back of the crowd, with Rubie and the other kids. None of us know what's go'n on but you ain't gotta be no rocket scientist to know that this must be someth'n really serious if they got all'a these police.

They didn't find my cell phone dure'n the search and I didn't tell' em about it either. Chile, my heart is race'n a mile a minute. And now, my phone vibrate'n, but I can't answer it.

26

DIAMOND

The bell rang and then the fasten seatbelt sign came on, follow'd by the pilot's voice, "Flight attendants, prepare for landing". *This is the part that I hate the most about flying, descending. I feel like I'ma throw up!* Diamond jerked the barf bag from the back of the seat in front of her. She want'd to be prepared in case she was unable to keep her insides on the inside. *Air, quickly.* She reach'd to fully open the air duct above her head. Then she placed her tray table in the upright position, complying with the instructions the flight attendant had given the passengers. Three minutes after departure and eight minutes before landing are the most crucial times during a flight. Actually, the majority of crashes occur during this brief window of opportunity.

Instead of preparing a written evaluation, a pro and con comparison, of her life with Duane, she spent almost the entire flight with her eyes closed, sipping wine while feeling a bit under the weather. Normally she would get a little queasy at the landing phase but this was different and it began too soon and is lasting much too long. Not only did she feel nausea and dizzy but her energy level was declining and she also had this persistent pain in the lower part of her back. A couple of times during the flight, she was tempted to alert the flight attendant but she didn't want to bring attention to herself nor cause a scene. She figured she would feel better once the plane got through all of the turbulence and the medicine that she took about twenty minutes ago started working.

When we stop, I remain seated in first class. I need the extra time to gather my composure and make sure I can walk off this plane by myself. It took the passengers about ten minutes to exit the plane and that was just enough time for me to start feeling better. The wait really helped. I thanked the flight attendant for her service and head straight for the bathroom in the terminal to freshen up. I prefer the extra large stalls designated for the disabled or baby chang'n stations because they're spacious and often times have a private sink. Luckily, no one else in line and the stall that I want is open. OMG! I've broken out in a cold sweat and my stomach feels as if someone is inside of me with a pair of vice grips ripping my intestines apart. *Is this a hot flash?* There's no time to cover the toilet seat, I sit down! Awwww....good.... This may sound strange but actually, the coolness of the porcelain is helping to regulate my body temperature and the pain subsides as my bowels release.......... Thank God, I'm feeling normal again but still I hope I don't catch a virus from seating on this unprotected toilet seat. Mama will have a hissy fit, she always cautioning us about using public toilets. *My back still hurts.* Afterwards, I wash my face and hands and proceed to baggage claim to retrieve my luggage.

I'll call Mama just as soon as I check-in and get settled at the hotel.

A physically fit, attractive olive colored gentleman with Italian features held a sign with my name printed in large bold letters. I made myself known to him and he gathered my luggage. Although the hotel provides a free shuttle, I much rather prefer this private limousine service. However, I'm sure Duane will be on the shuttle, he enjoys interactions with common strangers and I loathe such trifles. I frequently have to remind him of our status in the community. To be honest, this whole weekend is going to be a challenge for me. I'm used to much finer hotels, restaurants, events and people. We're staying in the same hotel as my relatives but I've requested a suite for me and Duane, everybody else either has a single or double room.

"How long is the ride to the hotel," I ask the driver?

"Less than twenty minutes, if we don't happen upon any accidents. Otherwise, it could take over an hour but it rarely takes *me* that long, I know many alternate routes."

"Will we be there by seven o'clock?"

"We most certainly will, Madame." He closed the door, circled behind the car and got inside the driver's seat.

Great! That'll give me enough time to relax before the buses from St. Louis arrive. I found comfort on the butter soft leather seat and pulled out my folders, pad and pencil. I need to review the details for this weekend. The smoke grey partition between driver and passenger opens and the driver came into view. "Good Evening, my name is Armando. Please help yourself to a cool drink from the refrigerator. Or, if you fancy, there's wine and spirits on the bar. Also, fruit and snacks are located in the trays to your left. Would you like for me to make any additional stops before going to your hotel?"

"No thank you, Armando."

"In that case, we'll be on our way, Madame. Enjoy your ride."

I reach to open the first manila folder. I'm a visual learner and therefore, if I am to retain it, I must write it down. At the top of the sheet of paper I write, TO DO! Speaking from experience, I know how poor and unreliable my family can be so I require all of the monies necessary to secure this hotel, in advance because I am not going to be responsible for anybody's bill but my own. While all of the financial obligations have been satisfied, I still need to confirm talent show participants, prepare the souvenir bags and decorate the hospitality suite. Yesterday, I shipped an overnight box with supplies and the hotel agreed to hold the package until my arrival. Jade and Jennifer can help make the bags tonight. Rubie's in charge of registration and Mama is taking care of distributing the T-shirts. I'm in charge of the banquet and Baby Boy's responsible for the liquor. A couple of weeks ago when I sent in the final payment, I provided the hotel with a list of names and they in turn, sent me a roster to use for the room assignments. Once I check in, I'll receive all of the keys. There's no need for anyone to check in unless they chose *not* to prepay the required celebration fee. However, everybody will be required to check out and settle any additional charges incurred. The hotel, tours, and the celebration banquet are all included in the fee. Admission to Six Flags is the only activity not included but we were able to secure ample discount coupons.

My final note, be downstairs with room keys when the bus arrives.…... Deep in thought and unaware of my surroundings, I nearly jump outta my seat when the bellman opens the car door. Needless to say, I got papers spread all over the seats. By the time I gather my things, the doorman has loaded my luggage on a cart and Armando is waiting to assist me inside. I wink, say goodbye and give him a $20 tip.

"Thank you Madame and enjoy your time in Atlanta."

Armando held the door open for me to enter the hotel. *Well, this doesn't look too bad after all. If this is any indication of how lovely the room's decorated or the level of service, I'll be more than pleased. What a relief!* As soon as I enter'd the build'n, a huge floral arrangement caught my attention. Rich, shiny marble floors accentuated the magnificent rustic rectangular wishing fountain in the center of the lobby. The oversized tan leather chairs complimented the warm caramel tones in both the carpets and the sofas. There are several large plants in terra cotta pots. This hotel has a relatively charming setting. Planes are taking off in the fore ground and green foliage sprawls overhead around the balcony. I hope my relatives mind their manners and not embarrass me this weekend. But I just know somebody, who was s'pose to pay and didn't, is going to show up and I'll have to send 'em back home. I will not tolerate any drama this weekend. No one is going to ruin Reverend Daddy's birthday. This is going to be the best centennial celebration ever!

Check-in is a synch, as promised, they gave me all of the confirmed room keys and I go to my room, hoping for a much needed cat nap. After the bellman arranged the luggage and adjusted the room temperature, I tip again but this time, only $10. Immediately, I kick off my kitten heel pumps and place my suit jacket on the back of the desk chair. It is almost 7:15 pm , I'm tired and I haven't even put up one piece of decoration but first, I need to call my mama. I locate my cell and then press the send button twice to reconnect to her phone. Five rings, no answer, voicemail. I decide not, to leave a message. *I'll try again in a few minutes but right now I need to go to the hospitality suite to make sure er'ything's in order.*

To my surprise, when I entered the suite, it was in shambles with portions of the ceiling exposed, wide open. "Excuse me but I have this room reserved for tonight but it doesn't look as though the hotel's planning on us being here," I said to a young guy perched on a ladder. The child looked confused and before he could think of an answer, an older gentleman, standing behind me in a suit, responds, "Oh......,"

I turn around to walk toward him. He extends his hand and I politely accept his handshake. His silver name plate indicated Event Manager.

"I'm sorry ma'am, but we called your cell and left a message. Unfortunately, somehow our paths didn't cross, there's been some miscommunication. You see, apparently, this morning maintenance discovered that the air conditioning unit in this suite is not working properly; therefore, we made arrangements for your group to use a larger room, at no additional charge. Actually, we reserved the entire Club Lounge to accommodate your family registration and the Biltmore III for the Meet n' Greet. I apologize for any inconvenience but I think you'll like this alternate location just as well, if not better. As a matter of fact, it's being prepared for you as we speak. This way, please follow me." We walk a few more paces and he continues, "Upon arrival, your guest will be notified of the room change. Also, we've posted signs in the hotel lobby and parking lot."

When we arrived at Club Lounge on the twelveth floor, I was pleased to see that my overnight package arrived safely. This room has character; it reminds me of a fancy library equipped with private coves. Big plush furniture and a wide screen television mounted on the wall. The atmosphere plus this awesome view of the airport is certainly a bonus to our festivities. In the Biltmore III, the hotel staff is setting up the hor d'ovuer buffet I ordered for tonight. I stood there for a moment to absorb the environment. This place is twice as big as the hospitality suite. Well, it's safe to say our Meet n' Greet won't be as quaint as we originally plan'd but, we'll now be spread out, which is really great because that means I won't have to talk to erverybody, just a few and I'll make sure they all sit close by me.

I took items out of the box and began decorating the tables with runners and confetti. I used a rented helium tank to blow up one hundred gold balloons with black ribbons which I attached to the metal arch positioned near the entryway. Another fifty gold and black balloons were used in the centerpiece design. I tied a couple of balloons to the bottle of Olde Spice cologne on each glass table topper. Yes, these have a dual purpose, decorations and attendance prizes but who wears Olde Spice, Rev. Daddy, who else? By the time I finish with everything it's almost 8:30pm and I only have thirty minutes left to rest before the bus arrives. I hurry to my room to finally get off my feet for a few minutes and also, to call Mama. *My back still hurts.*

I heard her phone ringing but I was so anxious, I just started talking and I didn't wait for her to say a word! "Hello. Mommie.., Mommie, where are you guys now? I just finished decorating. You think you'll be here by 9 o'clock?"

No answer, silence.

"Hello. **HELLO!**" I shouted.

27

CAN WE GO NOW?

There it go again, my phone vibrate'n. I start walk'n nonchalantly to the back side of the store, reach in my bra, open the phone and look around to make sure the coast is clear before I start talk'n. I can hear Diamond shout'n "hello" and I'm afraid someone else will hear her too. So, I cover the phone with my hand and speak in a low yet stern voice. "Shhhhh… Shhhhh….Diamond, shut up and listen to me verrrrry carefully. We been detain'd by the sheriff and the po'lice. Baby Boy ov'a there try'n to talk to 'em now. I'll call you back as soon as I can. Don't worry, we's all safe!" Umph, I didn't wait for her to respond, rather I snap'd the phone shut and put it back in my hide'n place, 'fo anybody sees me with it.

Just as I came from behind the build'n, I saw Baby Boy walk'n in my direction. Good. Perhaps he got some information 'bout what's going on and how much longer we gon be here. Since they hadn't beat up or cuffed any of us, I figured we not the folks they look'n for but then I see those men, in black outfits with SWAT wrote across they back, get on our bus.

"What's going on? How long we gotta stay here," I ask Baby Boy.

"Calm down. Don't get all excited and work up your blood pressure. I recognized one of the officers from a law enforcement workshop, he knew me too, so I went over to talk to him and he told me that earlier today three men escaped from the Kentucky State prison. Two of 'em already been caught and the other one is still on the loose but they got a tip that he might of hitchhiked outta Kentucky. That's why the police set up this road block. But once they verify our identification and search the bus, we should be back on the road. So, just relax Mama."

Annoyed but try'n my best to conceal my frustration, I whisper to Baby Boy, "Well, when was they plan'n on tell'n us? If you had'na went ov'a there, we'd still be wonder'n what was go'n on. And anyway they don't need to search our bus, I can tell 'em we ain't pick'd up no hitchhikers. The onlyest people been on that bus is the folks sit'n right there. And not to mention, the other bus was just in front of us and I didn't see them stop and pick up nobody neither." I had barely finish'd my sentence when I heard, "We got 'em!" Then there was a lot of commotion on the bus for several minutes but once er'ything quiet'd down, I saw the police escort a handcuffed man, in a blueish grey jumpsuit, off'a our bus. *He must'a been hide'n….. but when did he get on? I'm sure I would'a noticed the outfit!* I was sit'n right up front all'a the time and I would'a swore on a stack of bibles he what'n on that bus. Embarrassed that I had stuck my foot in my mouth, once again, I walk'd away to find Jade and Rubie and more importantly, sumthin cool to drink.

Chile, ev'n though the sun was on its way down, just about gone as a matter of fact, my skin felt sticky like somebody done pour'd honey all ov'a me. I know'd it must'a been at least 90 degrees outside and with us on top'a this black asphalt, I'm sure that pushes the temperature up anuth'a few degrees. I was sweat'n and pant'n like a whore on nickel night. Shucks, I'm old and too much heat causes me to get a dizzy headache and weak in the knees. Oh Lord, now my heart beat'n real fast. I need to cool off. And quick or else they gonna hav'ta call an ambulance too. I barely made it to where I was go'n but when I got there, I plop'd down on the edge, open'd a cool bottle of water that they had put in a cooler for us and began move'n my hand up and down, hope'n to produce some kind'a air flow. The water from the outside of the bottle drip'd all ov'a my blouse but I didn't care. Maybe it'll help cool me down. Jade was sit'n next to me and I reach'd ov'a and tap'd her on the shoulder.

"Baby, please get my fan outta my bag and bring it to me."

"Grandma the bag, with your fan, is still on the bus and we can't go back on the bus yet but wait a minute, I'll get you something else."

Jade got up, went inside the store, grab'd a newspaper, separated it into sections and start'n with me, she pass'd them papers out to all'a the older relatives. You would'a thought she gave 'em sumthin' special by the wide grins and sincere thank you's she received, a couple of 'em ev'n tried to give her some money but she politely refused. Thank God, I began to cool down but the po po made us stay put for anuth'a thirty minutes before they said we could leave. By the time we got back on the bus it was almost eight o'clock, which meant we really was gonna be late for the Meet n' Greet that was s'pose to start at nine. You ev'a heard people say, we can all sing together but we can't all talk at the same time? Well, er'ybody on that bus was talk'n at the same time. They was either talk'n amongst theyself or on they cell phones about how we almost got kilt. Black folks know they can exaggerate a story or should I say embellish it so that folks are interest'd in hear'n the whole story. With all the commotion go'n on, I could hardly hear myself talk. It was sooo loud on the bus and there what'n no way I was gon ax them to be quiet, especially, after what we just went through. So to keep from yell'n, I lean'd forward and ax'd the bus driver a question.

"Richard, what time do you think we'll make it to Atlanta?"

'Well, we're a little over a hundred miles away and I speculate we'll be there around nine thirty or so. If it what'n' for that runaway convict, we'da been there waaay before nine. I'll try to make up some lost time but I sho' don't wanna get pull'd ov'a."

"Please, please don't speed, do the speed limit. I definitely don't want us to get stop'd by the cops again. Take ya sweet time. And by all means, get us there safely. We'll be there when we get there!" *That reminds me, I need to call Diamond.* I sat back in my seat to think about what I'm gonna tell her, she such a drama queen and to be honest I'm not in the mood to hear all'a that. Perhaps I'll do a puzzle to calm my nerves before I call her. I brung all kinds of things to keep me busy dure'n the ride but recently I had taken to do'n crossword puzzles whenev'a I what'n work'n on my legacy tape. I'll admit when I first start'd do'n 'em, I what'n that good and had to peak in the back of the book for most'a the answers but now I'm pretty good and I get better with each puzzle I do. It's sumthin' how they use the same clues ov'a and ov'a again in different puzzles. For instance, a five letter word for a desert animal is camel and the opposite of SSE is NNW. It used'ta take me all day to finish a puzzle, without cheat'n that is, but now I can get one done in less than an hour, sometimes a half an hour if it has a lotta familiar clues and I hardly ev'a hav'ta cheat now, only when I'm really stump'd on a clue do I cheat.

I was on a roll. I finish'd three puzzles and we only had thirty miles to go so I open'd my cell phone and press'd #1 speed dial for Diamond.

"Hey baby, it's me."

"Mommie I recognize the number and I already know it's you. What happened? Why did you hang up in my face? You didn't even give me a chance to say nuth'n nor ask questions about my child. I knew I shouldn't have let her ride on that bus without her own cell phone. Are you ok? Where are Rubie and Baby Boy? I can't take all'a this stress; just put Jade on the phone!"

"Excuse me but who the hell you think you talk'n to in that tone and what stress you talk'n about? Seems to me you're confused, I'm still yo' mama and *we* was the ones with the police, not you. So I suggest you change your attitude young lady."

"I'm sorry Mommie but I just need to know what happened and also make sure my child is alright. I been trying to call erverybody and no one is answering their phone."

I thought to myself that's because they see it's you on the line and they don't want to deal with your hysterics. But instead I said, "Apology accepted. Jade is fine, we all are fine. If I recall, I *did* tell you that I couldn't talk *and* gave you as much information as I could. I'm sorry if you thought I should have done more but I didn't have a choice. I was already using my cell phone when I was s'pose to have given it to the police when they search'd us. Anyway, some men broke out of prison and one of 'em got on our bus without us know'n but the police got a tip that one of em might'a snuck on our bus while we was at that truck stop in Kentucky. And luckily they was right. The police set up a road block and found him hide'n in the bathroom on our bus. I'll give you the full story when I see you but for now, I was call'n to say we'll be there in thirty minutes. Is er'ythang ready?

"Yeah almost, about an hour ago I finished decorating the room but I'ma need some help with the giveaway bags. I haven't had time to stuff any of them. So, when you get here, send Jade and Jennifer to the registration area after they put their luggage in the room. Oh, I almost forgot, one of the hotel managers changed the hospitality suite to a larger room at no extra charge."

"Why they do that?"

"Because the air conditioner broke in the other room but this new room is a lot bigger and we'll be more comfortable in there anyway. It even has a *real* stage. See ya in a few. Goodbye."

"Bye Diamond."

I took the microphone from the cradle to make anuth'a announcement. I tap'd on the mic and then blew in it. "Can I please have your attention? Listen up er'ybody! We'll be in Atlanta within the next thirty minutes and I need you guys to start clean'n up this bus. We ain't get'n off'a here till er'y crumb and piece of paper is in the trash. Also gather up all'a your stuff, make sure you don't leave nuthin on the bus because it will be clean'd tonight and they ain't responsible for your belong'ns. Jade is gonna come by and tell you your room assignments. Also I need you to dig in your pockets and come up with a tip for our wonderful bus driver. We want the kind of money that folds, not jingle. I'll pass a cup around for you to put it in."

Afterwards, I call Rubie to make sure she gave the same spiel on her bus. She did.

28

DIAMOND

I hung up the phone thankful that I had finally spoken to my mama and she confirmed all's well. Plus they'll be here in a few minutes. God knows I'll be so glad when this whole celebration mess is over with, then I can concentrate solely on me, cause I really need to get my life back on track. I feel as though eveything's slipping away. I repositioned myself in the chair and look down at the pad that I had been writing on for the last hour. I hate to admit it but the list of reasons why I should divorce Duane is a lot shorter than my reasons for not wanting a divorce. Actually, I had only written one reason why I want a divorce and that's, CHEATING. Under the column why I don't want a divorce (not in any particular order), just whatever came to mind, I wrote, MONEY, LOVE, SEX, FRIENDSHIP, SECURITY, COMPANIONSHIP, HOUSE, BILLS and of course, JADE. I've been happily married for almost twenty years but Duane's behavior these last couple of months has got me to thinking about ending it all. *Is he have'n an affair or am I just be'n paranoid?* I can't believe I'm asking myself that question when I have the proof. The detective already gave me several pictures, one with them sitting at a restaurant, another one with them eyeing fine jewelry in a department store and the most hurtful of all was them going into her apartment. Duane hates to shop, he'd rather cut off his arm and how dare he accompany another woman to her apartment!

Yes, I know I have my moments and can be difficult at times but I swear to you, I've NEVER cheated on my husband. There's no doubt in my mind that I love him but the real question is how far will I go to salvage this marriage? I put the pen down, got up from the desk and began pacing the floor. Is he still in love with me or is it too late for us? Maybe we should try marriage counseling. The pain in my back is getting worse so I took some more pills and decided to stretch across the bed for a few minutes, hoping for relief. As I was lay'n there with my eyes closed, thinking about my situation, our favorite song, *Saving All My Love For You* by *Whitney Houston* came on the radio. I couldn't help but smile and right away my mind drifted back to the good times, when we first met. I affectionately remembered this as the first song we danced to.

#   #   #   #   #

Most people go to college to get an education and subsequently secure employment. Not me. My main reason for going to college was to find a rich husband so I didn't have to work. For me, being a housewife, volunteering in the community, getting my name in the society column and traveling the globe seemed a much better fate. But if it wasn't for my friend tutoring me for the entrance exams, I wouldn't have enrolled in any college. You see, I never liked high school and therefore didn't apply myself. To a certain extent, I considered it a waste of time because compared to me, the kids were so immature. Of course, Mama didn't know what I was doing. She always swore I was a good Catholic girl but actually I began skipping school and hanging out with boys when I was a mere sophomore. Luckily for my sake, I never went *all the way* (to get pregnant like Rubie) and Mama never found out I was skipping school either.

Many of my classmates didn't like me because all'a the boys wanted to go out with me. Back then if you had light skin and long hair you were in high demand. I'm not only light skin but I also have what is refer'd to as *good* long hair. Therefore most of the girls were jealous of me, except one, Lorraine. She was my friend and that was probably because we had known each other since the first grade. It didn't matter to me that her skin was darker than mine or her hair was nappier than mine, all through grade school, high school and college we consistently had a good time together whether we were playing, singing, laughing, talking or day dreaming about our future. To this day, she is still my closest, and quiet as it's kept, my only true friend. I know loads of people but no one compares to Lorraine. She's my confidant, my bff (best friend forever) and I'm disappointed that she won't be able to attend the festivities. If it wasn't for prior commitments, I know she would be here.

Throughout my childhood, I lived for summer to come around. This was the most exciting time of the year. It even out ranked Christmas because summer lasts three months and Christmas is only one day. Like all children I was glad to be out of school but I especially look'd forward to my anticipated adventures of summer. In addition to our annual family vacations wherein we visited relatives in Mississippi, Florida or Michigan, I was also allowed on several occasions to accompany Lorraine when she went to visit her relatives. Lorraine was not what you would call rich nor was my family considered poor but her family by far was wealthier than mine. They use to take *real* vacations to places I could only dream of as a child. They went to New Orleans, DC, Harlem, and Philadelphia. She also went on a cruise to Mexico one time. I would be on pins and needles waiting for her return so she could share pictures and stories with me. It made me feel as though I had been with them. I envied her family's vacations because they didn't have to pile up in a station wagon like we did; instead they traveled by plane or boat, stay'd in a hotel and ate in fancy restaurants. Not us, we always drove, parked on the side of the road to eat food Mama packed at home and slept on pallets that our relatives made for us on the floor. However, we did get to go to *Universal Studios* one year when my sister was in the national spelling bee contest but that was definitely no match to all of the *real* vacations Lorraine and her family took.

Although Daddy always made sure we had fun on our road trips and I truly enjoyed being with my family but I really felt special every time I was invited to go anywhere with Lorraine, even if it was just to go over to her house and play. She *had* and got to *do* all of the stuff I wanted to *do* and *have* but knew my family couldn't afford. Her house was finely decorated and both the front and back yard was landscaped, which was unheard of back then. We only had Daddy and Baby Boy to cut our grass. To me, her pink bedroom was absolutely enchanting because unlike my mix'n match furniture everything in her room was a match; the canopy bed, dresser, chest, desk, bookshelves with all the colorful books and a toy box full of the best toys. In my bedroom no two pieces of furniture were from the same set or from the same relatives for that matter. Plus she had her own bathroom and closet! She actually had clothes hanging up in color coordinated fashion. Shucks, everything I owned was folded up in my drawers and one of the drawers didn't even have a front cover. If empty, you could see straight through to the back of it. I kept that same bedroom furniture til I was in high school.

When I was younger there were many times when I secretly wished I was in her family instead of mine. She had everything. Lorraine took dance lessons, had a private foreign language tutor, went to charm school and always had the most lavish birthday parties of the whole neighborhood. I mean complete with cake, ice cream, balloons, clowns and magicians who gave prizes out to everyone. Her parties were nothing like the homemade parties my mama gave us. She had a monkey at one of her parties but I didn't like that though because he picked boogers outta his nose and ate 'em. That was sooo nasty. It gave me the cooties.

I remember one day when I was about seven or eight years old and we were playing in her room and she said to me, "I wish I could live with you and your family. That way I would have somebody to play with all of the time."

I eyed her fun filled room and replied, "Girl, are you crazy? If I had all of this stuff you got, I wouldn't need no body to play with!

Ironically with all of the stuff she had, it seemed as though Lorraine was forever envious of my family and our relationship with each other. I guess she felt lonely since she was an only child. Not me. I couldn't imagine what it might feel like to be lonely because I was never alone. My brother and sister and most of the times some of my cousins, usually Aunt Tootsie's children, was always at our house. Whenever she could, Lorraine loved to spend the night over my house and go to church with us. For the life of me, I couldn't understand why anybody would want to go to church, especially Catholic church. It is so boring, no one ever shouted like they did when I went to my uncle's Baptist church in Michigan. I considered church something you did because you were told to do so. Period! You should have seen my mouth drop wide open when she told me her parents never went to church. Not go to church, that was hard for me to believe because I thought all adults went to church and took their children with them. At least *my* relatives did so I assumed everybody else did too.

Well, as the years passed on and we grew older, I became less and less envious of Lorraine and all'a her stuff. Given that she was an only child, her parents frequently let her bring a friend along to keep her company. The summer we completed the eleventh grade her parents planed a trip to France and Lorraine was to stay with her aunt in Savannah while they were gone. I was invited to go to with her to Atlanta. By then I was used to going places with them but this was the first time I was asked to go out of town.

I ran home, bust through the door and almost stepped on Rubie sitting on the floor watching TV. "Where's Mommie?" I ask while looking around the room.

"In the kitchen cook'n dinner", she replied. "You was s'pose to be home an hour ago, where you been?"

I didn't even bother answering her, instead I ran straight into the kitchen. I was too excited and tired from running the three blocks, I could hardly catch my breath. It took me several tries before I was able to speak. "Mommie, guess what? Lorraine asked me if I could go to Savannah with her because her parents are going to France and she gotta go stay with her aunt while they gone." Mama didn't say a word, she kept frying chicken. It only took me a split second to figure out why she wasn't responding. You see, we were taught to always greet adults upon entering a room. So I started over, "Hi Mommie. Sorry I'm late."

She turned around, "That's better. Hello to you too. Now, what's this you talk'n about go'n to Savannah?"

I repeated what I had said before but this time I said it at a lot slower pace. Then I said, "Mommie, please can I go. I'd give anything to go out of town with her."

"I don't know Diamond. Chile, I can't give you an answer right now. I gotta give this a lot more thought and, what does Lorraine's folks hav'ta say about all'a this? Did they ask you to go or is this sumthin' you and Lorraine thought of yo' self? Do I know this aunt in Savannah? Umph, I need to talk to her parents before I can ev'n consider a thing like this."

I didn't want Mama to become too negative so I rattled off, "She *did* say *her* mama is gonna call and ask you but I wanted to tell you about it first. While I was over Lorraine's house she told me that last night her parents told her about their travel plans and asked her if she wanted to go. Since she doesn't want to go, they said she had to go to Savannah

171

to stay with her aunt. But her aunt don't have any children so she asked if I could come with her. Her parents said they would check to see if it was ok and then her mama is gonna call you. That's all I know so far. Cross my heart." I was talking fast again and outta breath.

She rolled her eyes, "So you really ain't been ax'd yet? Anyhow, Lorraine is welcome to stay with us while her parents go outta town. How come you didn't ax her to come ov'a here? She ain't gotta go all the way down south. Chile, them people travel more'n anybody I know. They act like money grow on trees."

"Mommie please don't tell 'em that. I mean, I know Lorraine's welcome here and all, but I really wanna go out of town this summer. Without y'all! I already passed all'a my classes and I'm seventeen, I'll be a senior next school year. I promise to be good and I'll be sure to go to church every Sunday while I'm there. Plus, I need to get away from this house for a while, start preparing myself for when I go away to college." I even shocked myself with that last line because that's the first time I ever used the words *college* and *me* in the same sentence. But if it was gonna help me get to Savannah, so be it.

"Diamond don't start worry'n me girl. I'll let you know my decision if'n when they ask me. Now, go set the table and tell your brother and sister to get wash'd up. Dinner'll be ready in a few minutes."

At supper I picked over my food, didn't participate in the table discussion and I asked to be excused way before dessert was served. I wasn't hungry. I had to think of some way to get Mommie to let me go with Lorraine. That night and every night afterwards when I said my prayers I prayed real hard to God to do His magic and soften up my mama. I told Him I would do my chores without being reminded to do so, never skip school anymore, study real hard and try to get all A's, but more importantly, I would pay attention in church. I ended my prayer, as was my custom, (and still is) with a special message to my father; I love you Daddy. He had died two years before and I missed him terribly.

I kept my promise to God and I did mine, Rubie and Baby Boy's chores. They didn't know what had got into me but they weren't asking either. They didn't care, they were just glad I was doing their chores. I also stopped sitting in the back of the church eating candy and talking with the rest of the teens. I took to sitting up front, close to Mommie and the elders. I could tell she was soooo proud of me for doing that!

I have to admit, it made me feel good too. As they say, hard work and prayer pays off. I knew Lorraine's mother had call'd my Mama the previous week but now, two weeks had passed and Mommie still hadn't said if I could go.

During the month of June, to earn some spending money, I baby sat my neighbor's son while she took a class at the university. This particular day, as I was walking home that afternoon, I decided today is the day! I'm going to ask her again if I can go to Savannah. I grabbed the mail out of the box on my way in the house. Clutched in my hand were a couple of circulars and four familiar brown envelopes. After my father died we started getting money from the government. All of us got a check, me, my sister, my brother and my mama but mama was the only one who cashed the checks. That money helped support us and pay my siblings tuitions. However, Mommie regularly made deposits into our own savings accounts. Once a year she would show us the blue savings pass books with our own names wrote on the inside. For every month, there would be a new entry under the credit column. There was never anything written on the debit side. She said it was for our future but one time I tried to take some money out of my account and the teller told me that this is a custodial account which meant my mama had to sign the withdrawal slip too. I wasn't about to ask her to do that, I knew she would never agree, so the money just kept piling up. By then, we each had almost $500.

"Mommie, the checks are here." I said, still pondering how I was gonna bring up the subject of me going out of town.

"What else come?" Mommie rhetorically asked as I handed everything to her. She looked through the stack. "Good, no bills today. I think we ought to do sumthin' different with your check this month. Yeah, I speck we should go to the mall and buy you some new clothes to take to Savannah with you."

I look askance and shout, "Are you serious? (I immediately started doing the happy dance.) I can go! I can go! Oh, thank you Mommie. I love you so much." *And yes, silently I thanked the Lord too.* I almost tripped running up the stairs to call Lorraine with the good news. We talked on the phone for hours, making all sorts of plans. My mama had to holler up twice to tell me to get off the phone and come eat. The next day Mommie took me shopping like she said she was and I got new clothes, complete with sandals to match. You couldn't tell me a thing. I was gonna be the best dressed girl they ever saw. The citizens of Savannah had yet to see a true Georgia peach!

We were scheduled to travel the same day as Lorraine's parents, July 3. I spent the entire week leading up to our departure preparing for my trip. I ironed clothes, picked out accessories to go with my outfits, gave myself a manicure, polished my toenails and washed and set my hair. The night before we was to leave, I had everything laid out on my bed to compare with the notes I had previously made. Satisfied that I hadn't forgotten anything, I began packing my suitcase and checking off the list. I read in a book that you should also pack the list to ensure everything comes back. The floor squeaked and then there was a knock at the door. "Come in." Mommie came in the room holding her bible. She sat on Rubie's bed and motion'd for me to come and sit next to her. Look like she had been crying so I readied myself for some bad news. Walking slowly towards her I ask, "What's wrong, Mommie?"

She shook her head, retrieved the laced handkerchief from her sleeve, wiped her eyes and said, "I'm sorry I'ma bit emotional but this is the first time one'a my babies is go'n outta town without me or one'a my relatives. Your father and I used to talk about the day when our children would leave home. We expect'd to be ov'a whelm'd with joy but right now I'm dread'n for tomorrow to come. I know you'll only be gone for three weeks but I'ma miss you so much. Diamond, you make sure you mind your manners and don't you forget how you was raised. Don't go down there embarrass'n our family name. It's important that you keep phone money in your pocket at all times. You nev'a know what might happen. Also, I expect you to go to church while you're there. It don't necessarily hav'ta be a Catholic church, as long as it's the house of the Lord, that's good enuf for me. You got your bible?"

"Yes ma'am, that's the first thing that I packed. Mommie, you can bet I'ma be on my best behavior and I'll be sure to call home every few days."

"You'd betta. Now don't you stay up too late, we gotta leave early in the morn'n", she replied.

We hugged and kissed, and then she left me to finish my packing. As she was closing the door, I heard her say, "Lord please watch ov'a my child." The next morning I awoke to the smell of smothered potatoes, bacon and biscuits. I hurried up and brushed my teeth and washed my face. That's all I had to do because I took my bath last night. By the time I got downstairs, Aunt Tootsie was pouring scrambled eggs in a skillet. I walk over to the table where my mother and uncle were sipping on hot tea and coffee.

"Good morning everybody," I said.

"Hi Diamond," Ant Tootsie continued, "I was just get'n ready to tell Earl to go wake ya'll up." My uncle was reading the paper so he just tipped his head.

I sat down at the table and Mommie leaned over and kissed me on my cheek. "Hey Pooh, I should'a known you'd be up. You so excited you prob'ly didn't get any sleep but don't worry, you'll have plenty of time to sleep on the plane if you feel like it. Go make sho Rubie and Baby Boy up. We need to leave in about an hour."

Before I could get outta my chair, they entered the room. I guess the smell of food woke them too. All of us took our places and Uncle Earl said grace. We ate a good breakfast, got dressed and left on time. It was 6 AM. My aunt and uncle didn't go to the airport with us because they had to get back home before their children woke up. My whole family walked me to the gate. Lorraine and her folks were already waiting when we got there. A short while later her parents left to go catch their flight but Mommie, Rubie and Baby Boy stay'd til after we got on the plane. I could still see them waving when we backed away from the gate.

Since this was my first time flying, Lorraine gave me the window seat. I stared out the window the whole flight. I was amazed at how small everything looked. When we stepped off the plane it was very hot but not as humid as St. Louis is in the summer time. It was mid-morning; the noon sun hadn't yet peaked. We at least could feel a mild breeze. Ms. Ella Mae met us at the gate. "This is my friend Diamond", Lorraine said.

"Hey baby", she replied in such an incredibly regal southern drawl.

"It's so nice to meet you," I said. Ms. Ella Mae was as tall as she was round. Her hair was cut short and she sported a jheri curl. Some of the activator got on my face when I bent down to hug her and my nose was aroused by her scent. She smelled like a rich lady, similar to the free expensive perfume samples at Famous-Barr department store. And, her make-up was flawless. Her lips were big and her mouth seemed too crowded with all of them big teeth but she had the most jovial smile that you ever did see. Right away I observed that she kind'a waddled when she walked. But for a heavy set person, she had a quick stride and loads of energy. We could hardly keep up with her stumpy little legs. I instantly liked her. After we identified our luggage in the baggage claim area, we proceeded to the car and the skycap put our bags in the trunk. She tipped him $15 which confirmed (for me) she was as wealthy as Lorraine's family. Nobody ever gave that much money away in exchange for a few minutes of work.

Once we were situated in the car and on our way out of the airport parking lot she asks, "How was the flight? I hope there wasn't too much turbulence, especially since this was Diamond's first flight."

I answer, "The flight was absolutely wonderful. I didn't get sick not one single bit." Lorraine agreed but she was used to flying. She had told me she never gets sick on planes.

"Are you ladies hungry? It's almost lunch time. We ought'a stop and get ya'll somthing to eat before we go to the house."

I was still full from breakfast plus the food they gave us on the plane but there was no way I was gonna say no. I'll just order a snack or fruit, somthing on the light side. I was not going to ruin an opportunity to experience any and everything I could about that city.

"Yes Aunt Ella Mae, I'm hungry" Lorraine replied.

She flashed that big smile of hers and said, "That's settled. We'll stop for lunch."

We went to *Wang's*, a small family owned restaurant in historic downtown Savannah. That was my first time eating authentic Asian food and I thought the food at the Chinaman in St. Louis is tastier. I experienced numerous firsts during my summer with Lorraine and her aunt but my most memorable occasion was going to a party at the YMCA. Amongst teenagers, this was the summer talk of the town. Everywhere we went, the movies, bowling alley and at the skating rink, kids would ask if we were going to be at that party. "Why, of course," was our reply. Well, as luck would have it, Ms. Ella Mae had made other plans for us to attend a social event with her the same night. Lorraine and I want'd to go to the "Christmas in July" party at the "Y". In an attempt to persuade Ms. Ella Mae into letting us go, we explained how much more fun we would have at a community dance with youth our age. Another time we told her that several chaperones would be present. But what finally won her over was when we said that all of the proceeds are donated to an emergency shelter so that they can purchase

Christmas gifts for abused kids. It was the truth! Ms. Ella Mae didn't have any children of her own but she really loved children, anybody's child. At last, she agreed with us. And she also arranged to drop us off at the "Y" before going to her event at the country club.

I had never been in the YMCA at home. In fact, I assumed you had to be male to go in there. I found out that's not the case here in Savannah. This place is packed with girls and boys. The gymnasium was decorated in red, green and gold. In the far corner of the room, a large Christmas tree was adorned with the same colors. Two chaperones had on elf costumes. Get this! They even had Santa in his sleigh with reindeer and fake snow. For me, this environment is an oxymoron. Standing in a winter wonderland dressed in summer attire with the air conditioning on.

I'm not what one would consider shy but it does take me a few minutes to loosen up when I'm in unfamiliar settings. Lorraine already knew most of the kids from previous visits but I only recognized a couple of the people from the mall. She immediately went to dance and while she was gone, I strolled over to the refreshment table to get something to drink. I was minding my own business, drinking punch when I caught eye contact with this real cute guy standing on the side talking with a bunch of other guys. He winked at me and I winked back. The whole night I kept stealing looks at him and I saw him checking me out a few times too. Each time a fast song came on I hoped he would ask me to dance but other boys asked me instead. I danced so many songs sweat was running down my face and my hair started sticking to my neck. I went in the bathroom to "use it" and get some wet paper towels to cool off with. When I came out of the bathroom he was standing right there, looking straight at me.

"Hi, I'm Duane. What's your name?"

I was so nervous I had to swallow hard before I could speak, "Uh, Diamond."

"Well Ms. Diamond, I've been waiting to dance with you all night. You're pretty popular and you can dance. I watched you go into the bathroom and figured this is my only chance." Within seconds, before I could respond, the lights dimmed and the music began. "Can I have this dance?"

My wish was to fast dance with him, *not* slow dance. I didn't know how to slow dance Savannah style plus it look like a whole lot of grinding to me.

"I'm from St. Louis, we don't slow dance like ya'll."

He grabbed my hand, pulled me along and said, "No problem, I'll teach you."

"Wait, wait. I don't want to embarrass myself." I said, walking awkwardly to the dance floor.

"You won't, I promise," he said as he put his arms around my tiny mid section. He was absolutely right. I felt as though we had been dancing together for years. I had no trouble following his footsteps but I made sure I kept plenty of space between us. Once he realized I had the hang of things he asked, "What grade you in?"

"I'll be a senior in the fall when we go back to school. What about you?"

"I'll be a senior too but I'm going to graduate at the end of the first quarter and then go to college in January. When I finish there, I'm going to med school."

A doctor! I knew I had to carefully select my words if I want to make a good impression on this guy. "Oh, and what school will you be attending?" I ask with a quick glance at my feet to make sure I stay'd in step.

"Savannah State College, my family's alma mater. My relatives have been going there since it was first established in 1890. The original name was Georgia State Industrial College for Colored Youth. In case you didn't know, it's the oldest public historically black college in Georgia. Are you planning on going to college?"

"Yes" I answered, "but I haven't decided where I would like to go." That's the second time in my life I spoke about going to college. Mimicking the love scene from a movie, I gave Duane my most admiring look into his eyes and said, "Perhaps now, I'll consider Savannah State." **Yes, I will be saving all my love for him.** The *Whitney Houston* song ended and the lights came on, much brighter than before. Then the DJ announced that the next song would be the last song of the evening. We decided not to dance. Once we maneuvered through the crowd and located an open spot near the exit, I said, "I'm leaving Monday to go back to St. Louis. You seem like a nice guy. I wish we had met sooner."

"St. Louis? I go to school in St. Louis, we can still keep in touch," he said and reached into his pocket and pulled out a small notebook and pen. *This guy is too smooth.* He scribbled down his name and phone number, tore off the page and handed the piece of paper to me. I borrowed his pad and pencil, and did the same. He gave me a swift kiss on the cheek and out the door he went to catch up with his friends. "Call me," I said.

#   #   #   #   #

Knock, knock. "Who is it?" I ask in a startled voice.

"It's Jade. Grandma sent me up here to get you? Hurry up Mama, everybody's downstairs."

"Ok, go ahead, I'll be right down." I jumped up, grabbed my copy of the master list along with the big stack of keys and left the room. Fortunately, my back pain has subsided and I feel much better.

29

AT LAST, THE PEACH STATE

Once we pass'd Marietta and Smyrna, I-75 start'd to get wider and by the time we got about a mile or so from downtown the expansion grew to about eight lanes with cars in er'y lane. It's hard to believe this part of the in'rstate was only two or three lanes wide when Reverend Daddy first moved down here. Right after Atlanta got approved to host the 1996 Summer Olympic Games they did a lot of construction on the highways and practically er'ything else too. I remember traffic out this way used to get heavy at certain times of the day, especially dure'n rush hour but chile it's almost ten o'clock at night, where's all these people go'n this time'a night? I sho want'd to tell the driver to take that North Avenue exit so I could get me a couple of them famous *Varsity* hot dogs but I knew we need'd to get to the hotel, we already behind schedule. You can bet I'll be sure to come back down here and get one of 'em before we leave on Monday.

On the way to the hotel we see exits for the *King Center, Centennial Park* and the *West End*. We also got a glimpse of where the *Braves* stadium used to be and the new *Turner Field* plus we saw the *Centennial Olympic Stadium* with its symbolic torch. Given that there was an accident at the I-75/I-85 split, it took another fifteen minutes before the bus pull'd into the Sheraton Gateway Atlanta Hotel, our home for the next few days. Jade had just finish'd count'n the money we collect'd for the bus driver. She slid across the aisle and sat in the seat next to me with the money tightly in both hands.

"Grandma, we got a hundred and ninety eight dollars."

I grab'd my purse. "I'ma give you anuth'a two dollars so it can be a ev'n two hundred. Let's put the money in a thank you card. That way he'll think we only gave him a card and he'll really be s'prised when he sees all'a the money we collected." I gave Jade my extra bills and one of the cards that I had brought with me. She sign'd the card, "From All of Us", seal'd it and address'd the front of the envelope. I pick'd up the mic again, hopefully for the last time this day. "Hello folks. Can I have your attention? Before we get off the bus, I think we should say a prayer of thanks to the Lord for our safe arrival. Ev'n though it was eventful, we made it here safely!" Right then er'ybody stop'd do'n what they was do'n and positioned they body for prayer. I bow'd my head and continued, "Father God, we thank you for allow'n us to arrive here without physical harm to anyone. Please bless us throughout this joyful celebration weekend. We know that it is because of You, all things are possible. " Then I made the sign of the cross start'n with my fo'head, then my chest and conclude'n with my left and right shoulder as I said, "In the name of the Father, Son and Holy Spirit." Most replied, "Amen." And some said, "Ashay."

I bent ov'a and whisper'd in Jade's ear, "While we empty the bus, you go up to your mama's room and tell her to bring the keys."

As soon as I got off the bus, I saw Rubie. She was walk'n in my direction so, I figure she gon stop and talk but instead she ask me without ev'n break'n her stride, "How much money did your bus collect for the driver?"

"Two hundred, what about yours," I said as she whisp'd by me.

She turn'd her head back to me and said, "We only had seventy five dollars. Perhaps we should switch buses on the way back so our driver can get a nice tip too. Can't talk right now, I gotta go help Diamond distribute the room keys."

"Sounds like a plan." It didn't take long for er'ybody to remove the trash from the bus and claim they luggage. Baby Boy put me and Jade's stuff on a hotel luggage rack and we proceed'd to the hotel. Jade was stand'n at the entrance tell'n relatives to go to the registration area, Club Lounge, where Diamond and Rubie was wait'n for them with they room keys. We had previously advised folks from other cities who didn't ride on the bus to check themselves in. They didn't hav'ta wait on us. By the time we arrived, there must'a been about 50 people already there.

Diamond took care of the details so you know er'ything is beautifully organized. As you step off the elevator, on the nineteenth floor you hear Daddy's favorite music. Alternate'n genre, one jazz song and then the next song was gospel. Church incense permeates the environment. A huge ticker tape neon sign flashes HAPPY BIRTHDAY REVEREND DADDY! The long registration table in the center of the floor is draped with kente cloth and fresh flowers. Contemporary, modern and African art work is beautifully display'd throughout the registration area. While Opal, Amy and Rubie give out room keys, Jennifer and Jade stand close to the end of the table pass'n out souvenir bags. Within a few minutes, most'a the folks have they room key but some are still wait'n for they bag. A noisy crowd ensues, many kiss'n and hug'n and laugh'n and talk'n. I see Diamond tap the side of a small Chinese gong two or three times to get our attention. It didn't work. She then pulls out an old fashion whistle and blow it several times. They heard that! The room got quiet real quick.

"May I have your attention, please? For those of you who don't know me, I'm Diamond, Rev. Daddy's granddaughter and Pearl's eldest daughter. First, I would like to thank each and everyone of you for coming and I thank God for your safe arrival. Folks, we are going to have a fabulous celebration this weekend! Please remember to wear your T-shirt tomorrow and don't forget to sign up for the talent show. The guest of honor should be arriving soon. Meanwhile, I know some of you want to freshen up and others want to mingle with relatives so I'm going to ask that we make our way downstairs to the Biltmore room for the official Meet and Greet. We'll be more comfortable there and also we can get a bite to eat and a cool drink."

I, Pearl Ann Johnson, inconspicuously head for the elevators, I what'n gon be wait'n with the others. Instead I'ma be one of the ones who go and freshen up. Chile, I been on that bus or in the Tennessee heat for the betta part of the day and my Secret is about to tell on me. Plus my teeth feel like they got little sweaters on 'em. A bell ding'd announce'n the elevator's approach and I wait for the people to get off. Then I dash on and push two buttons, my floor and the close door button. It seem'd to take a long time for the doors to close. Good, nobody got in the elevator with me. I'll join er'ybody in a few minutes. Right now I need to brush my teeth and take a shower. I remembered that Baby Boy had already took my things to my room. *Did he give me my key back?* I walk off the elevator relieved to find the key card in my pocket and a directional arrow indicate'n the path to my room.

Since Lorraine couldn't come, I got a room all to myself cause she 'bout the only person, other than my children, that I'd ev'n consider share'n a room with. The older I get the more I like be'n in my own space. I'm too out spoken, inconsiderate and set in my ways for change. That's one'a the perks of be'n old, folks expect and pretty much accept whatev'a we say and do. Think about it. Children and old people are naturally honest but unlike children, old people rarely get chastised or punish'd for they truthful yet often times outrageous comments. I can see it hap'n this weekend, for instance, a young relative greet they great aunt with a kiss, "Hey Antie, I love you. How do you think I look in my new glasses?" The aunt replies (without bat'n an eye), "Very educated, now you just need to get your teeth fixed and lose some weight. And, Antie loves you too. Please go o'va there and get me anuth'a slice of that pie."

The ev'n numbers on the right and odd on the left, my room's half way down the hall on the right. I gently ease my card in the metal slot, pull it out quickly, wait for the green light, turn the door handle and enter the room. The first thing I see is my luggage sit'n on top'a the collapsible guest rack that's normally stored in the closet. As I walk further into the room, I admire a large bouquet of flowers and a basket of fruit on the desk. I pick up the card and read it, "Welcome to Atlanta". *That was nice of the hotel.* My shoes come off before I make it to the thermost'aat located across the room. I don't like the temperature in my room to be too cold, actually I prefer the windows open but that ain't an option in most hotels, include'n this one. I change the dial to a more comfortable set'n, especially since I'm get'n ready to take a shower. Usually I'm not one to turn the TV on as soon as I enter a room but I like to watch the news er'y day or so and I haven't seent it since yesterday morn'n. So, I turn on the set and walk back towards the bathroom to start my water.

After shower'n, I brush my teeth, comb my hair, put on more deodorant and lip stick and decide on a colorful loose caftan to wear tonight. Before leave'n I call Diamond's room again but still no one answers. *It's 10:30 pm, I need to get go'n.* I walk to the elevator and wait two full loads before space is available in the third car. Since I what'n go'n straight to the event, I push the button marked "L" for lobby. Ev'n though I don't plan'on make'n any phone calls from the hotel phone in the room, I do frequently use room service when I stay in hotels. Therefore, I need to give 'em my credit card for incidentals. The elevator doors open and several guests step aside to let us off.

I what'n really watch'n where I was go'n cause I was try'n to get my credit card outta the badge holder they gave us at registration. I find it's simpler to put my money and credit cards in here instead of lug'n a big purse around all weekend. *This shouldn't take long, there's only one other person in line ahead of me.* Incidentally, I can ov'a hear a conversation behind me and I swear it sounds like Sam but before I can do a subtle turn around, I hear my name.

"Pearl Ann Johnson, you can't hide from me. I can pick you out anywhere, in a dense crowd, from behind or just by the scent of your sweet perfume."

I turn around and there Sam stands. We embrace and share a friendly kiss, "Well now Mr. Ashley Wilcox, what a pleasant s'prise see'n you here!" I step back to get a betta view of my dear friend. He has aged well. "It's good to see you. Are you in town for business or pleasure?"

"Strictly pleasure my dear. Please drop the formalities. Obviously, you don't know?

"Know what, I insist'd.

"I spoke with Diamond and told her I would be arriving tonight. Not sure why she didn't pass the message on to you but I'm here for Reverend Daddy's birthday celebration. So, if you don't already have an escort, I'd be glad to oblige for the weekend if you promise to call me Sam."

"It's a deal! Look, I gotta go take care of some business at the front desk, why don't you join me at the meet and greet upstairs in Club Lounge?"

"I got a better idea, I'll wait for you and we'll go up together," Sam said.

"Sounds good, I'll only be a minute." The person in front of me completed his transaction within five minutes and while the clerk was handl'n my request, I look to see where Sam wait'n for me. I spot him and he motions for me to join him at the fountain in the center of the lobby. I wave back, he turns around and then I see him toss a coin in the fountain.

I sneak up behind him. "Boo! What'd you wish for?"

"If I tell you it will never come true, right?" Sam and I begin walk'n towards the elevators.

"No my friend", I replied, "That's just some old myth. The truth is whatev'a God has set aside for you is for *you* and can't nobody take it from you. Haven't you heard tale of a person get'n they dream job or a new house when the odds was not in their favor? Chile, God can make'a way outta no way."

"Well then, I guess it's ok to tell you." He intentionally lower'd his voice and moved closer to me. "I wish I could steal you away." I roll'd my eyes at his familiar adolescent tease but he continued on. "I know you'll be busy this weekend and I do truly understand but nonetheless you asked me and that was my wish. Did they deliver the welcome package to your room? I remember how much you like flowers."

I stop dead in my tracks. "That's from you?" Sam nods his head yes and I reach up and kiss him on the cheek. "Thanks, that's very thoughtful but I assumed it was from the hotel that's why I hadn't said anything. I didn't ev'n know you were here and the card included with the arrangement was basically anonymous, a welcome to Atlanta but no signature. Please forgive me and thanks again for the flowers and fruit. Since you've agreed to be my escort for the weekend, how about we head to the Biltmore and get ourselves a nice hot cup of tea."

"Pearl, I'd be honored to escort you to a cup of tea or for that matter, to the ends of the earth. All you have to do is say the word."

"The tea'll be fine for now," I replied with a smile. I enjoy'd our chat while we was walk'n. When we get there I quickly scan the room and I knew we was in the right place cause the same ticker tape neon sign that I saw in the reception area is hang'n on the wall directly above the ice sculpture of the bible with pray'n hands off to the side. I like the theme Diamond got go'n but she forgot to do sumthin' with cars and how much he likes to fix 'em up. Oops....I spoke too soon, right across from where they got the coffee and tea set-up, there's a large cake decorated like an auto repair shop, complete with little black mechanics work'n on cars and trucks. Looks like more people here than was downstairs, I thought the crowd would'a thin'd out by now. I tell ya, that Diamond is, what's that the kids say, off the chain when it come to plan'n events!

A loud trumpet fanfare commands our attention. Then a deep prestigious voice says, "Ladies and gentlemen, please stand and help me give a warm welcome to our guest of honor this weekend, the Reverend

John Bishop Gooch, better known to his loved ones as Reverend Daddy."
Diamond is his escort and he looks so handsome in that tuxedo. Of
course, she looks good too. Er'ybody is clap'n and I feel my eyes begin to
sting. That mean I'ma cry any second but the young folks start shout'n
"Dad-dy, Dad-dy", and we all join in, "Dad-dy, Dad-dy." Chile, they
so crazy, I just love be'n with my family. As soon as he sits down people
surround him. I'll catch up with him later, first I need to find Ant Hattie
and Jade to make sure they got they equipment. I plan on take'n a lot of
pictures then I'll use they audio to help me finish my legacy tape.

Sam turns to me and says, "Pearl, I'm going over there to say hi to
your father and a few other folks. See you later." Sam what'n no stranger
when it came to my family, he practically know all of 'em. Anyway,
you know how us blacks folks are. We genetically predisposed to good
manners. Ev'n though we rarely receive the same courtesy, generally
we're welcome'n and respectful to other cultures. Do I have scientific
proof of this? No, but Africans are such a hospitable people, we had to
get it from our ancestors.

I look at the clock, its get'n late. *Where's Ant Hattie and Jade?* I see
both of 'em sit'n at a table with Tootsie. Ant Hattie is talk'n when I
walk up so I had to wait for the opportunity to politely interrupt. "This
place is really nice. I can't wait to see all'a the things they got plan'd for
us this weekend but honestly I hope they don't last this long. It's almost
midnight, way past my bedtime."

"Hello er'ybody. Tootsie, will you excuse us a minute, I wanna have
a word with Ant Hattie and Jade."

"Sure. Anyway, I need to go help Diamond with the night
crawlers."

"Night crawlers," I ask. "What's that?"

"Don't worry, you'll see." And off she went.

Ant Hattie cut her eyes at me and said, "Girl you betta make this
quick. It's late; I'm tired and ready to go to my room. I need to put my
feet up. Perhaps I'll make myself a cup of tea before I go to bed."

"They got hot beverages right ov'a there next to the desserts. Jade
please go get your grandma and your great-great aunt a cup of tea. You
want some dessert too," I ask Ant Hattie.

"No, but bring me a sweetener." Ant Hattie tells Jade.

"Pink, blue or yellow," Jade asks.

"Yellow." And to me she says, "I can remember when we only had one choice, sugar. Funny how some things change and others remain the same." Jade came back carry'n a tray load'd with er'ything we might need, hot water, cups, stirrers, lemon, cream and variety of teas and sweeteners.

"Thanks Pooh, have a seat." I told Jade. "Again, I want to thank ya'll for agree'n to help me. If you don't mind, I'd like for ya'll to take a few pictures too. I got about 10 disposable cameras in my room and I'll make sure you have one for er'y occasion. Let's meet for breakfast each morn'n, my treat of course, and map out our plan for the day. If that's all ok with you ladies, we're done here."

"Good. I can finish my tea and head up to my room."

Jade asks, "What time are we meeting for breakfast?

"How about 8am," I ask.

"Fine with me," Ant Hattie said.

"Ok. Good night Grandma and Ant Hattie." Then she leaves to join some'a her teenage cousins. Me and Ant Hattie finish the tea and retire to our rooms. *Oops, I forgot to tell Sam goodbye.*

30

DIAMOND

"Reverend Daddy, please hurry, it's time." *Why is he back there having a conversation with Baby Boy?* Yes, it was Baby Boy's responsibility to get him here tonight but now is not the time to chit chat, the music has already begun and the doors are open. I quickly link my arm inside of his and when we step in the room, the applause erupts and cameras start flashing. WOW! I feel like a star walking the red carpet at a movie premiere. Reverend Daddy looks around and sees familiar faces, some he hasn't seen in years. A single tear cascades down his face. Our walk is at a slow but continuous pace. He has excellent mobility for his age. We arrive at our table and within seconds, people come from all directions to greet him. I decide this is a good time for me to check to make sure everything else is ready and in order.

My nephews Onyx and Topaz are, quote, unquote "producing the talent show", everything from getting folks to sign up to organizing and managing the show. The reason why I agreed to give them this assignment is because both of them are responsible boys. Rather, should I say males? Onyx is a metro sexual senior in high school and loves anything that has to do with music or the theatre. Topaz is a sophomore jock that wants to be a pro foot ball player. They make good grades and are also active in the youth program at their church but they're still young and inexperienced at this sort of thing so I'll go and see how things are come'n along, just to be sure.

Out of the corner of his mouth, Onyx slyly tells Topaz, "Here comes Antie Diamond."

"I bet she tell us the same thing, don't she know we got this!"

"You know how she is, everything's gotta be perfect. She don't mean no harm though," Onyx replied.

"Well now, how are my two favorite nephews come'n along?" Jokingly I continue, "I would thank you not to tell my other nephews that I gave you that title because it could be easily taken away."

We both smiled, "Everything's fine, Auntie Diamond." Topaz didn't say anything so I continued talking, "Ten people signed up. The show will be a blend of picture, song, dance and poetry. We are scheduled to rehearse tomorrow morning right after breakfast and then again to slate the performers when we get back from the outings at 3pm. Don't worry we'll be ready in time for the eight o'clock curtain call."

"Topaz, why is Onyx doing all'a the talking, don't you agree with what he said?"

"Yes."

"Then say so or shake your head or do somthing. Don't stand there like a bump on a log. Just make sure you guys keep it clean and entertaining. Remember this show is to be a tribute to your great-grandfather not a Rapp concert. I'm counting on you guys, don't let me down."

"We won't. Promise." said the boys. And off to prevent the next fire I went. It didn't take me long to locate my mother's sister who was supose to help me.

"Ant Tootsie, are you still available to help?"

"Yeah but what did you say the night crawler is again?"

"You know how when you're on a cruise and they provide your cabin with written daily announcements and agendas. Well, that's the same concept with the night crawlers. We'll be slipping customized agendas under folk's door while they're asleep."

"What time will this be take'n place?"

"It'll have to be late but not too late because we still gotta get up early the next day. How about we do it at midnight every night?"

"Sounds good, I'll meet you in your room at midnight. Is there anything you need done to get ready?"

"No, I got somebody to take care of all'a that. You just show up on time!"

"Please."

"What?"

You forgot to say please," Tootsie reminded Diamond."

"I'm sorry Ant Tootsie. Please. I don't mean to sound like I'm barking orders because I really do appreciate all your help. See you at midnight." *Wa-wa-wa. I got a big celebration to pull off this weekend. I don't have time to stroke people's egos.*

I mingle with relatives for a while and then I go to my room to rest for a few minutes and wait for Duane. His flight landed half an hour ago, he should be here in a few minutes. *Anyway, my back's starting to hurt again.*

31

DUANE

I've wanted Diamond to be my wife from the first time I saw her, the summer before starting under grad school, at a party at the "Y". While Georgia is famous for pretty girls and beauty pageants, Diamond was a pleasant change for me. She was not just another pretty face in Savannah but a strikingly beautiful, funny, witty, strong traditional black woman. I liked the way she carried herself. Initially my family didn't think she was good enough for me because she hadn't come from a historical wealthy southern heritage like us but over the years they've grown to love her as much as I do. Sometimes, they can be so bourgeoisie, it's embarrassing.

I attended a private Catholic boarding school from the time I was in the sixth grade till I graduated high school. Then I went away to college. The only time I was at home was for the holidays, Thanksgiving and Christmas, spring break and of course the summer hiatus. Even then there were times I didn't come because I was visiting friends from school or we were vacationing elsewhere. My parents spared no expense for me and my siblings. Yes, my childhood was very different than Diamond's but I'm not say'n my life was any better or that I'm better than her. I may have had more material things but she definitely had more intangible things like love, trust, pride, friendship and loyalty. And I believe those qualities are far more important than the *stuff* I got because without them you don't truly appreciate your *stuff* but rather you come to expect the *stuff* and what's even sadder is you can't imagine life without it. Through God's grace I've been able to move pass that but I can't say the same for my parents. However, I do love them dearly; they are the best people they know how to be.

I'm grateful for them providing me with a *free* education. Not many people can finish medical school and not have any student loans to pay back. My parents agreed to pay off all my loans if I became a doctor. It is because of their love that I'm a successful pediatrician today. They may have provided the money but I put in the time, discipline and sacrifices. Medical school and residency is very hard on a family. Doctors spend long hours at the hospital and consequently you're absent for the precious milestones of loved ones such as recitals, games, dances, awards or simply dinner at home as a family. You realize years later that you don't know your own family. One day you see your infant daughter in her crib and the next time you get significant time off work, she's crawling, then walking, talking and before you know it, it's first day of school.

Prior to college, I lived a sheltered life, void of black. I had very little contact with the "outside" black community. On the contrary, I was surrounded by whiteness and I only dated white girls. If it was white, it was right! We lived in a white neighborhood and I was usually the only black child in a sea of white students. I rarely saw other black children and I was never allowed to play with "those" poor black kids. That was prohibited. I was ignorant to anything "black", whether it pro or con. From an early age I was taught our fair skin made *us* different from *them,* a gift from my paternal Creole lineage. Furthermore, I was misinformed by all of media; I *really* believed their stereotypical portrayal of black people. And plus, the news wouldn't lie! Consequently, I witnessed but didn't question white male privilege nor did I acknowledge the existence of systemic racism. While I credit the expensive schools for book and theory knowledge, Diamond was the one who taught me street smarts and introduced me to the middle class black family experience. I'm ashamed to say this but back then I didn't know how to support black because I was not allowed to. I was not exposed to it and I didn't truly understand the plight of the African American 'til I went to a HBCU, Savannah State College. That's when I sought out resources to increase my knowledge of black folks and I also began to advocate for people of color living in white America. I painfully remember the first time racism personally reared its ugly head up at me. It caught me by surprise; I had lived with a veil over my eyes for so long, I didn't even see it coming.

#   #   #   #   #

My senior year was not a full school year but rather a few short months. At the end of the first quarter, I had already earned enough credits to meet the requirements for a diploma as well as been accepted to Savannah State College. Instead of sticking around and taking more high school classes, I'm going to start college early. In all honesty, I'm anxious to live and go to school with black students. Especially since I met Diamond, we've become good friends and we try to keep in contact. When time permits we meet at Northwest Plaza for a movie or just to walk around the mall. Even though I'm excited about moving to a different environment, I'm still going to miss the crew, my friends Ben, Robert, Mike and Paul. I've known Ben the longest, though. We met in the fifth grade but didn't start going to school together til the sixth. I met Robert and Mike in the seventh grade and Paul in the eighth. All of us are from Georgia but Ben and I are the only ones from Savannah.

I attend Chaminade College Preparatory School, a private, all boy Catholic school, grades six through twelve, located in St. Louis, Missouri. Most of the students are local but about a hundred of us, representing seven states and four countries, live on campus. Our parents are doctors, lawyers, stockbrokers, engineers, CEO's and other wealthy professions. Ninety-nine percent of the students enter and complete college. With statistics like that you may think all we do is study but I beg to differ. We have plenty of extracurricular activities, track, water polo, swimming, tennis, golf, baseball, football and basketball, plus a whole slew of academic clubs. We also hold a national and state championship in soccer.

The last week of school seem to fly by. After I finished my last final, I went to my room to pack. It feels strange. As usual everybody is leaving for Christmas vacation but this time I won't be coming back. I've spent the last six years of my life here and it's all about to be over with. I'm leaving comfortable familiar surroundings for unfamiliar territory. The movers'll be here early tomorrow morning but my flight isn't scheduled to leave til late in the afternoon. I should be back in Savannah by night fall. It's bitter sweet. Well anyway, some of my friends from school have invited me to come and hang out with them in Stone Mountain to celebrate my accomplishments and to say good-bye to the fellas.

Unfortunately, the weather delayed the flight for a couple of hours and we didn't land til almost eight o'clock. I was so exhausted by the time I made it home, I unpacked a few things and went straight to bed. Early the next morning the private line in my room rang.

I answer the phone, "Hello."

"What's, up? Did I wake you," Ben asked.

"No, I had to get up to answer the phone anyway," annoyed I continue, "What are you doing up so early?"

"Talking to you, did you ask your parents?"

"Not yet. I plan on asking them today or tomorrow. It all depends on what kind of mood they're in. It's not like I've never been over Robert's house before but I don't know how they're gonna feel about his parents being out of town."

"Then don't tell 'em that part. I didn't tell my parents," Ben said.

"What did you say to them?" Intrigued, I propped my pillow up.

"I said that Robert invited me to his party next week. Is it ok if I stay for the weekend? It was easy; they didn't even ask questions because they know Robert's folks. Besides it's just gonna be the five of us hanging out and saying farewell to our buddy. I can't wait for the summer, by then we'll be eighteen and we won't have to ask anybody anything."

"I don't know, Ben. I don't like lying to my parents."

"It's not lying, you're only withholding information."

"Yeah, but it's, crucial information. I'll let you know what they say. Now can I please go back to sleep? It's seven o'clock in the morning. Bye." I drifted back to sleep and had a dream about being trapped in a burning house. I awoke with a decision; I'm going to tell my parents the whole truth, *if* they ask. But, they didn't.

The following Friday, which was yesterday, Ben rode with me to Stone Mountain. Last night, the crew minus Paul, ordered pizza, watched sports, played Atari and listened to some music. This morning, actually it was after twelve by the time we left the house, we went to Mc Donald's, pigged out and came back here to look at ESPN for the rest of the afternoon. Several good football games are come'n on.

"I wish Paul would have come," Mike said.

"Me too," Robert concurred.

Ben asks, "What are we going to do tonight? This could be our last time together for a while. We need to celebrate. Duane is the first of us to go to college. Congratulations, man."

"Thanks. You guys'll be graduating soon too. May is only five months away and then we'll all be in college come fall. Let's vow to stay in touch with each other once we go our separate ways. Perhaps an annual event, meet each year for the weekend in a different city," I suggest.

"I'll vote for that but what are we doing to-night?" Ben asks again.

Mike answers, "We can go to a movie, shoot some pool or I know, go to this party I know about. A friend of mine's girlfriend is throwing a big bash. She's got a lot of cute friends that will definitely be at the party. I was hoping ya'll want to go."

"What kind of party, *invitation* or word of mouth?" Robert ask'd.

"I'm telling you, she invited us and what's even better is we don't have to dress up. We can wear jeans," Mike said.

Ben stomped his foot and got up from the sofa, "Then I say we go to this party. You guys are cool and all but I don't want to spend another night stuck in the house with ya'll. I need to see some la-dies. But since this celebration is for Duane, he should decide." He points in my direction and they all look at me.

I reply, "Well then, I say we check out the Ohio v. Michigan game that's getting ready to come on and then we grab a bite to eat before going to the party. Cool?" Now it's my turn to look askance at them. They nod in agreement. We watch the game, freshen up (some of us) and leave by six-thirty. Robert's car is bigger and newer so, we took his and left mine.

"Where to, guys?" Robert asks after backing out of the driveway. Again, my friends look to me for an answer.

I'm enjoying this, making all the decisions. Too bad it's only for one night. "A celebration like this shouldn't be a hamburger event. Let's go some place that has a variety of food, like seafood, chicken and steak. Some place where we can sit down and have the food served to us on real plates and use flatware and stemware. I don't want my celebration at McDonald's. How about we go to Red Lobster, my treat? *My folks won't mind, I haven't used my Visa card in months.*"

"Red Lobster it is!" they respond. Ten minutes later we arrive, drop Mike off at the door to get in lineue while Robert parks the car. When we get inside, he tells us the wait is fifteen to twenty minutes. We wait for thirty minutes and are seated. Me and Ben order the crab legs, Mike ate chicken and Robert had steak. The food was good. I was waiting for the check when all of a sudden the staff start clapping and singing happy birthday while walking to our table carrying a free dessert for *me*. Somebody secretly told the waitress it was my birthday. It is not! They laugh at me til tears roll out their eyes. *It was pretty funny.* I paid the check and we left the restaurant at nine o'clock.

"Hope you're not sore about our celebration for you back there," Ben said after we got back in the car.

"Of course not, but can we go to the party now?" I ask.

Robert shouts, "Next stop, party!" Mike provides the directions. We hear the music before we even get to the house. We park. Before making our way to the door, we hang outside to talk amongst ourselves for a few minutes. There's a line to the door. I can see a big guy at the door, a bouncer or a relative, we won't know til we get up there. Mike's leading the way and I'm standing directly behind him. His body over powers my small frame. Before you know it, it's our turn.

The big white guy at the door stops Mike and says "I'm Mary Jo's father; you fellas make sure you mind your manners tonight. I don't want no trouble." I step from behind Mike and said, "You bet, sir."

The man points at me and says, "Oh, I didn't see *you*. They can come in but you can't."

Mike speaks up, "Why not, he's with us sir. And we were invited by your daughter."

The man steps within inches of Mike's face, "I don't give a damn who he's with or who invited him. Spooks and jungle bunnies ain't welcome in my home. Now I suggest you take your friend outta here before I get my shotgun and blow his ass away."

He's not being very polite, so much for manners! Did he just threaten me? I once heard tale of blacks being lynched in Stone Mountain but I dismissed it as myth or rumor. *This is for real, my life is in danger.* It's useless for me to challenge this man's way of thinking. Words cannot adequately describe how hurt and embarrassed I felt but it's not worth the chance of risking a senseless death. I chose the non-violent route. Instead, I keep quiet, turn around and go back to the car. My friends follow. I get in the front seat and slam the car door so hard I'm surprised the window didn't break. *How dare that man judge me and my purpose in life solely based on his prejudice beliefs.* "Let's go!" I said. Then we left. Needless to say, the trip back to Robert's house was awkward for everybody. I did a lot of shouting and asked rhetorical questions. They didn't know what to say so they didn't say anything. Shortly after returning, I decided to drive back to Savannah, alone. Ben remained at Robert's. I never told my parents about that horrible experience but surprisingly that one incident sparked a change in my whole perspective of life. On my drive to Savannah that night, I thought about all the injustices of the world and I couldn't get over the fact that *I* had been a victim of racism! The next week, I arrived at Savannah State with a vengeance to eradicate hate and a lifelong promise to advocate for human rights.

# # # # #

Regardless how much money or education I have, ultimately, I'm just another person of color living in white America. None of us are totally free from racism and we must continue to fight for equality of all God's people. My flight arrived on time. When I finally get to the hotel room, Diamond is awake, lying across one of the beds fully dressed. I presume, waiting for me.

"Hi. How was your flight?" She asks.

I tip the bellman; he exits and I walk over to kiss my wife. Smack! "It was good. I expected you to be asleep by now. How was your event?"

She gets up. "It was fabulous. Everybody liked it, especially Reverend Daddy. I've got one more thing to do before I can call it quits tonight."

Then there's a knock at the door. "Who is it?" I ask.

"It's Ant Tootsie." I open the door. She comes in complaining, "Hi, Duane. I don't know if I should say good ev'ning or good morn'n. Then she turns to Diamond and says, "I'm sleepy as all get out, we gon hav'ta change this to a earlier time or you need to find yo'sef anuth'a partner.

"What are you two getting ready to do?" I ask.

"Distribute these agendas to our guests. Here's one for you." Diamond said and picks up a stack of flyers.

She kisses me on the cheek and they leave the room. I scratch my head. *She can stay up all night if she likes. It's late, I'm going to bed.*

32

THE BIG DAY!

Today is June 29th, my daddy's actual birthday. The banquet and talent show we got plan'd for tonight is in his honor. He's one hundred years old. I saw Diamond in the hall and she told me that her and Tootsie didn't finish pass'n out the night crawlers till late. They agreed to start an hour earlier tonight. Good. Looks like people read'n them flyers too, cause er'ybody I seen this morn'n got they t-shirt on. In addition to the t-shirt reminder, the flyer outlines the day's events. We have a choice between *Six Flags* and *Raging Rivers* or *Underground Atlanta* and the *King Center*. Transportation provided for both, meet in the lobby at nine. *That gives us a whole hour for breakfast.* When I get off the elevator, I see Ant Hattie and Jade sit'n on a bench outside'a the restaurant, wait'n for me. "Good morn'n ladies." We greet each other with kisses.

The hostess asks, "How many?"

"Three." Ant Hattie said.

"You ladies prefer a booth or a table?"

"Booth, please, if it's not too low." I say. She leads us to a tall booth. Jade sits on the inside and me and Ant Hattie sit across from each other. We have the option to order from the menu or partake of the buffet. I chose the menu, a continental breakfast and they have the buffet. We all order hot tea. Once they fix they plate and sit down, Jade says grace and I begin the discussion, while we eat our meal. "I'm so excited this morn'n. All the things we been plan'n for will finally take place. It's gonna be a great centurion celebration! Which one of the events are you going to?" I ask Jade.

"I'm going to Six Flags and Raging Rivers but I'm not gonna get wet! I'll walk through the parks, make sure everybody's having fun and take pictures. Then when I'm on the bus, waiting in line, on the rides or sitting around just people watching, I'll record."

Ant Hattie took a sip of tea and said, "*Six Flags* sounds like too much walk'n for me and I don't want to be outside all day. I think I'll do the other one."

"What about tonight, will both of you be at the talent show and banquet?"

"Yes, but I might not stay to the end," Ant Hattie said.

"I'll be there all night. I promised Mom that I'd be available to help out if she needs me."

I pull the fourth chair out from under the table so that they can see the Walgreens bag in the chair. "Make sure you get a couple of these cameras," I said point'n towards the bag."

"I'm sure you'll remind us if we forget," Ant Hattie replied.

I ate just enuf. I don't wanna be look'n for no bathroom er'y few minutes. I'm go'n on the bus with Ant Hattie but I need to go to my room befo' I get on the bus. Diamond is gonna ride on the same bus as Jade. We finish our breakfast and they each take three cameras. "You can always get more if you need to. The buses are due back at the hotel by 3pm. After then, I'll be in my room rest'n before the banquet." We kiss goodbye and go our separate ways.

#   #   #   #   #

Diamond and Duane awake at the same time. She still hasn't confront'd him about his alleged infidelities. *Perhaps this is not the time, nor the right place to have a big confrontation, because that's exactly what it'll be.* I feel refreshed this morn'n, not a pain in my body. I get up, shower and dress, all while trying my best to ignore him without being blatantly rude. I do not initiate any type of conversation. I only respond to his questions.

"Would you be interested in having breakfast with me this morning?" Duane charmingly asks me.

I might as well make the best of this weekend; it may turn out be our last weekend together. "Honey, I'm already dressed and you're still in the bed. How long will it take you to get ready?"

"Twenty, maybe thirty minutes, I need to shower."

"Fine, I'll go check on the excursions and then I'll meet you downstairs in the restaurant at eight fifteen. Is that ok?"

"Yes. What's the weather forecast?" He asks.

"The high is seventy-eight degrees today. Dress cool and comfortable. See you downstairs." I was on my way to Jade and Jennifer's room when I ran into my mother at the elevator. "And where are you on your way to?" I ask her.

"To see if your grandfather needs anything this morn'n. Then I'm go'n to have breakfast with Ant Hattie and Jade. Where you go'n?"

"To check to see if the girls are up, OMG, I'm turning into you. Remember how you used to check on me and Rubie?" We smile and I continue, "Ant Tootsie and I stayed up late last night but I was able to get up on time. I hope they did too. How'd you like it? Didn't they do a good job designing the flyer? DING! Here's my ride, I'll see you in the lobby at nine. Don't be late," I said and got in the elevator.

"Awwww," I'm startled when Jenn quickly thrusts open the door, she must'a been standing right next to it when I knocked. "Good morning, sweetheart. Where's Jade?" I ask and walk further into the room.

"In the shower," she replies, "Antie Diamond, I don't mean to be rude but I was on my way out when you knocked on the door. Excuse me, I gotta go, me and Uncle Bubba's kids going to breakfast together. Please tell Jade I'll see her on the bus." And out the door she went. I pick up the remote to lower the volume on the television so that I can be heard. "Jade, what time are you meeting your grandma?" *I'm hoping we can find time for a serious talk **and** listen.*

"In fifteen minutes. Why?" She asks from the bathroom. "Mom I know I said I will help you all day today but technically that doesn't start til after we get on the bus. Breakfast is considered free time! Is Daddy here yet? She asks as she exits the bathroom half dressed, only in her bra and panties.

"Yes he is. As a matter of fact, I'm meeting him in a few minutes. Jade, it's been a long time since we ate a meal together as a family, you sure you don't want to change your plans and join us?"

"I'm more than sure, I'm positive. Now please go, Mama. I gotta finish dressing. I can't be late for breakfast."

I kiss Jade on her forehead, tell her what Jenn said and remind her, "Meet me and your father in the lobby at nine." It must be my lucky day because the doors open as soon as I approach the elevator. I step in, "Lobby please," I say to no one in particular but more so out of habit than anything else. The doors remain open and I realize I'm the only one in the elevator. I had to laugh at myself, *push the button, girl.* I go to the restaurant but I don't see Duane however, I put our name on the waiting list anyway. Then I head out to the parking lot to talk to the bus drivers. *God please let them be professional and already know what they're s'posed to do.* They did, *thank you God.* I return inside to meet my husband for breakfast.

#   #   #   #   #

BABY BOY

I can't afford for my boys to have their own room so we compromise and the four of us share space, a suite. My sister, Diamond offer'd to pay the difference but I wouldn't accept it. I'm awakened by loud music. I put on my robe and come out of the bedroom, "Can you please turn that music down, son? It's too early in the morn'n; nobody wants to hear that mess!" I bellow.

"Why does it have to be labeled mess?" Topaz challenges his father.

My glare is equivalent to the look of the evil step parent in fairy tales. "Because I said so, you got any more questions?"

"No sir." Topaz said and mumbled under his breath, *I thought he said we was gon have equal rights while we're in Atlanta.* I heard him but I wait til he strolls in front of me to thump him on his head. "Stop play'n Dad, I just did my hair," he whines.

Onyx pull'd his t-shirt over his head and guided his arms through the sleeves. Then he smoothed his shirt and paused to admire his frame in the full length mirror. *Damn I look good.* He likes the design on the shirt and the color, black, is his favorite. . He and Topaz have already decided that they were gonna stay at the hotel, order room service and play video games all day. He's expecting the day to go as *they* have planned.

I go back in the bedroom to talk to my wife, "Peaches," I say, loud enuf for my sons to hear in the other room, "you think one'a us needs to go to Six Flags?"

"No Charles. They'll be fine by themselves. Anyway, I want you and me to spend the day together, touring *Underground Atlanta* and *The King Center*. Maybe we can even go to Little Five Points, too if you feel like riding the MARTA train."

It's my turn to set the ol' man straight. I peak around the door frame, "Thanks Mom for have'n our backs. Dad acts like we little kids or somthing. He forgets that both of us are old enough to drive, which means we're old enough to go to an amusement park, unsupervised." Onyx mocks.

I gave him that, don't get smart with me look and he cowers back to the common area. My wife's the only person I allow to embarrass me and she's also the only person that calls me, Garnet. My co-workers call me, Johnson, my relatives call me, Baby Boy and my children call me Dad. Most'a of my relatives don't even know what my real name is, they assume I'm namd after my daddy, Charles Le-Roy Sr., but that's not true, I have his first name as my middle name. Folks always say I look just like him. Now that I'm thinking about it, I haven't seen those, *his* folks in a long time. They haven't invited us to a family reunion or any kind'a celebration on that side'a the family, in years. I only saw them a couple of times after the funeral. Our contact slowly drifted after daddy died.

I holler above the music, "If ya'll plan on eating breakfast, I suggest you go with us downstairs to the restaurant." My next statement is a significant blow to the plan, the one that I overheard last night. "I'm not gonna pay for you guys to lie around here and eat and do nuth'n all day. But on the other hand, if you want to participate with the family and come help celebrate your great grandfather's birthday, you're more than welcome."

Both thought, *"Like we got a choice!"*

"Call your Aunt Rubie and see if they wanna go to breakfast with us," Peaches instructs the boys.

\#   \#   \#   \#   \#

RUBIE LEIGH

RING, RING…! Rubie answers the phone, "Hello."

"Good morning, Antie Rubie."

"Good morning, Topaz," she replies.

He continues, "Mom told me to call to see if ya'll wanna meet us downstairs for breakfast?"

"When, what time?"

"We ready to leave now. So, I guess in a few minutes."

"As usual, your uncle's outside smoking a cigarette. Get us a seat and we'll meet ya'll down there as soon as he comes back."

"Ok, bye."

I said "Bye," too and hung up the phone. Me and the girls been nagging Stan to stop smoking for a long time now. I've almost given up! Ever since Opal and Amy moved out and Jenn started driving, I have a lot more free time and sometimes I sit and think about stuff… Like…I want somebody to be around to share my golden years with. Shoot, Stan's educated and he knows very well what smoking's doing to his body. But I'm afraid if he doesn't stop, I might end up by myself. *Rubie, you can't tell him how to live or die.* He gotta want to do it himself. Why do people start smoking? Ain't nobody ever see a crack head and say, I wanna be like that. Smoking is an addiction and I don't care if you smoke crack, weed, cigars, or cigarettes, it's all linked to a highly addictive oral fixation acquired at birth, Sigmund Freund theory. Plus my mama told me. That coupled with the environment is also the reason for obesity. Most people can stop, some cold turkey but others need medicinal or psychological help to quit. The key to success is to accept it as a life change. You might have to change the people in your circle, the places that you frequent or the food you intake. It requires extreme discipline and for the most part people aren't willing to make those sacrifices, not even for their health. It's a blessing and just shy of a miracle that Reverend Daddy has lived for a hundred years. He smoke and drink!

Jenn called earlier to say that she would meet us in the lobby. I pick up my purse when I hear Stan put his card in the slot and open the door. "I told Baby Boy we'd meet them for breakfast. You ready?" I ask before he's too far inside of the door.

He takes a peppermint ball from his pocket, unwrap it and put it in his mouth. "Yeah, let's go."

And we leave for the restaurant.

#   #   #   #   #

PEARL

It's exactly 8:45 AM by the time I make it back to the room. That's still enuf time for me to get my i.d. and money. I search my purse for the items. Then as I bent down to put the purse away, I see that my feet are begin'n to swell. You'd think I'd feel it first, but I don't. To help keep my feet from hurt'n and swell'n any more than they are now, I take a couple of *Advils* and look for my other pair of shoes. See'n that we gon be do'n a lot of walk'n, I decide on my support tennis, put 'em on and leave. When I get there at nine, the lobby is pack'd with all'a my relatives in they centennial t-shirts. I'm just thrill'd to see my children and my grandchildren and aunts, uncles, nieces, nephews and cousins. Where's daddy? *I want my family to take a picture!* I manage to assemble my box of jewels and we pose for a centennial birthday picture with Reverend Daddy. CLICK! Several other relatives also use this opportunity to take they family portraits.

Our bus arrives back at the hotel, as promised, by three o'clock. Since I didn't hav'ta pay any admission fees, I splurge and buy myself a copy of the original record'n of the *I Have A Dream* speech, a ML King flag, mouse pad and magnet. Chile, this was a fun fill'd educational activity plus it what'n too hot outside but now, er'ybody is really look'n forward to rest'n before tonight's festivities. Well, at least I am. Baby Boy had brung Reverend Daddy back hours ago, 'cause he got tired. Right now, I'm tired! And, it's a long laborious walk to my room, I'm ache'n er'ywhere but I must admit, I did have a good time today. We went to *Underground Atlanta* and *The King Center*. I were disappoint'd when it was time to leave the center. You see, I especially love museums; really, I love any kind'a information that increases your knowledge. I can spend hours on end absorb'n a single exhibit.

Actually it took me thirty minutes to ev'n enter the build'n because I was so impress'd with the grounds and the statue of *Mahatma Ghandi* that was donated by the Embassy of India, USA. It's located just before the entrance to the *International Civil Rights Walk of Fame.* As I stroll down tribute lane, I feel a personal connection to one'a the preserved footprints they got along the pathway of many Trumpet Award recipients and civil rights activists. *Dr. Otis W. Smith* a respect-able black physican on Simpson Road who used to treat my kids back in the 70's whenev'a we need'd a pediatrician when we was in town visit'n Reverend Daddy. I distinctly remember him be'n rather intel-ligent and have'n an excellent rapport with parents and children but I had no idea that he was *that* involved in the civil rights movement.

I had hoped more of our young people would'a went with us today 'cause they need to know how crucial the youth were to the success of the civil rights movement. The young folks made it possible for parents to keep they jobs because the adults would get fired if they went to jail so instead, the children , from as young as age 6, began to protest segregation and consequently they were arrested by the hun-dreds. The nation watch'd in horror as the police turn'd fire hoses and dogs on young non-violent marchers. The follow'n year in Montgom-ery, Alabama, at the foot of the *Edmund Pettus Bridge*, blacks were attack'd by police and an angry mob when they challenged the right to vote. Boycotts and sit-ins were other effective strategies Dr. King and his aides used to respond to the financial dispairity blacks suffer'd under *Jim Crow.*

Adjacent to the national historical site is the *Martin Luther King, Jr. Center for Non-violent Social Change* that *Coretta Scott King* founded. And, all sorts of King family memorabilia is in there. They ev'n got some real letters on display that the four King children received from children around the world who express'd great sadness and fear upon hear'n that they daddy had been assassinated. Like Dr. King once said, "Injustice anywhere is a threat to justice er'ywhere." Chile, the entire complex has several exhibits that speak directly to your soul! The double internment of Dr. and Mrs. King along the *Freedom Walkway* and the *Eternal Flame* are equally touch'n. I also got a chance to tour King's birth home and *Ebenezer Baptist Church*, both on *Sweet* Auburn Avenue. You know, just about er'y place I visit, I usually look to see if I can find a Catholic Church nearby and guess what? There's a Catholic Church and school right across the street from the King Center. The name of it is, *Our Lady of Lourdes.*

While *Underground Atlanta* has some unique restaraunts, nite clubs and speciality shops, *for me,* it's no comparison to the King complex. We merely walk'd around and shop'd. Ant Hattie had a cone from the ice cream place and I bought a caramel apple at *Southern Candy Company.* If you go to *Underground Atlanta, Okoye's Art Gallery* is a must see plus several vendors outside'a *Underground* have nice things too, especially the lady that sits near the MARTA Five Points entrance who sells handmade brass jewelry. I took pictures throughout the day but a few of the exhibits didn't allow the use of cameras or cam corders.

When I finally return'd to my room, I took two more *Advil* and sat on the bed to pull my shoes off. The banquet starts at sev'n and the talent show begins at eight. Unlike Ant Hattie, I plan on stay'n till the end of the show. I'ma be right there clap'n for all'a 'em. I really think it's important that we support our young folks in positive ways. Howev'a, to make sure I'ma have enuf energy, I gotta take a nap for a couple of hours. Give the medicine time to take affect and plus the rest will do me some good. I'll be refresh'd when I get up. After I take off my clothes and pull the covers back on the bed, the phone rings.

"Hello." I say on the second ring.

"Hi Grandma, it's me, Jade. Can I come by and get a couple more cameras for tonight?"

"Only if you come right now, I was just get'n ready to lay down."

"Our bus is pulling into the parking lot as we speak. I'll be right there."

"Bye." I said and walk'd to my door, opened it and put the night latch in its lock position to keep the door from closing entirely. This way she can let herself in and I can get in the bed. Jade came about ten minutes later. I was relax'n in bed. She talk'd about what they did at *Six Flags* and *Raging Rivers* for a few minutes, then she took four more cameras on her way out and promised to go by Ant Hattie's room to see if she need'd anuth'a one. I turn'd the light off on the nightstand and got comfortable for sleep but the darn phone rang again. *What now!* "Hello."

"Hi Pearl. Sorry, I wasn't able to go with you this morning. How was your day?" Sam asks me.

"I had a wonderful time but it was rather exhaust'n. Can I call you back when I wake up?"

"Didn't mean to keep you, just want'd to know what time I should pick you up tonight?"

"How about six forty-five?"

"Fine, see you then." Sam said.

I hung up the phone and look'd at the clock to see what time it was, told myself, I had two hours to sleep and went to sleep. I slept good too, didn't wake till six o'clock. Exactly the time I want'd to wake up, a hour is plenty'a time for me to get ready.

#   #   #   #   #

Topaz and Onyx prepare the slate of performers on the bus ride back to the hotel. Their bus was s'posed to get back to the hotel at three but it didn't get back till three thirty so they had to push the rehearsal back to four o'clock. Most of the people in the show rode the same bus, so Topaz gave an update on the bus and asked Diamond to get the message to all the others who signed up but aren't on their bus. Once the bus arrive, they go straight to the Biltmore. Maintenance had promised that the stage would be ready and it was. Onyx marked center stage with his masking tape and looked out into the empty ballroom. The size of the room was a bit intimidating but he longed to perform in front of a crowd of people. "Do you think people will be mad because I'm first in the show?" He asks Topaz.

"Who cares? We didn't have selfish thoughts when we decided the line-up, right? He continues, "We agreed to start the show off soft and end it with a bang. Poetry is the softest in the line-up, that's why you're first, end of story."

Topaz always displays a macho tough personality but he's really a softie once you get to know him. I say to him, "I think the old ladies gonna steal the show."

He responds, "They are pretty good aren't they?"

207

"Yes but the dancers got it going on too," I remind Topaz. "I'm glad we decided *not* to have a winner. This way it'll be a celebration not a competition. Everybody should just go out there and do their best for Reverend Daddy. Remember, it's his big night."

The performers arrive on time and Onyx reads the lineup, pointing to individuals as he goes along. "This is the order of the show. First up, poetry, then song, dance, rapp and we'll close the show with instrumentals. If anybody has objections, raise your hand." No one did. After they had rehearsed the whole show, Onyx told everybody to be back stage, dress'd and ready to perform, at seven forty-five.

"This is a wrap! Let's go back to the room and chill." Topaz says.

When they get there, Peaches' gone and Baby Boy's asleep. They agree that the noise from the shower will probably wake their father so they decide to play videos games til he wakes up.

\#   \#   \#   \#   \#

Stan's sitting at the bar in the lobby, smoking cigarettes.

Rubie and her girls gather in her room touching up their hair while talking about the day's events. For one reason or another, none of them went on *The King Center* or the *Underground Atlanta* tour. Amy and Opal both have small children, Jenn want'd to be with her newfound relatives and Rubie promised her sister they would spend the day together. Diamond wants to talk. So, they walk around *Six Flags* holding hands while talking mostly about their past and futures. It was some serious sista to sister bonding time.

"Mom, where did you and Antie Diamond go? We didn't see you guys again til we got back on the bus." Opal asks.

"No where special, we just strolled around and talk'd. If something caught our attention, we went in but mostly we walked the park and ate a bunch of stuff that we shouldn't have."

"Did you get on any rides?" Amy asks.

"Of course not, you know good and well I don't do rides." I said to her. "But Diamond got on a couple, the roller coaster and the merry-go-round. I took pictures. Speaking of pictures, I want the four of us to take a picture tonight. Me and Jenn wearing black, what color are you girls wearing?" I ask them.

"I'm wearing royal blue," Amy says.

"Me too," Opal concurs. They often dress in the same fabric or colors without ever having discussed it. It's amazing how much alike they are.

"Good. That should make for a nice picture, me and my girls! Let's all sit together tonight. I'll get Topaz to save us some seats."

"Mom, you forgot there's going to be a head table for Reverend Daddy with Grandma Pearl and other senior family members. We can't *all* sit together."

"No not them. I was referring to my immediate family, ya'll and ya'lls families. We haven't spent an evening together in a while. It'll be fun." I tell my children.

"Fine with me," Opal says. Amy nods her head in agreement.

Someone knocks on the door. It's Peaches. She enters and greets us with kisses. Then she asks, "Can someone freshen up my curls?"

"Have a seat. I'll hook you up once I finish with Mama," Amy replies.

# # # # #

Diamond didn't know whether to expect Duane to be in the room or not. Lately, he seem'd to disappear frequently. Regardless, she wasn't going to confront him with the pictures til they got back home. She figured he probably wouldn't be there but to her surprise, he was there, watching a *CSI* rerun and drinking a bottle of beer. *Patience, Diamond, remember don't confront him til you get home!*

"Hey Baby. I see your bus was late getting back. Did you have fun with your sister?"

"Yeah, we had a nice time. How was *Underground Atlanta* and *The King Center*?" I ask him.

"*Underground* ain't nothing but some restaraunts and shops so I wasn't that impressed with it, but *The King Center*.....well, even though I'm up on the civil rights history, it was my first time visiting King's resting place and I was moved....almost to tears. It's because of King, that the young black senator from Illinois, you know, the one who gave the speech at the democratic convention, will probably run for president. In his speech he talked about citizens of America. He said and I paraphrase, "I'm not advoacting for Irish Americans or African Americans, Mexican Americans, or Chinese Americans. I'm for a United States of America." What's his name?"

"I saw him speak at the convention but I don't remember his name."

"It's an odd name…...like *Babick Alabama*…………No, I remember now…, it's *Barack Obama*. I know it's only a rumor but I hope he runs for president. What's even more hopeful is there's a good chance he can win too. Diamond, my dear, people are ready for a change. They're tired of the Bush-Clinton-Bush era."

Duane is such the opposite of his parents. He's down for the cause, no matter what, when or where. He adopted Malcom X's motto, *by any means necessary.* I guess that's one'a the reasons why I love him. I walk over to the desk and kiss him gently on the lips. "No argument from me, I agree Duane. And I'm so glad you enjoyed your day. I had a good one too but right now I feel like I need a power nap if I'm going to make it through the night." I proceed to take off my clothes and get in the bed. "Wake me at six if I'm not up." Once I find a comfortable spot and start to relax, Duane gets up from the chair and come and stands next to the bed. *What now?* I had to scoot over to make room for him to sit.

We look at each other in silence for a few seconds. "What?" I ask him.

He keeps looking at me and then he says with such sincerity that it caught me off guard, "I love you, Diamond."

"I love you too, Duane." With concern and, anticipating a testamony, this time I caringly ask, "What's wrong, honey?"

"Nothing, I just want to tell my wife that I love her."

We kiss briefly and he goes back to the chair to finish watching *CSI*. I don't know what brought that on but I don't spend a whole lot of time pondering it either, instead I fall fast asleep.

33

HAPPY BIRTHDAY,
REVEREND DADDY!

The big celebration gon be in the same room as the Meet n'Greet but they gon open up the other two sides of the partition. Then it'll be twice as big. Last week, Rubie and I went to several stores look'n for outfits to wear tonight. I finally found sumthin' at *Dillard's* in the *Galleria*. I really like how this dress make me look so slim. That's the reason why I bought it; the full bodice and the dark color helps to camouflage my broad hips. By the time I take a shower, get dress'd and put on my makeup, it's six-thirty. Sam should be here in a few minutes. Meanwhile, I call Diamond's room. I know she's gon say she got er'ything taken care of but nonetheless, I call anyway.

Duane answers the phone, "Hello."

"Hey baby, let me speak to Diamond."

"She's not here Mama." Duane's been call'n me Mama ev'a since they got married, Stan too for that matter. "You're late; she's already gone down to the Biltmore."

"When you go'n downstairs?" I ask him.

"In a few minutes, I just got out of the shower but don't worry, I'll be on time."

"O.k., I'll see you down there."

"Bye." He said.

I put my finger on the button to disconnect our call and then I dial Reverend Daddy's room. The phone rang five times, I was just get'n ready to hang up when he finally answer'd.

"Hello."

"Happy Birthday, Daddy. You ready for tonight?"

"Yep but I'm still wait'n on yo' brutha, Bubba. He can't stop stand'n in the bathroom show boat'n. I keep tell'n him no matter what he put on, he ain't gon nev'a look as good as me." Us laugh and he continues, "We shouldn't be too much longer, soon as he can pull hisself from in front'a the mirror we'll be head'n downstairs."

"Alright then, I was just call'n to see if ya'll was dress'd. Don't forget you s'pose to sit at the reserved table."

"I'm not gon be sit'n up there look'n stupid all by myself am I?" He asks.

"No, all the elders, well at least those who want to, will be sit'n at the table with you but since you the guest of honor, I need you to sit in the middle so er'ybody can see you." Sooner than Reverend Daddy could respond, there was a knock. I yell, in the same direction, "Just a minute," and immediately end'd my conversation, "Daddy, I gotta go, Sam's at the door. We'll continue our talk downstairs."

I heard him say "Bye," as I was put'n the phone down. I go open the door and Sam stand'n there in a tailored tuxedo. "Wow, you look so hansome!" I say.

He replies, "Thank you. And you look simply georgous in that dress. Did you loose some weight, Pearl?"

"If so, you can look right behind me and find it." I jokingly say while glancing at my backside. We both laugh and leave the room to go to the celebration.

By the time we get to the ballroom its almost six forty-five and several people have already scoped out and claim'd they spot. And you know how us black folks are 'bout punctuality. Chile, I'm scared of them! Diamond ask'd me to give the welcome so I gotta make sho I keep track of time. Since the festivities don't start til sev'n, I still got time to look and mingle. Sam and I walk around and do just that.

As expect'd, the decorations are awesome and I absolutely love the black and silver color scheme in this part of the ballroom. We made certain each table comfortably sits eight people and all the guest tables have black table clothes with antique or classic model cars as the center pieces displayed in different scenes. For instance, one table's decorated as a hardware store; another table is a gas station. Some of the others include a grocery store, an auto repair shop, a taxi stand, a car wash, tailgate party, campground site, church parking lot, barber shop and so forth. A massive arch made of silver and black ballons, which, by the way, are the same color as Reverend Daddy's tuxedo ensemble, span the reserved table. The stage is right in front of that. In the back of the room, a great big projection screen's set up in the far left corner and through the partition to the right of that, in the area where the buffets are set up, we got a whole different theme go'n on. It's a spiritual setting complete with gospel music, scriptures and fake animals, plus, the caterer and all our volunteers are wear'n biblical attire. When you back there, you think you're on Noah's Ark or in Jeruselum somewhere. Our decorations really did capture Reverend Daddy's true passions in life, cars and his faith. But he'd say, "not necessarily in that order."

To my s'prise, people are steady come'n in and at this rate, er'ybody gon be on time. Contrary to last night's casual attire, my relatives' is dress'd to the nines tonight! Ev'n the young people look exceptionally nice. No sag'n pants or hoochie mama outfits but rather sport coats, ties, ev'ning gowns and cocktail dresses are the majority here. Tootsie came in wear'n an adorable little peach palaaz pantsuit. Jenn, Rubie's daughter, got on a cute dress with a balero jacket but my Ant Hattie got 'em all beat in her strapless gown with sequined long gloves. I bet she made it herself too. It's so good to see er'ybody together and dress'd up and we ain't ev'n at no funeral, we have'n happy times. *God is good!* I see my children's families have arrived. Earlier, I promised Reverend Daddy he wouldn't hav'ta sit alone so if none of the elders wanna sit at his reserved table, I'll ask for volunteers from the young people. Right now, he and Bubba the onlyest ones sit'n at that table.

At five minutes to sev'n, I start make'n my way back up front. I got side track'd several times but I still managed to reach the stage by sev'n o'clock sharp. Delighted at the turnout, I began the welcome. "Good ev'ning saints. GOOD EV'NING SAINTS!" I said much louder this time.

Noise from feet shufflin' and private conversations eventually stop and the crowd respond, "Good ev'ning."

I wait'd a few more seconds before continue'n with my spiel to make sure I had er'yone's attention and that they was settled down, "Welcome

Kathy R. Jackson

to LA, Lovely Atlanta! And thank you for come'n to this Centurion Celebration." Immediately, cheers erupt from the audience. "We have a host of activities plan'd for tonight but before we get start'd we need to give thanks to the Lord Almighty...... Reverend Daddy, our most distinguished and honor'd guest, will you please lead us in prayer?"

"Why, certainly," he said but instead of walk'n up to the mic he stood up and support'd his weight against his table, which is a big accomplishment in and of itself when you a hundred years old. He start'd off, "Bow ya'll heads for God's bless'n. .....Father God, we thank you for bring'n us together one more time. Please bless those present and bless those who was not able to attend, where ev'a they may be, they here in spirit, cause we brought 'em in our hearts, right along with us..... Lord, we know it is through your mercy and grace that we live abundantly. Thanks for all you do for us.....Praise, glory and honor to you always." He end'd with a resound'n, "AMEN!"

And we all respond, "Amen," too.

I wait'd momemtarily to allow time for reflection and then I went back up to the mic and pick'd up where I left off. "Did ya'll have a good time today? I know I did. If you didn't go to the King Center, I suggest you put it on your list of things to do the *next* time you in Atlanta because it is truly sumthin' to see! Now I want you to relax, have some dinner, perhaps dance to a song or two and enjoy the entertainment." That's the caterer's cue to begin the food and beverage service. Since the hotel gave us permission to use a outside caterer, we chose Paschal's, one of Atlanta's oldest and most popular soul food restaraunts. You know, they famous for they fried chicken. At first Diamond didn't want to use 'em but when they told her they could make whatev'a she want'd she changed her tune. We decided on two buffets, a soul food and a gourmet buffet. The soul food buffet includes favorites like fried chicken, of course, with pork chops, hen & dress'n, mac n'cheese, green beans & potatoes, fried corn and collard greens. The gourmet buffet has prime rib, grilled salmon with mandarin orange glaze, asparagus, wild rice, ceasar salad, oysters on the half shell and shrimp cocktail. The servers brought rolls, cornbread and butter to the tables. For dessert they got a choice between homemade ice cream, cheesecake, pastries, peach cobbler and banana pud'n or they can have all of 'em, if they want. Er'ything looks so appetize'n, I'ma afraid somebody ain't gon wait they turn so I add, "Please be patient, remember, the caterer will advise you when they're ready for your table." I turn from the mic and mouthe to Rubie, *"Is somebody fix'n Reverend Daddy's plate?"*

"It's already taken care of," she tells me.

I continue. "Again, thank you for come'n to Reverend Daddy's Centurion Celebration…..Enjoy the ev'ning and don't forget to drop a little sumthin' sumthin'in the wish'n well, ov'a there by those beautiful balloon trees. At this time I'ma turn the mic ov'a to my daughter Diamond, our emcee for tonight." Then er'ybody start'd clap'n for me. Once I made it back to Reverend Daddy's table all'a the seats was taken, 'cept for mine. Good thing I left my purse in the chair but then again, Sam sit'n right next to me and I'm sure he wouldn't let nobody take my seat.

"Hello everybody," Diamond said into the mic, "As my mama said, I'm your emcee for the evening……. You would think with all of the technological and medical advances, more people would live to be a hundred but the reality is, we often times make poor lifestyle choices that result in early death…….. Will you live to be a hundred? Food for thought…Anyway…..we have a spectacular celebration planned for tonight and to start it off, while you're waiting to eat, we have a slide show of Reverend Daddy's many accomplishments over the last one hundred years. Please turn your attention to the screen in the back of the room."

Joyce Ann, Tootsie's daughter, the one who used to be a crack head but now she work at Purina, she put this presentation together as a gift to her grandfather. A few months ago I sent er'ybody an email request'n pictures and we received a tremendous response, a lot of priceless photos, pictures of folks we hadn't seen in years, since they died. Joyce Ann skillfully put all'a this in a *Power Point* and used a melody of songs, highlight'n *Celebration* by *Kool & the Gang*, as the background music. Some of the pictures are so old, they look more like draw'ns or oil paint'ns than photographs. Among them, are ones when Reverend Daddy was a young man, a family man, a farmer, a soldier, play'n with his grandkids, work'n on cars, open'n his first garage, preach'n in different churches and a few was of him smoke'n and drink'n with friends and relatives but the most shock'n s'prise of all was that Joyce Ann had somehow managed to get a picture of his wife, my beloved Mother. I think *this* might be the only picture Mother ev'a took, she didn't like cameras. Chile, we ooooo'd and ahhhhhh'd and laugh'd or

215

cried er'y couple of frames. Overall, I thought the presentation was real nice and thoughtful. And, it last'd a little ov'a twenty minutes, which was plenty'a time for er'ybody to fix they plate and start eat'n before we begin the talent show. Now that I think about it, I didn't see Diamond eat nuth'n, instead she been steady run'n around check'n up on er'ything else. She didn't eat nuth'n earlier today either, she gotta be hungry but I guess she just too busy to stop n'eat.

When the video tribute end'd, the crowd immediately stood to give Reverend Daddy a stand'n ovation. Once er'ybody sat back down, a full two minutes later, Diamond resumed her spot at the mic, "Now let's have a round of applause for Joyce Ann, she designed all of this." And, we clap again but not as long as we did for Reverend Daddy. "I hope everyone's enjoying their meal. The caterer asked me to announce that *seconds* are available for all who wish to partake....... but, I must remind you, don't forget to leave room for dessert. We have all sorts of sweets to satisfy your pallet. If you haven't done so yet, I would advise you visit the dessert table now because the talent show will start in approximately ten minutes, at eight o'clock sharp and believe me, you don't won't to miss ANY of it!" The DJ then puts on some *Dottie Peoples* and several people head in the direction of the desserts.

All'a the performers backstage were anxious and ready to go on. I went back there to see if I could be of any help and my grandson Topaz, ask'd me to go sit back down. So I did. At exactly eight o'clock, they turn'd the house lights down and the spot light beam'd on Diamond. "Folks, it's time for the talent show, but this is not your normal everyday talent show. Here, there's no winner or runner ups, we're not gonna be judging at all. In *this* show, Reverend Daddy's relatives, young and old, have come together to honor him with the gifts and talents that God gave them. First up, we have his great grandson Onyx, with spoken word." Some of the older people in the audience look askance but Diamond clear'd it up right away. "For those of you who don't know what that means, he'll be reciting poetry." Laughter permeated the space. I didn't dare laugh, cause a year or so ago I didn't know what it meant either, the kids had to tell me too. Back when I grew up, anytime someone ev'a *spoke the word,* they was preach'n or read'n from the bible. And Onyx, did just that. He read from the Catholic bible, two of Reverend Daddy's favorite Psalms, Psalm 139 and Psalm 23......The Lord is my Shepard. He read both with such feel'n and compassion that it brought tears to er'yone's eyes. He also perform'd some'a his original material, include'n a poem he wrote for his great grandfather, entitled *The Great Centurion*. It was truly awesome!

"In a word, *wow*, pretty much sums up that performance. Ya'll give another hand for Onyx", Diamond instructed the audience. And we clap'd again. "Our next performer is actually a duet and they have been married for ov'a forty years. They used to sing at all'a the Baptist churches in Mississippi. Please welcome to the stage Uncle Bubba and Ant Clarice, Reverend Daddy's son and daughter n' law, singing *How Great Thou Art.*" My brutha' know he can sang. Clarice sound good too but the best part was when they got Ant Hattie to come up on stage and sing a song with 'em. Chile, they was harmonize'n up a storm...... sing'n old spirituals...... remind'd me of when I was a child. I look ov'a and saw Reverend Daddy sho' nuf have'n a good ole time, he just'a rock'n to the beat and smile'n from ear to ear. If someone outside was to pass by, they'd think we's have'n church up in here. It took a few minutes for the audience to regroup after all'a that shout'n but once they did, Diamond began, "God is good" and we respond, "all the time!"

She continues, "I'd hate to be the act that follows them but without further adieu let's give a warm welcome to *JJ & CC*, Reverend Daddy's great granddaughters, Jenn, Jade, Carol and Cynthia."

Ya'll already familiar with my granddaughters Jenn and Jade but you haven't been introduced to Carol and Cynthia, they my baby brutha' Clyde's grandbabies. *JJ & CC* did a praise dance to *"Eye on the Sparrow"* and they was equally entertain'n. Then Topaz, my youngest grandson sung a catchy little rapp tune about cars that he composed for his great grandfather. He had graphics to go along with it. The young folks *really* enjoy'd his performance. I tell 'ya, his song'll be stuck in my head all night long, *My Pops Rollin'!*

"Thanks Topaz." We all clap and Diamond continues, "In case you didn't know, that's his older brother who opened the show for us........ Moving right along....Last but certainly not least, we have Reverend Daddy's younger sister and two of his cousins. They call themselves, *The Mature Ladies* featuring Joyce Ann's son, Jamaal with a solo on the sax."

We, in the audience, clap as they enter the stage. I know we in for a good performance cause most'a our relatives on my Daddy's side'a the family can sing or play a musical instrument. Tonight's jazz trio consists of, Ant Annie Mae on vocals and keyboards with cousin Gertrude on the upright bass and her sister Elaine's play'n the drums. They ages range from sixty-two to eighty and just as predict'd, these old ladies stole the show! They sound'd betta than the record when they sang *At Last* by *Etta James* and Jamaal impress'd er'ybody with his *Grover Washington* rendition.

Diamond clear'd her throat a couple of times before she spoke again but her voice what'n as strong as it were at the begin'n of the show, she sounds a bit hoarse and looks a little parch'd. That girl need to eat sumthin', she too thin.

"Did you all have a good time?......That's good.....Well, before we leave, I need you to stand and fill your glass with champagne or sparkling cider so that we can properly toast Reverend Daddy. Please hold up your hand, our host and hostesses are come'n around to replenish your glass." Diamond grabs her water bottle and takes a long swig. She ev'n dabs a few drops on her forehead. Then she continues to address the crowd, "When your glass is filled, please stand up so I'll know you're ready for the toast to begin."

Within a couple of minutes er'ybody is stand'n up with they glass in the air. It's time for the toast.... Diamond's hold'n her glass in one hand and reach'n for the mic with the other and I see her sway to left and then to the right. We make eye contact and OMG, I see that same look of fear that I saw in her Daddy's eyes when he died, twenty years ago. Then she hit the floor, hard too. I scream so loud and jump up, Sam's steady try'n to hold me down but I'm determined to get loose but I couldn't get outta my chair fast enuf and when I finally make it to the stage she's lay'n on the floor unconscious but I can feel a pulse, she still breath'n. I franticly yell, "CALL 911, CALL 911.......*Lord please don't take my baby......Lord please don't take my baby.* Er'ybody move back away from her." I sit down closer to her on the floor and scoop her up in my arms. She doesn't respond.....I rock back and forth with her next to my heart, just'a pray'n for God's mercy. Then Duane comes and prys my hands off of her so he can begin CPR til the paramedics arrive. Chile, this all happens in a matter of minutes but it seem'd to take an eternity for me and Sam to get to that hospital.

PART V

PICK'N UP THE PIECES

When God leads you to the edge of the cliff, trust Him fully and let go. Only one of two things will hap'n, either He'll catch you when you fall, or He'll teach you how to fly!

34

THY WILL BE DONE!

The paramedics told us they gon take her to the nearest hospital, Southwest Atlanta Area Hospital. I've nev'a heard of it but they tell me it's a small community hospital. We was follow'n the ambulance but got cut off at a traffic light. It didn't make sense for us to have anymore folks in the hospital, so we wait for the light to change green and lost our escort. Duane rode in the ambulance with Diamond. It was so hectic get'n outta the ballroom and the park'n lot, er'ybody want'n to know what happen'd and if she's gonna be alright? Right now, that's the million dollar question and honestly, I'm afraid to hear the answer.

Me and Sam arrived a minute ago and he let me outta the car while he go park. Chile, my hands is trembl'n sumthin' fierce, I hav'ta grip 'em together just to keep 'em still. I'm so incredibly nervous. *Lord, please let my child be alright.* I rush through the ER doors to inquire about my daughter's condition and ask to see her. The security guard at the hospital entrance must'a seen the panic on my face cause he said, "Check with the ER nurse to your right," and point'd in that direction, before I could ev'n ask a question. Despite my best efforts to remain calm on the outside, on the inside, my mind is about to go biserk not know'n what condition my child in. When I get to the triage station, initially, I'm irritable and impatient but the Spirit within me speaks and I take a deep breath and calm down, *Diamond needs me, I can feel it!* The nurse is put'n a ice pack on a young boy's ankle while his parents look on. She then asks them to return to the lobby and listen for his name to be call'd.

As soon as they turn they backs to the nurse, indicate'n they finish, I politely interrupt her before she can call the next patient. "Excuse me miss, can you tell me where I might find my daughter, her name is Diamond Roberts, she arrived by ambulance a few minutes ago?"

"I'm sorry but visiting hours over, what kin are you to her?" The nurse asks in a professional manner.

"I'm her mother. This is an emergency, please, is she here?"

The nurse puts data into a computer and says, "Yes but she's still with the intensive care doctors. Her husband's already here, would you like to join him?

Intensive Care..."Yes, please," I say but actually my mind's race'n a mile a minute. *Thank you Jesus, Diamond's still alive! Diamond's alive!*

Then the nurse points her finger and whispers, "Go through these doors and turn left when you get to the end of the hall. You'll see the Intensive Care family waiting room on your right. However, we ask that you keep the noise and patient visits to a minimum, we have very sick people on this floor." She push a button and two doors automatically open. Once we go through, the doors immediately close behinds us. We locate the room, Duane's the only one in there and he's sit'n on the sofa with his head in his hands. I go sit next to him but he don't ev'n realize I'm there til I put my arm around his shoulder and ask about Diamond.

"How is she, did you talk to the doctor yet?"

He lifts his head, "Hi Mama. No, they haven't told me anything and I'm anxious to hear something. You know I wanted to stay with her, I'm a physician too, but they insist I wait here…. About ten minutes after we arrived, a nurse came out and said the doctor will give us an update as soon as possible…. This waiting is nerve racking." Then he turns towards Sam, who is sit'n on the other side of 'em and says, "I love that woman with all my heart and soul."

Sam puts his hand on top'a Duane's hands and look him straight in the eye, "Hang in there man, don't worry, she'll be alright. Plus the two of you have the best support system there is, a loving, caring, family."

Family. That reminds me; *I promised Baby Boy and Rubie that I would call them as soon as we got here,* so I did. Afterwards, I call Diamond's, best friend, Lorraine. She'll be here first thing in the morn'n but my chil'ren and my grandchil'ren on they way out here now. Ev'n though we don't know exactly what's wrong with her, none the less she *is* in *intensive care* and that's a pretty good indication she won't be come'n home tonight. Chile, I need to assemble some prayer warriors! I immediately send a text message to one'a the ladies in my Claver Auxiliary court and ask her to spread the word amongst our members. Also, know'n Reverend Daddy and Ant Hattie, they already got er'ybody back at the hotel pray'n. Meanwhile, I sit back, close my eyes and proceed to give thanks to our Lord and Savior and ask for His mercy upon my child. A few minutes later, the doctor comes out.

"I'm Dr. Ronald Kwasa. Are you Mrs. Roberts' family?"

"Yes, I'm her husband, Dr. Roberts; this is her mother, Mrs. Johnson and a long time family friend, Sam. Now, enough with formalities how's my wife, doctor?"

"Are you a medical physician, Dr. Roberts?" He asks.

You can tell Duane's annoyed by his question, "Yes, a pediatrician, what does that have to do with anything? Just please tell me what's wrong with my wife and when can we take her home?"

The doctor responds, "I apologize, I didn't mean to upset you but it would be helpful if I could ask a few questions. Unfortunately, your wife is in a sedated coma and she can't tell me what happened. She's stable, I've given her something to make her sleep but I still need to run a round of scans and test before I can accurately provide a diagnosis. Are you willing to sign the consent forms?"

"What type of test.....Regardless....., yes, I'll sign." Duane said.

I raise my hand, "Can I say sumthin'?"

"Sure," Dr. Kwasa says.

"Well, I know for a fact Diamond's been loose'n weight and have'n back pain for a while. She was s'pose to go to the doctor's the other day but she didn't.... I was look'n right at her when she faint'd. First she broke out in a sweat then she sway'd a little bit, her eyes roll'd back in her head and bam! She hit the floor, all within a matter of seconds."

"How long was she unconscious?" The doctor asks us while review'n her chart. "No known allergies or trauma."

Duane answers, "That's correct. I administered CPR till the paramedics arrived, then they took over, she didn't wake up in my presence and I stayed with her until we arrived at the hospital.

Dr. Kwasa continues, "Well, from my external examination, I suspect some internal bleeding and perhaps complications with her kidney but tests will confirm or rule out my suspicions. You can see her now but only one visitor at a time, in two hour intervals. And please, do try to limit your visits to five minutes. I want her to get plenty of rest. We'll talk again once the results are ready. Do you have any questions?"

"Yes, one, how long's the test?" I ask the doctor.

"I've placed a stat order which means rush, as soon as possible. I imagine they'll be ready within the next couple of hours. In the meantime, I suggest you people try and get some sleep. It's gonna be a long night. We'll let you know if her condition changes."

With that, the doctor shook our hands and left the room. Duane went right behind him to go see Diamond. When he came back, I could tell he'd been cry'n again. All's he said was "be prepared." I look at Sam as he goes ov'a to console Duane.

It's my turn. I leave the wait'n area and head down the hall to see Diamond for the first time since she collapsed four hours ago. Once I open the door to her room, I know exactly what Duane was refer'n to when he said "be prepared." Chile, you wouldn't believe how many tubes and wires they got my baby hook'd up to. Also I'm s'prised to see a breath'n tube, don't remember the doctor say'n anything about that. I walk close to the bed and sit on the edge. I just look at her for a couple of minutes. "Mommie's here baby." She look weak, awfully thin too. And they got a lotta Vaseline or sumthin' around her mouth and on her eye lids. I hardly ev'n recognize her. I pick up one'a her small frail hands, the one without the I.V., and rub'd it back and forth like I used to do when she was a little girl. This would calm her down whenev'a she was in pain. This is too much! I can't stay back here, it's kill'n me see'n her like this, plus I promised myself I wouldn't cry in front'a her. "Pooh, if you want Mommie, just tell one'a the nurses; I'll be sit'n right out front. I ain't go'n nowhere til it's time to take you home......... I love you." Then I get up, kiss her on the forehead and proceed to leave the room. Diamond didn't open her eyes not one time, I'm not ev'n sure she knows I'm here. As soon as I get outside'a the door, I break down in tears but somehow on the way back to the wait'n area, I manage to recapture my composure. I know I gotta be strong for Diamond and the rest of my family.

Thank you Jesus for your continuous love in help'n me get through this ordeal. Please have mercy on my child. In case you didn't know, prayer encourages me, hope enables me to go another day, er'yday.

Ten minutes later Baby Boy and his clan arrive. Then Rubie and Stan show up with Jade, Diamond's daughter and they kids, Amy, Opal and Jennifer. I told Ruby and Baby Boy to go back there and visit for a couple'a minutes but the others had to wait two more hours before they could go back. One by one, Duane gave 'em each a medical update. Seems he had a private talk with the doctor on the way to see Diamond.

For me, times creep'n by, it's only been a few minutes since the last time I look'd at my watch. Minutes turn into hours…..I gotta do sumthin' to fill up this empty space. "Let's pray ya'll. Remember, a family that prays together, stays together." So we all stand up, make a circle and hold hands. "Instead of just one person pray'n, how 'bout we go around the circle and each person say a little sumthin' for Diamond. Ev'n if you think you don't know how to pray or find the right words, just tell'a you love her." A few minutes after we finish pray'n Dr. Kwasa comes back in the wait'n room.

He asks Duane, "Is it alright to talk here or would you prefer we go somewhere a bit more private?"

"No, here's fine, everybody's family."

"Well, I have good news and bad news. The bad news is your wife needs a kidney transplant and the good news is, there's no internal bleeding and the odds are very good for a match with family members. If your relatives are here, we can test them all. That is, if they give consent. Otherwise she could possibly remain on the national list for months or even years, waiting for a kidney."

Again, I'm the first to ask a question, "If one'a us is a match and we agree, how soon after is the transplant?"

"If all goes well, meaning, we find a match, get authorization, complete pre-surgery tests and transfer, I would say perhaps by the end of the week."

"Transfer, where, St. Louis?" Duane asks.

Dr. Kwasa goes on with his explaination, "This hospital is not equipped to handle such a procedure and I will not release her for travel to St. Louis, that's too far. I recommend we transfer her to Emory Crawford Long Hospital in midtown Atlanta. It's one of the top transplant hospitals in the country and I'm on staff there as well. Don't worry, my office can make all the necessary arrangements for her transport and admission to Emory but first things first, we've got to start her on dialysis right away and begin searching for a donor." He looks around the room and continues, "If anyone's interested in donor consideration, please check in at the nurses' station. I'll be back in the morning or should I say later today since it's already 3AM. Good night folks." And he left the room.

I stand up, "Ya'll heard what he said. We need to find a kidney donor.

Duane stands and says, "I'll cover expenses for anyone who is willing to be tested. That goes for relatives at the hotel too. So spread the word, I'm sponsoring a donor drive for Diamond."

Rubie and I have a quick meet'n and decide its best we continue with the celebration plans. Church is scheduled in the morn'n and Lord knows we can use all'a the prayers we can get! I'm sure Diamond would want us to go on, she put a lotta work into plan'n er'ything so we gon go ahead, not me though, I meant what I said, I ain't leave'n this hospital without my baby. Duane's not go'n tonight either. The nurse brings us pillows and blankets, take our blood and we camp out in the wait'n room while er'ybody else go back to the hotel. Baby Boy, Rubie and Sam give blood too before they leave the hospital. Ev'n though Sam and Duane not family members, they volunteer just the same. Each promises to get others to come fourth.

Lorraine check'd in my room at the hotel and came to the hospital around ten this morn'n. She also gave blood. Once she finish'd her visit with Diamond, we all had church together, right here in this little wait'n room. Afterwards, Duane went to the hotel to shower and change clothes but I stay'd here. I'm grateful that Rubie and my granddaughters make'n sure the rest of the celebration continue as plan'd, start'n with church, then the swim party and tour of the historic colleges and universities. Since I what'n leave'n Rubie had Stan bring my suitcase and I freshen'd up in the bathroom. Duane kept his promise and assembled a whole bus load of folks (at the hotel) to either visit the family or test. The donor drive ended at five o'clock and we got some really good news; more'n thirty people actually test'd......hurray...... hopefully somebody will be a match but the best news of all is, Diamond's been upgraded from critical to serious. After receive'n plenty'a fluids and two full rounds of dialysis, she's awake and alert, she no longer in a medically induced coma. Her color's return'n to her natural hue and she able to communicate but we *not* outta the woods yet, she still needs a kidney, howev'a, she look a hellava lot betta than she did yesterday. *Thank you Jesus!* Dr. Kwasa will see her daily and he anticipates have'n a list of all'a the eligible donors in a couple of days but meanwhile, if we got any questions, we shouldn't hesitate to ask the nurse or give him a call. That same eve'n they moved Diamond from the intensive care floor to a private room, anuth'a good sign. I were so happy when Fr. Mahoney, the priest on staff at the hospital, came and anoint'd her, (one'a the catholic sacraments). He also arranged for us to receive Holy Communion er'yday.

The next two days are routine but uneventful. Ev'n though she gotta do dialysis er'y other day, she's improve'n, I can tell. Diamond sleeps a lot and I'm a permanent fixture, the gustapo, in her room. It's important she rest, so I'm limit'n visitor's time. I only had to do that one day because the majority of people went back to St. Louis on Tuesday. Ant Hattie stop'd by yesterday and gave me the used cameras and small tape recorder. She didn't test though, she way too old to donate, perhaps me too, but they gon hav'ta tell me to my face! Lorraine check'd outta the hotel on Tuesday, ne'vatheless she stay'd in Atlanta, she got relatives here. Since she works from home and she brought her computer with her, she can do her work and stay with her relatives for as long as necessary. She come visit Diamond for a few minutes er'yday. Duane flew back to St. Louis last night and he'll return on Sunday. *What's today, Thursday?* Baby Boy and Rubie already went home too.

Chile, I told er'ybody to leave, I understand they got jobs and responsibilities. If her condition worsens or they find a match, I'll call 'em all back. The only reason why Sam's still in town is because he had some kind'a business conference in *Buckhead* most'a the week but he s'pose to go home tonight also. He say he gon stop by, on his way to the airport, to say goodbye. As usual, he's been such a good friend. He's kept me company; we had dinner in the hospital cafeteria er'y night this week.

Diamond's eat'n dinner when Sam walk through the door carry'n a bouquet of flowers and a humongous *get well soon* card, grin'n from ear to ear. "Well, well, look at you, sitting up and eating solid food." She got a mouthful of food so all she do is smile and wink at Sam. Over the last couple of days she built some'a her strength back up and that's good, she need to be strong for the transplant. Today is the day Diamond s'pose to find out if anybody test'd positive for a match. We'd hope Dr. Kwasa would come early but no such luck, it's almost six o'clock and he's still not here. He's ne'va been this late before, so I call the nurse.

"Hello, this is Pearl Johnson,……. Diamond Roberts, mother,…. in room 5352….. Fine, thank you. Are you expect'n Dr. Kwasa today?"

"Yes, he's making rounds now. He should be in Mrs. Roberts' room within the next few minutes. We apologize for the delay but he had several emergencies today. We thank you for your patience." *Such professionalism, I like that.*

"You welcome", I say and hang up the phone. "He's on his way", I tell Diamond. And sure enuf, the doctor was here in five minutes.

"Good evening, folks."

"Good eve'n doctor. We was begin'n to wonder if you was come'n or not." Sam didn't say nuthin', he just nods his acknowledgement.

Dr. Kwasa places a stethoscope in his ears, walks ov'a to Diamond and listens to her heart and lungs. "How are you feeling today?"

"Actually doctor, I feel pretty good today, all things considering…. And I'm so glad to be able to eat again, even if it is only soft food. Any news about the results," she asks.

"Yes ma'am, pack your bags young lady, you're going to Emory! We have not only one but two potential donors. However, one may be too old."

I held up my hands in praise, "Two potential donors. Thank you Jesus, thank you Jesus! Who are they? Can you tell us?"

"Yes, but we still need to contact them." Dr. Kwasa turns back around towards Diamond and says, "It's your father and your brother."

"My father?"

"Her father?" Sam and I sing in unison.

Dr. Kwasa looks at the chart again and repeats, "Yes……, your DNA sequence is the same as your father and brother, a perfect match, as long as they are healthy." Chile, by now, all three of us got our mouths gaped wide open in amazement. The doctor's puzzled and confused, "Is something wrong?"

"Something definitely is." Diamond answers, rather curtly, "Your results are wrong. My father is D-E-A-D, dead! And has been, for more than twenty years, is this some kind of joke? If so, it is not funny. May I see that report?"

The doctor continues with his facts, "Yes, I'm very serious. This particular type of DNA/transplant, compatibility tests is 99.99 percent accurate." *Yeah, right.* Simultaneously, Sam and I move closer to the bed so we all can get a good look at the paper. "Right here," the doctor points to the report and all our eyes follow his finger as we scan the page together and then he stops midway and continues, "it lists all potential matches, Garnet Charles Johnson, relationship, sibling; Ashley Wilcox, relationship, father."

Now it's my turn to hit the floor! BAMM!!!!

35

SECRETS REVEAL'D!

Needless to say, I been up all night, ponder'n them results. After I faint'd they took me down to the ER, Sam went along with me. Initially, they say I was in shock then my heart and nervous stomach start'd act'n up. It took them a few hours to get a handle on er'ything but Sam stay'd right by my side. As a precaution, they kept me for observation and consequently Sam and I talk'd most'a the night (whenev'a I what'n pray'n). Yes, he miss'd his flight. Neither one'a us seen or talk'd to Diamond yet. By the time they release me and we get back upstairs to her room, its nine o'clock in the morn'n. And she already gone. *I wonder if she told anybody about the DNA….. Apparently, she gone.* Luckily, I see one'a her nurses in the hall who tells me they transfer'd Diamond early this morn'n and that surgery's scheduled for Monday. Of course, we leave and head straight for Emory. *I can only imagine what Diamond's think'n right about now.*

It's only a fifteen minute drive and we able to find park'n on a street lot instead of go'n up inside'a the hospital garage. If I can avoid enclosed public garages, I do. I'm scared'a those things. Sam gets out first and go put some money in the self serve kiosk. When I get outta the car, the first thing I smell is fried chicken. I look around to see where its come'n from. Several people told us Emory Crawford Long Hospital is in midtown Atlanta but nobody mention'd its right across the street from *Gladys Knight and Ron Winan's* restaurant, the one famous for they chicken and waffles. We in a hurry right now but you can bet your bottom dollar I'ma get me some'a that chicken while we down here, if not today, sometime soon. Chile, it smell sooo good! Anyway, once we get in the hospital we go to the information desk to find out what room she in. The desk is a massive marble, half moon shape structure with a clerk at both ends. I get in line and peak around the person in front'a me so I can count the number of folks in front'a them. All I see is one person and "Juanita Smith", engraved on a goldtone name plate attach'd to the desk. Once that person in front'a me leaves, I step up to the desk and the attendant greets me with a calm voice and welcome'n smile. I instantly like her. Plus I assume the information clerk would know plenty'a stuff about this hospital, be full of facts, information and history. Come to find out, normally all transplants are done at the Clifton Road facility, howev'a since there's been a recent increase in donors, more patients start get'n approval for transplants but they didn't have the space to accommodate all'a those patients ov'a there, so now, all'a the kidney transplants are done here on Peachtree Street, which helps address they patient ov'a load. *That's a bit more info than I need'd to know.* Anyhow, Diamond's on the floor designated for surgery patients, her room is 333.

I'm amazed at how big this place is. The ground floor itself with all the grandeur, look more like a fancy hotel lobby than a hospital. While follow'n the directions Ms. Smith gave us, we pass this gigantic open seat'n area with large mahogany tables and chairs on both sides of the aisle. I immediately notice a very diverse mixture of people and activities, young, old, short, tall, workers, visitors and a rainbow of colors, some people eat'n, while others talk'n, read'n, on they computers or simply chill'n. I like that! Once we round the corner I see the entrance to the *Seasonings Café*. I *had* to step in for a moment, just to see what go'n on there. And to my s'prise, this not just one place but four n'one, with different types of cuisine at each station, wraps, soups & salads, pizza, grilled items and traditional, er'ything from simple sandwiches to a full course meal. Plus, in the front, they got a wide selection of hot and cold beverages and a upright cooler with real *Edy* gourmet ice cream. Chile, this the biggest café I ev'a seen in my life! *One* station is the size of a regular café in St. Louis. We continue on to the elevators. A little further down the hall there's ev'n a florist, a bookstore and *two* gift shops. I tell ya, this place is huge. It's so many people walk'n around and so many different types of businesses make you think you in *Grand Central* station somewhere, instead'a hospital. I ain't ne'va seen nuthin' like it!

I can only imagine what kind'a medical equipment they got, you know this a teach'n hospital also, I bet'cha they got the best of er'ythang. *Good for Diamond.*

We finally make it to the elevator and get on. Sam looks at me and whispers, "You ok?"

I sigh deeply and shake my head yes.

He continues the conversation as we get'n off the elevator, "Don't worry, we'll talk to her together."

We start walk'n slowly down the hall to Diamond's room, "It's just so hard to believe…. All these years….I had no idea, did you?"

"Honestly, the thought did cross my mind once or twice but I only imagined what our lives would have been like if we had let that one night of passion in St. Louis lead to something else but I never thought in a million years I was Diamond's father."

"You know Charlie do'n more'n just roll'n ov'a in his grave, he probably do'n cartwheels or on a trapeze somewhere. I lightly chuckle to keep from cry'n…..At least I can say I ain't nev'a been unfaithful to my husband. Yes, I had sex outta wedlock a couple of times but that was way back before I learn'd the error of my ways. We all make wrong choices, major mistakes at one time or anuth'a in our lives. I've changed, grown in my faith, repent'd and I'd nev'a do anything like that again. Lord knows we ain't *always* the people He wants us to be but thank God I am not the person I used to be."

"Come on now, Pearl. I thought we agreed, you wouldn't beat up on yourself about this. Charlie will always be her daddy, I just *happen* to be her father, anybody could have done that."

I roll my eyes, "What are you try'n to say Sam, I don't like the sound of it. You make the whole encounter sound cheap and disgust'n."

"Pearl you of all people should know it wasn't nor could it ever be like that. I love you…… As I recall, we both were vunerable and went too far. Remember how awkward we felt afterwards. I admit, later that night, I was relieved when we agreed to erase and never speak of what we had done and just go back to being good friends. Who knows, perhaps we would have developed a romantic relationship and possibly even married if you hadn't met Charlie the very next day and (he put his arms up in the air, bent his index and pointer fingers, immolate'n quotation marks) "fell head over heels in love". I remember how much you two had in common and I used to envy you and your marriage.

Sure, secretly I was jealous but don't get me wrong, I think you and Charlie were way better together than you and I could have been back then. Pearl, I value our friendship and I highly respect you, I just hope Diamond can grasp all of this. This is a lot for any healthy person to process, let alone someone facing major surgery."

#   #   #   #   #

Last night Dr. Kwasa and I called my brother and now he's on his way back to Atlanta. Presurgery testing doesn't begin til Saturday but right after I talked to Baby Boy I called Lorraine to see if she'd accompany me here, today. Naturally, she agreed. Currently, she's downstairs getting something to eat. I told her that they found a possible donor but I didn't say who, though. I also stretched the truth a bit and told her that Mama had some personal errands to take care of this morning. I'm pretty certain she probably does but actually, I haven't spoken directly to her or Sam since they left my room last night but I did call the ER to get periodic updates throughout the night. It's not like I've abandoned my mother or anything, I just need some space and time to think. And despite the catalog of emotions that I'v recently conquered, from initial surprise to anger, then betrayal to regret and finally confusion to, at peace about the tests results, I absolutely wish no harm to anyone, least of all my mother. Life's too short! I love my mother and I can't even begin to imagine life without her, especially now, Duane yes but my mother, no way. True we don't always see eye to eye on everything but that's still my mama and I love her very much. As they say, blood's thicker than water. I can't even think of one thing that would make me stop loving my parents, no verse nor curse, no test or moving of the nest. *Honor thy mother and father.*

As soon as the doctors informed me of my diagnosis and impeding prognosis, my litany of personal priorities *immediately* changed and my new found marriage problems dropped to the bottom of my list. For the past few days, I've only been praying and thinking about my health. *If I don't get this transplant, I could die but what's even scarier is I could also die from possible complications during and/or after surgery.* What good is a husband if I'm dead! Yes, I admit, I have an indescribable ache in my heart caused by Duane's infidelity but I can't think about that right now. Honestly, I don't care what he does from here on out! I need to focus my energy elsewhere. My health is more important. Life's too short. So, if I somehow manage to survive this whole ordeal I promise to strive to live a more productive, Christ like life. Beginning with this DNA information......, there's no need to cause other folks unnecessary pain........ I don't even wanna know how *it* happened..... *And since the DNA only involves the three of us and we* **already** *know, why does anyone else need to know?* So, if it's ok with Mama and Sam I would like to continue to honor Daddy's memory and let sleeping dogs lay, so to speak. I even asked Dr. Kwasa not to reveal the name to Baby Boy and he said there was no need to because Sam's ineligible, he's too old. *But something also told me to request a copy of those results for my files... I ain't dead yet!*

# # # # #

"Mrs. Johnson, is that you?" A familiar voice asks.

I turn around and see Lorraine come'n up behind us, "Hi baby, when'd you get here?" Sam and I slow down our pace and wait for her to catch up to us. She walks ov'a to me first and plants a kiss on my cheek, then she kiss Sam. Er'ybody always treat'n him like family.

"I came in the ambulance with Diamond." We enter the room with Lorraine lead'n the way. *So much for us have'n that talk with Diamond, it'll hav'ta wait now.* I throw my hands up in the air as soon as she gets in front'a us. *Oh, well...* Sam and I look askance at each other then proceed in. "Diamond, look who I found in the hallway?"

"Good morning, Mama," I nod my head, "Sam....., I was wondering how long it would take you guys to get here. Lorraine's been excellent company. Sit down, relax, have a seat." I'm tired, we head to do just that and she continues to chat, "By the way, I spoke to the doctor again last night and I have some more information to share with you."

I stop dead in my tracks. "More information, are you sure you want to talk about this now. Can't it wait til later?" Chile, I ain't ne'va been one to put my business out in the streets and I ain't comfortable with start'n it right now either. I don't care if Lorraine is a long time family friend, some things is private and I think this should be classified as one'a those things.

"No it CANNOT! You see, Baby Boy's agreed to give me a kidney, that is, if he passes all'a the preliminary tests. He's on his way here right now. Ain't that wonderful?"

"Wonderful, that's the best news I've heard all week." I rise to congratulate her and then it dawns on me, *Oh my God*, I'ma have two children in surgery and at home recuperrate'n at the same time. *I didn't think about that possibility.* This means, I got double worry and concern. Life..... Its funny how any and er'ything can change in the blink of'a eye. *Lord please watch ov'a my babies.* I don't know what I'd do without my box of jewels.....We all spend the rest of the day visit'n with Diamond. We play scrabble, cards, some dominoes and watch a little television. We did er'ything *but* talk about them DNA results. At eight o'clock when visit'n hours was ov'a, Lorraine leaves, bound for an ev'nen with her relative's and Sam and I go across the street to *Gladys & Ron's* for dinner.

The restaurant's design is very fashionable, russet color leather and oak décor with spacious booths on either side of the room. One side'a the room's dedicated to *Ron Winans*, with photographs of him and famous people, gold records and memorabilia hang'n on the walls. The other side'a the room is decorated in the same way but with pictures of *Gladys Knight*, her friends *Tyler Perry* and *Stevie Wonder*, to name a few and countless awards. They also got two large LCD screens, one in the front and one in the back, where they show'n throw back music videos and short clips of old interviews and live performances. It's my understand'n they got several other restaraunts similar to this one in select cities around the United States. As soon as we sit down, the waiter comes ov'a to our table and I immediately look at his nameplate, "Yonte". Have you noticed I prefer to address strangers that I encounter by their names? "Hi, Yonte!" I say before he ev'n gets a word outta his mouth.

"Yes, my name is Yonte, I'll be your server tonight. Good evening, and welcome to Gladys and Ron's. Can I get you two started with some drinks, perhaps?"

My, my, what pretty teeth he got. And a nice smile to go along with 'em. I find myself feed'n off'a his positive energy. *Is that the cougar in me come'n out?* "Yes, I'll have a margarita on the rocks, with salt."

"Ma'am would you like that with Jose Cuervo or 1800 Tequila?" He then turns to Sam, "Anything for you sir?"

"Cuervo's fine unless you got Silver Patron." I answer.

Sam reviews the beer list, "I'll have a *Budweiser.*"

"Would you like draft or bottle, sir? And I'm sorry ma'am we're currently out of Patron but I promise you, the margaritas here are the best in Atlanta. Also, it's happy hour, two for one on our mixed drinks."

"Ev'n betta." I shake my head in agreement.

Sam decides, "Bring me a bottle." And we both spend the next couple of minutes cruise'n the menu before Sam breaks the silence. "What are you getting?"

"The shrimp and grits sounds delicious and I know I said how good the chicken wings smell'd earlier but I think I'ma try the chicken omlete made with a real chicken breast, how about you?"

"Definitely chicken wings and waffles for me."

Yonte returns to our table, serves our drinks and takes the food order. We both order a side salad. Within a matter of a few minutes, our salads come out and ten minutes later, we eat'n the main course. The service was excellent, the atmosphere was pleasant and the food was good! I really enjoy'd the whole experience and before I forget, kudos to the best waiter in midtown Atlanta, *Yonte Richardson.* We ate and indulged in small talk to camoflouge the seriousness of the last few day's events. Then Sam walk'd me to my hotel room down the street and we said our goodbyes. He's leave'n on the first flight out tomorrow. Oh, I almost forgot, prior to us leave'n Diamond, she ask'd me **not** to visit her tomorrow, she wants to bond with Baby Boy and have some alone time, so I'm free all day. One thing I'll probably do is sleep in late. Especially since Duane's not due to return til early Sunday morn'n.

I feel I need to have a talk with him before the surgery.

#   #   #   #   #

Sam call'd to check up on Diamond er'y day since he left…. By the time Sunday rollsaround, er'ybody's back in Atlanta, include'n Baby Boy's family and Rubie Leigh's. Duane and Jade got in yesterday morn'n, shortly after they told us er'ything was a go for today. Surgery's at ten but we all arrive at eight and gather in the hospital chapel to say the rosary and pray that Diamond and Baby Boy have a successful surgery and speedy recoveries. Perhaps you've heard myths about why Catholics pray the rosary. Some say we chant but that is the farthest thing from the truth. Typically, the rosary is said privately or in small groups but let there be no misunderstand'n about it, the rosary is a series of contemplative prayers regard'n Jesus' chronological journey here on earth.

Furthermore, we acknowledge the strong bond, the unique love, between mother and child, nuthin' can destroy it, not ev'n death. Like Christ, it's ev'a last'n. It's a relationship anybody can identify with, all cultures honor and respect it too. Other than the omnipotent one, who betta to ask to help us pray for God's mercy and grace than Jesus' mother, the ev'a bless'd Virgin Mary. In short, we ask her to intercede in our prayers; we seek her help in receiving God's grace and mercies, which only He can grant.

Rubie Leigh volunteers to lead us in the rosary and afterwards most of us decide to stay for the daily mass but er'ybody is back upstairs in plenty'a time for farewells. While Duane and Jade's have'n some private time with Diamond, the doctor comes out to see if the extend'd family, has any last minute questions about the procedures. He then gives us a brief overview. Essentially, the procedure will start with the removal of Baby Boy's kidney, and then it will be transplant'd into Diamond. This could take 6-8 hours to complete it all. Follow'n surgery Baby Boy'll be in ICU for a few hours and then transfer'd to his room for another three days before he can travel. He is expect'd to have a full recovery in a relatively short time but Diamond's recovery on the other hand's not that simple. She will also be in ICU, under constant observation the first forty-eight hours and then continually screen'd for infection and rejection ov'a the next few days. It could be another couple of weeks before she can go back to St. Louis. And ev'n then, with all the test'n they did, her body still might reject the new kidney but we pray that don't happen.

Chile, it's gonna be a *long* day.....I head to Baby Boy's room to see him off first.

#   #   #   #   #

Me, Duane and Jade sit and listen as Dr. Kwasa and the anesthesiologist once again advise me of all the risks involved, during and after the surgery, this time I sign the actual consent form, Duane does too. Seems like I should be nervous but for some odd reason, I am not. And I have yet to say anything to Duane about his infidelities but I don't want to take that silence to my grave, should it be God's will that I die, so I've decided to confront him (while I still got the strength) about the whole thing. Knowing within, however he responds I'm at peace!

"Jade, please baby, don't cry. I'ma be just fine, you wait and see. Come over here and give me a big kiss." We hug and hold on to each other a full minute before finally releasing. "I love you…..Now go wait out front with your grandmother….. I promise I'll see you in a couple of hours."

"Love you too, Mama." We blow more kisses and off she goes. *I hope this is not the last time I see my child but Lord knows I'm thankful I got to see her and everybody else too.*

"Diamond, my sweet, sweet Diamond. Please know that I love you more than life itself and I'll be waiting right here, for you, when you open your eyes."

We share the most passionate kiss I've ever experienced but I can't let it end like this, I gotta say something. Before we separate, I whisper in his ear, "I know your secret. I hired a private detective and I have pictures. How could you do this to me, Duane? I would have loved you forever!" I had intended not to cry but a single tear fell from the corner of my eye.

"Do what? And what pictures are you talking about? The drugs they gave you must be working because you're making absolutely no sense."

I pull open the cabinet drawer next to my bed and hand him the envelope as proof, the pictures are in it. "I know about your affair." *There, I said it. And I remained calm.* Now I can move forward, I'm ready for it all, come what may!

"Affair!" he looks at the pictures and starts laughing out loud.

"What? Why are you laughing?" I insist, pointing to the pictures. "Do you deny that's you and your mistress?"

"It's me alright but that's not my mistress, she's my wedding planner. You see, I've been secretly planning for us to renew our wedding vows for our 20th anniversary. This lady is taking care of all the details. We've been meeting for the last three or four months."

"Renew our vows? Oh, I love you Duane. I'm so sorry, please accept my apology. I feel like such a fool."

"You should but I still love you just the same." We kiss again and it's better than before. Wow! I can hardly wait to get this transplant thing over with if this is any indication of how it's gonna be between us. We have time to embrace once more before they come take me to surgery.

The next thing I know, I faintly hear sounds but I distinctly feel someone touching me, taking my vital signs. I awake and look straight into my husband's eyes and smile, "I love you.....God has kept me here for a reason. I survived because He has a plan for me. Through all my bad relationships, the addictions, the consequences, the negative thoughts, the illnesses, the death of my loved ones, the back stabbing from my friends, or the lack of support; I made it because I am blessed! I release and let go of all past hurts, misunderstandings and grudges because I am abundantly blessed! I recognize them as the deceptions they are and that they are sent from the enemy to kill my spirit, steal my joy and destroy my faith."

Duane's so emotional; he's cry'n tears of joy, "Hey baby, welcome back. The surgery went well."

Diamond closes her eyes in a jester of relief. Duane gently kisses her forehead and she whispers, "It's good to know my family loves me but its more important to know that God loves me! For God is all there is. All else is a lie!"

I pause, thank God and look at the both of them, "Ya'll wipe your tears and walk in the victory!!!!!!!!" Then I get up to go tell the others that Diamond's finally awake.

BOOK CLUB DISCUSSION QUESTIONS

1. Do you agree with how Pearl disciplines her children? Why or why not?

2. Do you think she has a favorite child?

3. When did the prisoner get on the bus?

4. Were you surprised to discover that Sam is Diamond's father?

5. Do you think Sam and Pearl will ever marry?

6. Will Diamond ever change her selfish behavior?

7. Name three things you learned about Catholics.

8. Did you enjoy the story? Why or why not?

Author contact: krj1359@yahoo.com

AUTHOR'S BIO

Kathy R. Jackson is a cradle African American Catholic and an avid reader of Christian fiction. Former human resources executive, she currently lives and works as a substitute teacher in St. Louis, Missouri. She has two adult children, Kris and Karmen, and one granddaughter, Khira.